Praise for the China Bayles mystery series . . .

"Mystery lovers who also garden will be captivated by this unique series." —*Seattle Post-Intelligencer*

"One of the best-written and well-plotted mysteries I've read in a long time." —*Los Angeles Times*

"An entertaining detective writer." —*The Dallas Morning News*

"A nice book to curl up with on a blustery day." —*Chicago Tribune*

"Albert has created captivating new characters and a setting dripping with atmosphere." —*Publishers Weekly*

"[China Bayles is] such a joy . . . an instant friend." —Carolyn G. Hart

"A treat for gardeners who like to relax with an absorbing mystery." —*North American Gardener*

"An appealing series." —*Booklist*

"A wonderful reading experience." —*Midwest Book Review*

"Gripping." —*Library Journal*

"Cause for celebration." —*Rocky Mount Telegram*

An Unthymely Death

And Other Garden Mysteries

SUSAN WITTIG ALBERT

BERKLEY BOOKS, NEW YORK

B

A Berkley Book
Published by The Berkley Publishing Group
A division of Penguin Group (USA) Inc.
375 Hudson Street
New York, New York 10014

This book is an original publication of The Berkley Publishing Group.

Copyright © 2003 by Susan Wittig Albert.
Cover design by Judy Murello.
Cover illustration by Joe Burleson.
Text design by Tiffany Kukec.

JUL   2 2003

PRINTING HISTORY
Berkley trade paperback edition / June 2003

Library of Congress Cataloging-in-Publication Data

Albert, Susan Wittig.
   An unthymely death / Susan Wittig Albert.—Berkley trade pbk. ed.
      p.   cm.
   Contents: An unthymely death—The khat who became a hero—The Rosemary caper—Ivy's wild, wonderful weeds—Death of a rose rustler—Mustard madness—The pennyroyal plot—A violet death—A deadly chocolate valentine—Bloom where you're planted.
   ISBN 0-425-19002-1
   1. Detective and mystery stories, American.   2. Bayles, China (Fictitious character)—Fiction.   3. Women detectives—Texas—Fiction.   4. Texas Hill Country (Tex.)—Fiction.
5. Herbalists—Fiction.   6. Texas—Fiction.   I. Title.

PS3551.L2637U67 2003
813'.54—dc21
                                                                    2002043933

PRINTED IN THE UNITED STATES OF AMERICA

10   9   8   7   6   5   4   3   2   1

PUBLISHERS NOTE: The recipes contained in this book are to be followed exactly as written. The Publisher is not responsible for your specific health or allergy needs that may require medical supervision. The Publisher is not responsible for any adverse reactions to the recipes contained in this book.

CONTENTS

*Written especially for this collection

A Note to Readers

THIS collection of stories began with a suggestion from an editor at *Country Living Gardener* magazine, where I regularly write a column called "The Herbal Thymes." *CLG* was expanding its Internet site and wanted to include some light and lively gardening mysteries designed especially for on-line reading, to be published in weekly episodes. "Would you be interested?" the editor asked.

I pondered the idea for all of two seconds and yelped an impulsive, enthusiastic *yes!* It would be fun to sidestep the more serious themes that are usually front and center in the book-length China Bayles mysteries. It would be especially interesting to include more gardening and herbal information, since many readers have told me how much they like that aspect of China's herbal adventures. I had come to understand that readers often read the books not just to be entertained, but also to learn. And since I've spent so much of my life as a teacher, that was just fine with me.

But when I hung up the phone, I wondered with a flash of panic whether I'd just talked myself into a corner. I'd never even read an on-line short story, much less written one, and I didn't have a clue as to how to go about it. However, I was intrigued by the idea of writing a short story in episodes, with links between story elements and herbal lore, garden information, recipes, and craft ideas. The mysteries would be light and entertaining, the structure and format would be fun to tinker with (especially all that supplemental linked material, which I was thinking of as "story enrichment"), and I would be able to bring in all the familiar Pecan Springs characters, as well as introduce a few who had not yet appeared in the already published China Bayles mysteries. A whole new adventure in story-telling!

The on-line garden mysteries were a great success, and over the next two years, I wrote six of them for *CLG*. But many readers asked if the stories could be put into a "real book" so they didn't have to read them on the computer, and they pointed out that their friends without computers couldn't read them at all. I discussed the idea with Natalee Rosenstein, my editor at Berkley Prime Crime, and we came up with the format for this book. In the process, I added four entirely new stories, substantially rewrote the six original stories, and developed a great deal of all-new "enrichment material."

As I've written and compiled these stories, I've had one purpose in mind: to show the many fascinating ways our gardens and what we grow in them can enhance our everyday lives. As you read each story, I hope that you will learn something new and unexpected about herbs, those plants we cultivate both for their delightful selves and for the many ways they have benefited us and our ancestors, back through the eons to the dawn of human culture. Remember, though, that before you use any herb to treat a physical or mental ailment, you should consult a qualified herbalist. Since China Bayles is only a fictional character, you can't take her word for it!

—Susan Wittig Albert
Bertram, Texas
March 2002

STORY NOTES

THE CHARACTERS

If you're not already acquainted with the books in the China Bayles mystery series, there are a few things you may want to know about the major characters you'll meet in this collection of short stories.

China Bayles is the owner of Thyme and Seasons Herbs. Some years ago, she left her successful profession as a criminal defense attorney and moved to Pecan Springs, a picturesque town halfway between Austin and San Antonio, on the eastern edge of the Texas Hill Country. She bought a century-old stone building a couple of blocks from Courthouse Square, started her shop, and began a kinder, gentler life that is enlivened by the occasional mystery. China is forty-something, has brownish hair with a wide streak of gray, and is always intending to go on a diet and exercise more. She's quick, clever, and (according to her intuitive, right-brained friend Ruby) far too logical and left-brained. She's always trying to find a balance between her need for personal independence and her desire to be connected to people she cares about, like Mike McQuaid. She and McQuaid were married in the book *Lavender Lies*. With McQuaid's teenaged son, Brian, and grouchy basset hound, Howard Cosell, they live in a large Victorian house on Limekiln Road, a few miles outside of Pecan Springs.

Mike McQuaid, China's husband, is a former Houston homicide detective, now a part-time professor in the Criminal Justice Department at Central Texas State University and a part-time private detective. He's six feet tall, broad-shouldered, and dark-haired, with a twice-broken nose and a been-there-done-that face that just misses being handsome. A shoot-out with a drug gang (in *Love Lies Bleeding*) left him walking with a limp. He collects guns, plays poker with his buddies, and is usually around when China needs him.

Ruby Wilcox is China's best friend and confidante. She owns the Crystal Cave, Pecan Springs's only New Age shop, where she sells such items as tarot cards, rune stones, crystals, and books on astrology, the occult, and the Inner Journey. Not long ago, she and China converted the apartment that adjoined their shops (where China lived until she and McQuaid moved in together in *Rosemary Remembered*) into a tearoom called Thyme for Tea. Ruby is a six-foot-something redhead with gingery freckles who loves weird, way-out clothes, although on her, weird looks wonderful. (And anyway, what's totally weird in Pecan Springs is probably your ordinary streetwear in New York or Los Angeles.) Ruby also loves to imagine herself as a private detective on the trail of a criminal—Kinsey Milhone, Stephanie Plum, and V. I. Warshawski, all rolled up together.

Sheila Dawson is Pecan Springs's first female police chief and one of China's and Ruby's best friends. She is a willowy, well-dressed blonde who looks like she'd be right at home at the Junior League. But Sheila, a former security chief at CTSU and a fifteen-year veteran of law enforcement, is more at home with a gun on her hip and a badge on her shirt.

AN UNTHYMELY DEATH

Thyme heals all wounds.

—Anonymous

Hey, China, what's that you're planting?"
Ruby Wilcox asked.

I patted the dirt firmly around the base
of the plant and straightened up. "It's
ginkgo," I said.

Ruby Wilcox is my best friend and partner. Her Crystal Cave, the only New Age
shop in Pecan Springs, Texas, is in the same
century-old stone building that houses my

herb shop, Thyme and Seasons, and our jointly owned tearoom, Thyme for Tea. The building is surrounded with herb gardens, and at this moment, I was working in the garden out front.

Thyme and Seasons and its herb gardens are a far cry from the Houston law office where I used to work as a criminal defense attorney. Leaving the law, moving to a small town, and opening my own business—these are the best things I've ever done for myself (second only to marrying Mike McQuaid, that is). And while some people might find small-town life limited or low on thrills and excitement, that hasn't been a problem for me. Between the shop, my family, and my friends, I have just about all the excitement I can handle. And if I want to kick up my heels in the big city, it takes less than an hour to drive from Pecan Springs to either Austin or San Antonio. Altogether, it's a nice arrangement.

Ruby bent over to peer doubtfully at the plant. "That dinky little twig is ginkgo? It's got a heck of a lot of growing to do. The last ginkgo I saw was a tree. A *big* tree." She looked up. "Taller than this building."

"Give it time," I said with a grin, and picked up my shovel. "Like about five hundred years. I started this little guy from a cutting, and it's got some growing to do." The oldest surviving tree on earth, ginkgo was once described by Charles Darwin as a "living fossil," because so many of its primitive botanical features are still intact. Extracts made from its leaves have been used for over five thousand years to improve blood circulation, treat asthma and bronchitis, and enhance memory. And even if it were entirely useless, I would still enjoy the dappled shade created by its fan-shaped green leaves. While this little fellow begins stretching up to his full height, I'm going to put up a sign letting people know that his ancestors were already ancient when humans were just beginning to rub sticks together.

From the back door of the shop, my helper, Laurel Riley, waved at me. "You're wanted on the phone, China," she called. "It's Hannah Bucher."

"Oh, good," I said, shouldering my shovel and heading for the shop, Ruby tagging along behind. Hannah is a seventy-something herb gardener who lives in Cedar Crossing, not far away. She specializes in thyme, growing and selling dozens of different varieties of this beautiful herb. She had promised to give me some plants of a new cultivar of lemon thyme, so I could try it in my garden. I'd been waiting impatiently for her call.

But Hannah hadn't phoned to talk about herbs. Instead, she'd called to ask me to come to Cedar Crossing to see her, and something in her voice prompted me to ask why.

"It's an urgent personal matter," she said. She lowered her voice, as if she were afraid she

Thyme is an aromatic perennial herb that's a favorite for culinary, landscape, and medicinal uses. Grow it from cuttings or root divisions, in a dry sandy soil in full sun. Harvest by cutting a few stems (or even the entire plant) and hang it to dry in a dark, dry place. In the kitchen, use fresh or dried thyme in stews, fish dishes, and with beef, lamb, pork, or poultry. (Lemon thyme is especially good with fish and chicken and in lemon desserts.) In the medicine cabinet, you'll find thyme oil in many commercial preparations, such as mouthwashes and hemorrhoid salves. The plant has a long association with the afterworld, and in some cultures, it was believed that after death, the soul found sanctuary in its blossoms. In non-Christian cultures, thyme was strewn on the corpse to ease the passage into the next world.

might be overheard. "I hate to say it, China, but I'm afraid someone is—" She stopped, and then in a lighter, brighter voice, went on: "I *do* hope you'll be able to come and get those lemon thyme plants soon. I've been saving them for you. When can you come?"

I glanced at the calendar. McQuaid and Brian—my husband and our thirteen-year-old—were going to Houston the next weekend to catch an Astros game. "How about Sunday?" I asked. Ruby and I had been meaning to visit our friends Barbara Thatcher and Ramona Pierce, who also live in Cedar Crossing.

"Sunday would be fine." Hannah's voice became low and urgent again. "Unless you can come sooner. And please bring Ruby. I need to talk to both of you."

Frowning, I hung up and went to the door of the Crystal Cave. As usual, Ruby was burning her own handcrafted herbal incense, which creates a perfect backdrop for the tarot cards, rune stones, crystals, and books on astrology and the occult that she sells.

"Want to drive over to Cedar Crossing on Sunday?" I asked.

Ruby pushed a curl of henna-red hair out of her eyes and looked up from the stack of books she was shelving. "Your plants are ready?"

"Yes, but that isn't why Hannah called. She wants to talk to us. It sounds like something's wrong."

Ruby gave me a curious look. "What do you suppose is going on?"

"I don't know," I said, feeling troubled. "I guess we'll find out on Sunday."

Since the early days of human culture, fragrant herbs have been burned to enhance spiritual experience or just to cleanse and sweeten the air. (Can you imagine what some of those closed-up cave dwellings might have been like without the fragrant scent of burning juniper?) Here is a recipe you can try.

RUBY'S HERBAL INCENSE

*4 parts powdered makko**
1 part powdered sandalwood
1 part powdered cinnamon
1 part powdered cloves
1 part powdered star anise
1 part powdered frankincense

Add enough warm water to make a pliant dough. Knead thoroughly. Shape into small cones and let dry for a day or so, at room temperature.

*Makko, the powdered bark of a small evergreen tree, acts as a binder and a burning agent, making the use of charcoal unnecessary. You can purchase it at herb or craft shops.

But Hannah never got a chance to tell us what was bothering her. On Friday, I learned that she was dead.

"A heart attack?" Ruby asked, her eyes widening when I told her.

"That's what the newspaper says." I handed her the obituary that Ramona Pierce had clipped out of the Cedar Crossing *Tattler* and faxed to me. "Apparently, she died the day after we talked. She's being buried tomorrow."

"What a shame," Ruby said sadly. "Hannah was such a lovely, vibrant woman. I had no idea she had heart trouble."

"Neither had I." I frowned, thinking about the tone of Hannah's voice when she had said that she needed to talk to us, urgently. "What would you think about going to Cedar Crossing anyway? I really would like to have those plants Hannah was saving for me."

"And I'd like to see Ramona and Barbara," Ruby said in a decided tone. "Let's do it."

Cedar Crossing is a pretty village, built on the bank of the Guadalupe River. Its chief claim to fame is a simple white-painted church with a delicate steeple, built by the German settlers who established the town 150 years ago. Hannah's house and gardens were just down the road from the church. On Sunday afternoon, Ruby and I drove slowly past, admiring the sprays of bright foliage that spilled over the stone wall. The sunny yellow blooms of St. John's wort were brilliant against the feathery purple leaves of a tall bronze fennel, and golden-leaved feverfew splashed at the foot of a sprawling gray-blue Russian sage.

When I saw a woman pushing a wheelbarrow down the path, I pulled over and stopped. I studied her for a moment, then turned to Ruby. "I'd like to talk to her," I said. "But let's pretend we don't know anything about Hannah's death."

Ruby gave me a curious look. "Why would we do that?"

"I don't know." I shrugged. "Just a hunch, I guess."

Ruby grinned. She is the kind of person who always trusts a hunch. "Go for it," she said. "Get that right brain in gear."

A Splash of Colorful Herbs

If you think of herbs as green or gray plants, uninteresting and nondescript, think again! You can use their blooms and their foliage to fill your garden with color — and reap the special benefits that each provides.

- St. John's wort (*Hypericum perforatum*) was traditionally gathered at the summer solstice to ward off evil spirits. This perennial herb has gained attention in recent years for its use as an effective antidepressant. Grow it for its beautiful yellow flowers, and steep its leaves and blossoms in vegetable oil (in a cool place) to make a soothing, anti-inflammatory massage oil that can speed the healing of wounds and bruises.

- With its striking, feather-plumed leaves, bronze fennel (*Foeniculum vulgare*) is a striking relative of dill, carrot, and Queen Anne's lace. Use fennel's anise-flavored seeds in salads and soups and, for a unique taste, in sausage dishes. As an endearing bonus, fennel will attract the colorful swallowtail butterfly to your garden.

- Feverfew (*Chrysanthemum parthenium*) is primarily grown as a medicinal herb, but its white daisylike flowers are also quite pretty — and healing, too. If you suffer from migraines, try chewing a few leaves every day. Recent research suggests that the herb is an effective treatment for some types of migraine.

- Russian sage (*Perovskia atriplicifolia*) is a wonderfully aromatic perennial, with long downy stems and finely cut gray leaves. It produces an airy cloud of blue-gray blossoms and will attract throngs of nectar-hungry bees.

The woman behind the wheelbarrow was tanned and athletic-looking, with dark brown hair twisted into a loose, thick braid down her back. She wore a red bandana headband, a sweatshirt and jeans, and heavy garden gloves. Her face was stern and unsmiling.

"Hi," I said cheerfully. "I'm China Bayles, and this is Ruby Wilcox."

The woman frowned. "China Bayles. Aren't you the person who wanted some of Hannah's lemon thyme?"

"That's me. Hannah said we could pick up the plants anytime." I shaded my eyes with my hands and looked around. "Is she here?"

"Hannah's dead." The woman pressed her lips tightly together. "She died early Wednesday morning."

Ruby's hand went to her mouth. "Oh, dear!" she exclaimed, as if this were the first she'd heard of it. "An accident?"

"They say it was a heart attack." The woman's voice was taut, and she wasn't looking at us. "The funeral was yesterday." She nodded in the direction of the church. "She's buried in the churchyard."

"I am *so* sorry," I said quietly. "Hannah was a lovely person." I looked around the garden, which must have covered at least two acres. The fragrance of honeysuckle and roses surrounded us. "It's so sad to think that she won't be here to take care of this beautiful garden. I hope the next person who owns it will love it as much as she did."

The woman's eyes flashed an enigmatic message. "I'll take care of it," she said roughly. "I promised Hannah I would."

"Managing a garden this size is a big job," I said. "It takes a lot of skill and knowledge. You really have to love it."

"That's why Hannah did what she did," the woman said. She turned toward the house and a look of something like hatred crossed her face. "And no matter what they say," she burst out passionately, "she wanted me to have it after she died."

"Who do you suppose 'they' are?" Ruby whispered to me as the woman strode away, pushing her wheelbarrow. "And who is she?"

"I have no idea," I said. I glanced toward the house. Another woman, short and plump and wearing a blue apron, was standing on the back porch, under the golden tangle of hops vines that covered the roof. At one time, Hannah had brewed her own beer, and had even given lectures on the subject.

The woman saw us and beckoned. "Let's talk to her," I said to Ruby. "Maybe she knows what's going on."

"You must be China and Ruby," the woman said as we approached the porch. "Aunt Hannah told me you might be here." She bit her lip. "I suppose you know that she died several days ago."

Hops

Before the advent of commercial brewing, beers were regularly brewed at home, from wild or cultivated herbs. Over the centuries, literally hundreds of plants have been used to make beer. Among the more familiar are dandelions, nettles, sarsaparilla, ginger, sassafras, borage, yellow dock, pennyroyal, and even mustard. Hops (*Humulus lupulus*) began to be added when it was learned that this herb could keep the beer from spoiling. For more on this fascinating subject, read *Sacred and Herbal Healing Beers: The Secrets of Ancient Fermentation,* by Stephen Harrod Buhner.

The kitchen was almost as pretty as the garden, with a cheerful red-checked cloth on the table and windowsills filled with pots of scented geranium. The woman introduced herself as Luella Mitchell, Hannah's niece. As we sat at the table and sipped glasses of iced tea, she told us about the circumstances of Hannah's death.

"It was very sudden," she said. Her round face was sad. "And quite unexpected. I've lived with my aunt for the past three years and even helped take care of her accounts, and I never even suspected that she had a bad heart." She sat down at the kitchen table and pulled a tissue out of her apron pocket to wipe her eyes. "It's so hard to accept."

I leaned forward. "Hannah told me that she wanted to talk to me about an urgent matter. She sounded terribly troubled. Do you know what was bothering her?"

Luella's face tightened. "I certainly do," she said. "She was afraid."

"Afraid?" Ruby put down her glass.

"Of that woman you were talking to, out there in the garden. Jessica Powell, her name is." Luella shook her head sadly. "Jessica killed somebody once, you know. She spent a long time in jail."

"She did?" Ruby breathed.

Luella nodded soberly. "Aunt Hannah realized that she'd made a dangerous mistake, giving Jessica a job and letting her live in the garage apartment. And worse, putting her into her will. The woman has a green thumb, there's no doubt about that. But she moved in and just took over." She shook her head. "Why, she pushed poor Aunt Hannah right out of her own garden!"

"It's true, then, that Jessica Powell will inherit this place?" I asked, remembering what the woman had said.

Luella's face was set. "Aunt Hannah called you, China, because she wanted some legal advice. She'd finally got up the courage to get rid of Jessica. But she died before she could change her will, so I guess—"

She was interrupted by a knock on the screen door. We turned to see two uniformed police officers standing on the porch.

"We're looking for Miz Mitchell," one of them said through the screen. "Hannah Bucher's niece."

"That's me." Luella stood, her face suddenly apprehensive. "Is there something the matter?"

"Afraid so, ma'am." The officer held out a paper. "We have a warrant to search the residence of Jessica Powell."

"My apartment?" Jessica Powell asked angrily. She had suddenly materialized beside the porch. "What are you looking for?"

"Please show us your living quarters, Miz Powell," the officer said without answering her question. The two men followed her through the garden, in the direction of the two-story garage.

"Why have they come?" Luella asked in a bewildered voice. "What are they looking for?"

"Evidence," I said. "They couldn't have gotten a warrant unless they had probable cause to suspect that Jessica Powell had committed a crime."

Ruby's eyes were large. "Murder?" she whispered.

"No, no!" Luella exclaimed. "That's wrong! Aunt Hannah had a heart attack!"

"We'll just have to wait and see," I said grimly.

Fifteen minutes later the officers were back. Jessica Powell was with them, stony-faced and silent—and handcuffed.

"But I don't understand!" Luella exclaimed. "Why are you arresting her? What's she done?"

One officer gave her a sympathetic look. "I'm sorry to have to be the one to tell you this, Miz Mitchell, but your aunt didn't die of natural causes. The autopsy report you requested indicates that she was poisoned."

"Poisoned!" Luella whispered. "But . . . but *how?* What kind of poison?"

The other deputy held up a plastic evidence bag. "Nicotine," he said. In the bag was a can of smoking tobacco.

"Nicotine poisoning?" Ramona Pierce asked blankly. "I've never heard of such a thing."

"I have," Barbara Thatcher said in a grim voice. "Wicked stuff. Terribly toxic."

It was Sunday evening, and Ruby and I and our two hostesses were seated at the table in the dining room of Ramona and Barbara's home, finishing a wonderful dinner of fresh garden vegetables and penne pasta with herbs—one of Barbara's specialty recipes. It was a pretty room, with a pair of French doors that opened out onto a patio bordered with rosemary, and the setting sun cast a golden light over Ramona's garden. The two women had bought the house together the previous year.

PENNE PASTA WITH ROASTED GARDEN VEGETABLES AND HERBS, À LA BARBARA

2 Roma tomatoes, seeded and coarsely chopped
2 zucchini, sliced in half-inch rounds
1 cup diced eggplant
1 small yellow bell pepper, seeded and sliced in thin rings
1 small green bell pepper, seeded and sliced in thin rings
1 cup fresh green beans, cut into half-inch pieces
1 cup sweet red onions, sliced in thin rings
½ cup fresh basil, chopped
¼ cup fresh parsley, chopped
2 tablespoons fresh lemon thyme, minced
3–4 cloves garlic, minced
¼ cup extra virgin olive oil
8 ounces penne or other tubular pasta
Freshly grated Parmesan or Asiago cheese

Toss tomatoes, zucchini, eggplant, bell peppers, green beans, and onions with basil, parsley, lemon thyme, garlic, and olive oil. Arrange in a single layer in a large baking pan. Roast in a 350° oven, stirring occasionally, for 20 to 30 minutes, or until vegetables are slightly softened. When vegetables are nearly done, cook pasta according to package directions, or until al dente. Drain. If you like, place roasted veggies under the broiler until they just begin to char. (Don't overdo it!) Toss roasted vegetables with pasta. Top with a generous grating of Parmesan or Asiago cheese. Serves four generously.

Because of its traditional medicinal and ritual uses, tobacco (*Nicotiana tabacum*) has long been considered an herb. Columbus found tobacco in the New World, where (as he wrote in his journal) he saw "native peoples carrying some sort of cylinder in which sweetly smelling herbs were glowing. The people sucked the other end of the cylinder and, as it were, drank in the smoke." The natives used the plant medicinally and in ritual celebrations, with care. Nicotine is addictive. Taken internally or applied to the skin in high concentrations, it is a virulent poison that can cause fatal cardiac irregularities.

Barbara practices law in San Antonio, and Ramona has her own interior decorating business.

I nodded, agreeing with Barbara. "Tobacco is toxic, all right. It's one of our most problematic herbs."

Ruby looked up from her plate. "You're saying that tobacco is an *herb*?"

"Sure," I said. "It's a member of the nightshade family, like peppers, tomatoes, and eggplant—and potatoes, too." I forked up a few veggies to demonstrate. "Over the centuries, tobacco has been used to treat all kinds of ailments, including cancer. But it is most definitely toxic."

Ramona frowned. "I know that cigarettes are bad news, but—"

"It's not just cigarettes," Barbara said. "When I was in the DA's office, we prosecuted a case where the killer poisoned his victim with a nicotine-based pesticide."

"Gardeners sometimes brew up their own pesticide by steeping cigarettes in water," I said. "Some people have been accidentally poisoned just by getting it on their hands."

Barbara looked at me curiously. "So the police, acting on a tip, searched Jessica Powell's room?"

"And found the tobacco can," Ruby said. "They think she made a nicotine concentrate and somehow administered it to Hannah. In her coffee, maybe, or in some strong-tasting food, like chili."

"But *why*?" Ramona asked, frowning. "Everyone liked Hannah. We'll all miss her."

"Because Jessica was the beneficiary of her will," I said.

"And Hannah had become afraid of her and was planning to change it," Ruby explained. "Jessica must have realized what Hannah had in mind, and decided to take action."

Barbara raised her eyebrows. "Hannah was planning to alter her will?"

"That's why she called China," Ruby explained. "According to Luella Mitchell, her aunt intended to make a new will and—"

"But Hannah just made that will," Barbara said, "not three weeks ago! I know, because I prepared it for her. I can't believe she'd decide to change it without consulting me."

I stared at her. "You were Hannah Bucher's lawyer?"

"For over two years," Barbara replied. "And she never said a word about being afraid. Hannah and Jessica were friends long before I came into the picture. Hannah gave her a place to live and a job right after she got out of prison."

"Jessica killed someone," I remarked. "At least, that's what Hannah's niece told us."

Barbara made a face. "Seven or eight years ago, she shot her abusive husband and spent the next six years in prison. But times have changed. If the case came to trial today, even here in Texas, she'd get a lighter sentence."

RAMONA'S LEMON MADELEINES

½ cup margarine or butter
2 large eggs
¾ cup sugar
¼ cup plain low-fat yogurt
1 teaspoon lemon extract
½ teaspoon vanilla extract
1 cup all-purpose flour
1 teaspoon lemon zest
3 tablespoons fresh lemon thyme leaves, minced
¼ teaspoon salt
Confectioners' sugar

Preheat oven to 400°F. Grease a madeleine pan (twelve shells). In a small saucepan over low heat, melt the margarine or butter; set aside to cool. In a large bowl, beat together eggs, sugar, yogurt, and extracts until blended, occasionally scraping the bowl. Continue beating until light and lemon-colored, about 5 minutes. Blend in melted margarine or butter, flour, grated lemon peel, minced lemon thyme, and salt. Spoon 1 tablespoon batter into each madeleine shell. Bake 10 to 15 minutes until madeleines are golden brown. Immediately remove from pan and place on wire racks to cool. Repeat until all batter is used, greasing pan each time. Sprinkle madeleines lightly with confectioners' sugar. If there are any left (there probably won't be), store them in a tightly covered container to prevent them from softening. Makes about two dozen.

Ramona frowned. "Maybe Hannah just didn't want to tell you that she was afraid of Jessica."

"Maybe," Barbara replied slowly. She didn't sound convinced. "But she *did* tell me that she was afraid of her brother. That was why she didn't want her property to go to him."

"Her brother?" I asked.

Barbara nodded. "Harold. He's Luella's father. When Hannah told him that the house and gardens were going to Jessica, he got so angry that she thought he was going to hit her." She poured herself a second cup of coffee and passed around a plate of lemon madeleines that Ramona had made. "If you ask me, the case against Jessica Powell isn't as open and shut as it might seem."

We could have asked the police to talk to Harold Bucher, but since they had already arrested Jessica Powell, they were probably satisfied that they had the killer in custody. Ruby and I were curious about Hannah's brother, though—and anyway, it was a beautiful Monday morning, and our day off. So we got directions to the Bucher ranch, and after breakfast with Ramona and Barbara, climbed in the car and drove north on Cedar Crossing Road for ten miles or so.

Cattle ranching isn't as profitable as it used to be, and in this part of Texas, a great many of the large ranches have been broken up and sold. Barbara had told us that the Bucher ranch—the B-Bar-R—had been a huge spread once. Now, all that was left was the old ranch house, built of native stone and nestled into a grove of willow trees where Harold Bucher lived.

Around it bloomed a wild garden, filled with wildflowers and herbs: echinacea, tansy, and Joe-Pye weed.

"Looks like Hannah and her brother shared one interest, anyway," Ruby remarked as we got out of the car. "They were both gardeners."

I glanced toward the house. A colorful flock of bantam chickens was chasing bugs through the grass, while a black dog napped on the porch. He raised his head when he saw us and gave a short, sharp bark. A moment later, we saw a stooped old man in denim overalls and a wide-brimmed straw hat, hoe in hand, going through the gate into a vegetable garden. Ignoring us, he began to chop weeds along a row of healthy-looking garlic.

"Are you Mr. Bucher?" Ruby called.

"That's me," the old man said shortly. "What d'ya want?"

We walked closer. "We'd like to talk to you about your sister," I said. "We were friends of hers."

"We were very sorry to hear about her death," Ruby said softly. "It must have been a terrible shock."

Harold Bucher went right on

Willow

Ginkgo isn't the only tree-sized herb. Some ten centuries ago, Egyptian, Greek, and Chinese herbalists recommended willow to lower fever and relieve pain. Now, willow's chief chemical constituent, salicylic acid, appears in every medicine cabinet — as aspirin. We take it not only for pain relief, but to help prevent heart attacks. Other herbal trees include juniper (its berries are used medicinally and to flavor gin), hawthorn (a cardiac tonic), chaste tree (once used to treat malaria, as well as respiratory ailments, although it was thought to reduce sexual desire), and eucalyptus (antibacterial and antibiotic, used to treat fevers and malaria).

hoeing. The man might have been in his late seventies, his face lined and gray, his eyes slitted against the bright sun. "She was an old woman," he said sourly. "People die when they get old."

"But your sister didn't die of old age," I replied. "You've heard the results of the autopsy?"

"Luella told me. Said the sheriff arrested that Jessica woman for poisoning her." The old man turned his head and spat. "Well, all I got to say is, Hannah's fancy new will won't do Jessica no damn good in jail."

He was right, of course. A murderer cannot profit from her crime. If Jessica Powell was convicted of killing Hannah, she wouldn't inherit. But who would?

"Are you Hannah's nearest relative?" I asked.

> ### Echinacea
>
> Many plants found growing in the wild have had important medicinal uses. Echinacea (*Echinacea angustifolia* or *E. purpurea*) is a native American herb with drooping purple petals around an orange center. It is said to boost the immune system and fight colds, flu, and yeast infections. The yellow button-shaped flowers of tansy (*Tanacetum vulgare*) are a pretty accent in the garden. A bitter herb, tansy was used medicinally as a blood cleanser and tonic. It is not native to North America, but became naturalized here when it was brought by colonists. Joe-Pye weed (*Eupatorium purpureum*) is another American native. It takes its common name from the Indian doctor Joe Pye, who publicized its many medicinal uses. Butterflies love all three of these plants.

"What if I am?" He eyed me obliquely. "How come you wanna know?"

I shrugged. "Just curious, that's all." I looked around the place. It must not be easy for a man his age to live so far from civilization. What if he got sick? "You ever think of moving into Cedar Crossing?"

Garlic

Garlic (*Allium sativum*) has been called the "herbal wonder drug" for its many medicinal uses. It has been found in Sumerian caves where early humans lived over twelve millennia ago. It has powerful antibiotic properties and has been used to stave off colds and flu, lower blood pressure, and reduce serum cholesterol levels. And of course, its flavor can't be beat. To make a tasty, heart-healthy spread, mince 4 cloves of garlic and stir into 1 cup of low-cholesterol margarine. Add 1 tablespoon each of minced fresh basil, chives, and parsley. Stir in 1 tablespoon of lemon juice. Keep tightly covered until used.

"My girl Luella's been after me to move," he said grudgingly. "Reckon I might, if I could find me a pretty place with a nice garden." He spat again. "Wouldn't feel right if I couldn't get dirt under my fingernails every day."

I nodded, knowing how he felt. My fingernails have dirt under them most of the time. I wondered if the "pretty place" he had in mind was Hannah's. "Did you visit your sister often?"

He stopped hoeing and straightened up. "Saw her the day 'fore she died. We had some fam'ly business to transact. Didn't get it done, though. Got interrupted by that nosy neighbor of hers. Mildred Rawlins." He reached into the pocket of his bib overalls. "You wanna know about Hannah, you see Mildred. Her an' Hannah was thick as a pair of thieves."

He took his hand out of his pocket. He was holding a can of chewing tobacco.

"Do you think Hannah's brother could have killed her?" Ruby asked thoughtfully as we drove back to Cedar Crossing.

"He seems to have had a motive," I said. "According to Barbara, he was furious about the will. And from what he said about wanting a place with a nice garden, I'd guess that he was hoping to inherit Hannah's house."

"Not just motive, but means," Ruby replied grimly. "Did you see that can of chewing tobacco? And he admitted that he was with Hannah the day before she died, so he had opportunity, as well!"

"It's certainly something to think about," I agreed. "Let's see what Hannah's neighbor has to say."

Mildred Rawlins's garden was smaller than Hannah's, but very pretty and bordered with a low, clipped hedge of german-der, a plant that was cultivated in many medieval apothecary gardens for its usefulness in treating rheumatism and gout. Ruby and I were knocking at the front door when she came around the house, carrying a tray of seedlings. She was a tall, thin woman with gray hair in short, tight curls all over her head. We introduced ourselves, but she already seemed to know who we were. She put down the tray and invited us in.

Ruby and I went into the living room while Mildred went for tea and cookies. She obviously enjoyed garden crafts, and the room was full of her work — bouquets of dried flowers, some small framed pictures made with delicate arrangements of pressed pansies, lavender, and dried herbs, and a sweet-smelling bowl of rose potpourri.

In a few moments, Mildred was back with a tray. "Hannah talked about you two often," she said, pouring a fragrant tea out of a china pot. "She was anxious for your visit. She hoped you could help her." She sighed heavily. "I certainly do miss her. We were good friends — it's hard to believe she's gone."

ROSE POTPOURRI

2 cups dried rose petals
1 cup dried lavender
1/2 cup rosemary leaves
3 bay leaves, broken
1 tablespoon ground cinnamon
2 teaspoons grated nutmeg
2 teaspoons whole cloves
1 teaspoon powdered cloves
2 tablespoons orris root powder (to serve as a fixative)
6 to 8 drops rose oil
Dried rosebuds for decoration

Mix dried ingredients together and toss with rose oil. Place in a covered container for 6 weeks, stirring or shaking daily, to blend the fragrances. Display potpourri in a pretty bowl or basket, and renew scent with rose oil when necessary.

"Did she tell you what she wanted to talk to us about?" I asked.

"Not directly," Mildred said. "But I got the idea that something odd was going on and she hoped you'd help her straighten it out."

"Her death was tragic," Ruby said with a sigh. "I'm glad they've caught the killer."

"I wouldn't be too sure about that if I was you," Mildred replied darkly. "Jessica Powell isn't much liked around here. Folks don't forget or forgive the past, and that husband she killed grew up in this little town. But Hannah gave Jessica a job and a place to live when she got out of prison. That took courage, and Jessica was grateful. She'd never have done anything to harm Hannah."

"They found a can of tobacco in her room," I pointed out.

"What does that prove?" Mildred tossed her head. "Lots of folks in this town have tobacco in their houses. Cigarettes, pipe tobacco, chewing tobacco. Even nicotine patches. I read somewhere that you can die if you put too many of those patches on yourself."

"But if Jessica didn't do it," Ruby asked reasonably, "who did?"

Mildred shook her head, tight-lipped. "I'm not one to accuse, mind you. But that brother of Hannah's—he's a devious old man, with a terrible temper. And he was here the day before Hannah died. I know because I walked in on them. They were having a fight."

"What were they fighting about?" I asked.

"About the house, that's what," Mildred said fiercely. "They'd been arguing about it ever since Hannah made that will." She stood up and went to a corner cupboard. "Hannah asked me to keep something for her until you got here." She turned, holding a large manila envelope.

"What's in it?" Ruby asked curiously as I took the envelope.

"Papers," Mildred said with a little shrug. "That's all Hannah told me—just some old papers."

It was almost noon by the time we got back to Barbara and Ramona's house. Barbara was still at her office, but we found Ra-

If you have room for only one herb in your garden, make it a scented geranium (*Pelargonium graveolens*). You can use the fragrant leaves for potpourri, teas, drinks, and desserts, as well as jellies, sauces, and even vinegars. Growing beside a path where you can brush against it, this generous plant will share its scent with you each time you pass. Among the popular favorites are rose, lemon, orange, apricot, grapefruit, and strawberry scents. Plan to bring these tender plants inside during the winter.

mona at the picnic table in the backyard, repotting several scented geraniums.

"Hi," she said, looking up from her project. "Did you learn anything new?"

Ruby shrugged. "We learned plenty—we just haven't figured out what it means. Let's have a look, China."

I opened the envelope Mildred Rawlins had given us and slid the contents onto the table. But if we were hoping to see something dramatic—a threatening note, or a map to a long-lost treasure, or old love letters tied with a faded pink ribbon—we were disappointed.

"Why, these are nothing but canceled checks," Ruby said, sounding disappointed. She picked up one of the two rubber-banded bundles and flipped through it. "They're all made out to the Texas Fidelity Investment Company. Looks like they go back about three years." She pointed to the signature. "They've all been signed by Hannah."

I glanced through the other bundle. "These are made out to Texas Fidelity, too." I looked closer. "There's an account number typed on the check." I read it aloud.

Ruby frowned. "But these checks have a *different* account number. Hannah had two accounts?"

"I wonder why she wrote the checks but typed the account

numbers," Ramona remarked. "If I were going to the trouble of typing anything, I'd type everything. Except for my signature, of course."

"Maybe somebody else typed the numbers," Ruby suggested.

"Maybe Hannah didn't know there were two accounts," I said slowly. "Maybe, when she signed the check, she thought she was depositing the money in her regular account. Then somebody else typed in the account numbers—making some deposits to Hannah's regular account, and some to a second account."

Ruby snapped her fingers. "And then maybe Hannah discovered the second account and figured out that somebody was stealing her money! And that's when she called you, China—to help her put a stop to it."

Ramona stood up. "I'll phone Barbara and tell her what you've found. As Hannah's lawyer, she can contact the investment company and get the names on those accounts."

Barbara called back in fifteen minutes with what she had learned. Ramona put the call on the speaker phone, so we could all hear.

"You were right, China," Barbara said. "There were two investment accounts. One is in Hannah's name, and has about thirty thousand dollars in it. When the other account was closed last Thursday, the balance was nearly seventy thousand."

"Last Thursday!" Ruby exclaimed.

"The day after Hannah died," I said. "That can't be a coincidence. Whose name was on the account?"

"Jessica's?" Ramona asked.

"Hannah's brother?" Ruby guessed.

"Hannah's niece," I said.

"That's right," Barbara said. "The name on the account was Luella Mitchell."

"But just because Luella was investing her aunt's money under her own name doesn't mean she's a killer," Ruby pointed out.

"Let's see if we can reconstruct what might have happened," I said. "Luella figured out that her aunt had discovered her scheme and was planning to expose it—and perhaps to have her charged with embezzlement. She brewed a nicotine concentrate and put a fatal dose into her aunt's coffee, or into some other strong-tasting food. Hannah died of cardiac arrest, and everybody thought it was a simple heart attack."

"Until," Ruby said, "the autopsy report came back."

"Right," I said. "The autopsy that Luella herself had requested. If she hadn't insisted on an autopsy, the death would have been put down to natural causes."

"So what are you saying, China?" Ramona asked, frowning.

"I'm saying that Luella wanted the autopsy in order to prove that her aunt had died of nicotine poisoning. Then she hid the tobacco can under Jessica's mattress and tipped off the police that it was there."

"But why incriminate Jessica?" Ramona asked in a puzzled tone. "If all Luella wanted was to get out from under a possible embezzlement charge—"

"Because," Ruby said triumphantly, "that's not *all* Luella wanted. If Jessica were convicted of Hannah's murder, she couldn't inherit Hannah's estate."

"Exactly," I said. "Hannah's property would go to her brother, Harold. And he's an old man. It wouldn't be long before everything belonged to his daughter."

"It makes sense," Ramona said reluctantly, "but it's just a theory. How are you going to *prove* it?"

"I wonder," I said, "where that can of smoking tobacco came from. It was an odd brand, as I recall. Duke's, wasn't it?"

"Yes, that's it," Ruby said. "You don't suppose Luella would have been careless enough to buy it around here, do you?"

As it turned out, that was exactly what had happened. It took us less than an hour to canvass three convenience stores and the only grocery in town. In the end, we found one that carried that particular brand of tobacco, and a curious clerk who remembered Luella's purchase.

"We don't sell that brand very often," she said, "so I remember. It was a lady that bought it, which kind of surprised me, since smoking tobacco ain't exac'ly what most women around here buy. They smoke cigarettes, y' know—and they don't usually roll their own. But I figgered maybe she was gittin' it for somebody else."

Once we had the clerk's statement, it didn't take long to convince the sheriff to arrange a lineup and persuade Luella to be a part of it. The clerk identified her without hesitation. Confronted with the evidence of her crime—the tobacco purchase and the second investment account—Luella broke down and confessed. The case became even stronger when the police found Luella's fingerprint on the inside of the tobacco can lid.

Not long after, Jessica was a free woman.

"I don't know how to thank you," she said to Ruby and me as we stood together in Hannah's garden—hers, now.

"We don't need any thanks," I said. Around us, the thyme that Hannah had planted was blooming, each bush covered with bees gorging themselves on the fragrant nectar. I thought of an old bit of folklore I'd heard once—that each thyme blossom contains the soul of a departed loved one—and felt glad that Jessica would be around to take care of the garden and carry on Hannah's tradition of growing thyme. "It's enough to know that the garden will go on, just as Hannah wanted it to."

Jessica's smile made her face almost pretty. "Yeah. Well, that'll happen, for sure. But in the meantime, don't forget these." She bent over to pick up a tray of sturdy lemon thyme seedlings.

So Ruby and I drove home. Hannah's untimely death was tragic, yes. But now I'd have a bit of her garden, growing in my own. And as someone said once, "Thyme heals all wounds."

The Khat
Who Became
a Hero

IT was a gray, drizzly Tuesday afternoon
outside, but inside Thyme and Seasons, the
air was sweet and lavender-scented, soft
music was coming through the open door
of Ruby Wilcox's Crystal Cave, and I had
just finished happily hanging a dozen bright
red chile-pepper ristras on the wall, carefully handcrafted by my friend Carmelita.
Every now and then, as I look around my
shop, I have the feeling that my life is
complete. A wonderful husband and son,
work that I enjoy in a business of my own,

Ristras are fun and easy to make. To create a small one, you'll need about 4 dozen fresh, unblemished red chile peppers, with stems; 3 pieces of cotton string, 24" long; an untwisted coat hanger; and a pair of rubber gloves. Don't use green (unripe) peppers or peppers with soft spots. And peppers can burn you, so be sure to wear the gloves and work in a place with good ventilation.

1. You will be tying five clusters of three peppers on each string. To assemble the clusters, hold three peppers by their stems and wrap the string around the stems twice. Pull the string upward between two of the peppers and pull it tight. Make a half-hitch with the string, loop it over all three stems, and pull it snug. Make the next cluster above this one. Continue making clusters about every three inches on the string, until you have made five. Then make two additional strings.

2. Suspend the untwisted coat hanger from the back of a chair. Form a large loop in the bottom end to keep the peppers from sliding off. Then twist or "braid" the pepper strings around the wire, pushing them down toward the loop. You will be working from bottom to top, layering trios of peppers on top of trios of peppers. Distribute the peppers for a balanced effect, and continue twisting until you've used all the peppers. Don't worry about the loops of string between the clusters—they'll be hidden in the center of the ristra. Cut off the excess wire at the top, make a loop for hanging, and decorate your ristra with a raffia bow.

3. Hang your ristra outside in the sun to dry, and bring it indoors if the weather is wet. (You don't want those peppers to mold.) As they dry, the peppers will lose most of their weight. When dry, you can remove them from the ristra as you need them for cooking.

and a quiet life in a pretty place. What more could anybody want?

Except that something was definitely missing from this state of perfection, and I was worried about it. Khat's kitty dish was full of his low-calorie kitty food, his catnip mouse was lurking in the corner, and his favorite kitty cat-nap pillow was waiting on the windowsill. But Khat himself was nowhere to be found.

Khat—an inordinately large Siamese who looks out on the world with a serene air of imperial authority—has been Top Cat at Thyme and Seasons for the last four or five years. He originally belonged to a lady who had the misfortune to die under mysterious circumstances. Alone in the world, without someone to look after, he appointed himself my guardian and declared that he intended to spend all of his nine lives making sure that I behaved properly.

At the time, I could take cats or leave them (preferably the latter), but my wishes apparently don't count for much. When Khat makes up his feline mind to something, no mere fallible human can dispute him. I did, however, reserve the right to give this animal a new name. His deceased owner had called him Pudding, which suited him about as well as a filmy Victoria's Secret bra suits me. But nothing else came to mind, and I fell into the habit of calling him Cat, or The Cat, which seemed perfectly appropriate. When Ruby objected that The Cat was not sufficiently distinctive for an animal with such a sovereign air, we compromised on Khat, which Ruby instantly amended to Khat K'o Kung. She is a great fancier of Koko, Qwilleran's talented Siamese cat-sleuth in the Cat Who mysteries, and has always wanted a cat who could tell time, read backwards, and had fourteen tales.

Khat K'o Kung adopted me when I still lived in my bachelor quarters behind the shop. After McQuaid and I moved together to the house on Limekiln Road, I tried to take Khat with me. But after a week's trial, he announced that he refused to share any part of his life with Howard Cosell, McQuaid's crotchety old basset hound, and preferred to live in the shop from here on out, thank you very much.

So that's the way it is. Every morning, I unlock the door, step inside, and Khat wraps himself around my ankles, purring loudly enough to be heard at the Alamo. If I'm late, he's waiting impatiently on the front stoop, charcoal tail wrapped around his four charcoal feet, blue eyes blinking his displeasure at my dismal lack of punctuality. Next stop, kitty food bowl, and just a little extra liver, please, to make up for your lateness.

Except that this morning, Khat wasn't waiting on the stoop, or in the store, or next door, in Ruby's Crystal Cave. He wasn't chasing grasshoppers in the gardens, either, or terrorizing mice in the stone stable behind the shop, where I sometimes teach herb classes. At first, I hadn't been very worried. But it was almost closing time, and since Khat was not only about to miss his breakfast, but dinner as well, I was beginning to get concerned.

"Here's the menu for the Friends luncheon on Friday, China." It was Janet, the cook who manages the kitchen at Thyme for Tea, the tearoom that Ruby and I opened nearly two years ago. Short and dumpling-shaped, with merry hazel eyes and a cheerful face framed by curly brown hair, Janet has the look of a cherubic Munchkin. A couple of months ago, she went to Dallas to a week-long school for gourmet cooks, and ever since, she's been trying out the new dishes she learned. From the look of her menu, she was about to spring some gourmet surprises on the Friends of the Pecan Springs Library.

> **Janet's Menu for the Friends of the Library Luncheon**
>
> **Spicy Tomato Juice Cocktail**
>
> **Herbed Breadsticks**
>
> **Fresh Green Salad with Cherry Tomatoes, Mushrooms, and Bocconcini**
>
> **Chicken in Sun-Dried Tomato Sauce, Served over Pasta**
>
> **Ginger-Peachy Melons**

"Makes me hungry just to read this, Janet," I said, scanning the items. I squinted at the salad. "Bocconcini? What's that?"

"Mozzarella balls," Janet explained. "Marinated in olive oil and basil vinegar, with red pepper flakes." She looked smug. "One of the gourmet tricks I learned in school."

"Maybe it's a little too gourmet for the Friends of the Library?" I suggested tentatively.

"We have to raise their standards," Janet replied. "Otherwise, I'd be flippin' burgers and fryin' up onion rings, like Lila Jennings over at the Diner." She frowned. "I hope I don't have any trouble finding those little balls in Pecan Springs. Guess I better give young Mr. Cavette a call and see if he can get them."

"Speaking of finding," I said, handing the menu back to her, "have you seen Khat? He wasn't here when I opened this morning." I gestured toward his dish. "His breakfast is still waiting."

"Oh, dear." Janet looked distressed. "Poor kitty, he'll starve."

"Not for a few months yet," I said dryly. Khat tops the scale at eighteen pounds, and although I feed him a low-calorie cat food and watch the snacks, he never seems to lose any weight. A few missed breakfasts might be a blessing in disguise. "But it would be nice if he'd check in so I could quit worrying about him," I added.

"I'm sure he'll be here in the morning," Janet said reassuringly. "You know how he feels about his security job."

I nodded. At night, Khat likes to pretend he's a Rottweiler, as one startled Pecan Springs patrolman discovered when he thought he saw somebody lurking in the shadows after midnight. Khat leaped off the arbor and sank his claws into the cop's shoulder. Trespassers, beware. Thyme and Seasons is patrolled by an attack cat who takes his work seriously.

But on Wednesday morning, Khat was still AWOL. I left Ruby to mind the store for an hour, climbed on my bike, and rode around the neighborhood, looking and calling. As I biked past old Mr. Cowan's house, Miss Lula, his yappy little Peke, dashed out of the shrubbery and snapped at my sneaker. I said a few nasty words under my breath, and Mr. Cowan rose up out of the bushes, a pair of binoculars in one gnarled hand and a bird book in the other.

"Don't you kick poor little Miss Lula," he cried.

I braked. "I wasn't going to kick her," I replied warily, as the dog danced around me, cursing me in Chinese. Miss Lula is about the size of a half-grown possum, but her teeth are like needles. "I'm looking for my cat. Have you seen him?"

"Nah," Mr. Cowan said. He pulled down the brim of his Texas Rangers baseball cap. "Lost, is he? Run away from home? Got smashed flat by a car, mebbe?"

I shuddered. "I hope not, but I haven't seen him since yesterday."

"Good riddance, if ya ask me," Mr. Cowan said cheerfully. "The birds around here 'ud be a whole lot chirpier if that durn cat was to take a hike. Why, just last week, I caught him stalkin' a grackle out in the alley. Woulda got him, too, if Miss Lula hadn't of broke it up." He cackled. "Damn funny, it was. The grackle squawkin', the cat cussin' and gnashin' his teeth, and Miss Lula so proud of herself she could spit. I heaved a zucchini at him."

Since the Pecan Springs City Council spends ten thousand dollars a year to make life unpleasant for the grackles, I hardly thought it was sporting of Mr. Cowan and Miss Lula to keep Khat from doing his little bit in defense of clean windshields. But I only sighed and said, "If you see him, let me know, will you?"

"Don't count on it," Mr. Cowan said. "I got a soft spot in my heart fer grackles." He frowned. "Janet said she wanted some of my cherry tomatoes for that party on Friday. Tell her she better get herself over here and pick 'em 'fore the coons do. I got a mama coon and two babies livin' under the garage. Cutest little guys on four feet — 'ceptin' fer you, Miss Lula," he added hastily.

"I'll tell her," I said, wondering if the presence of a mother raccoon in the neighborhood might have anything to do with Khat's extended absence. I don't think a coon would attack a cat, especially one as large and formidable as Khat K'o Kung, but you never know. I shook my head. It was something else to worry about.

Mr. Cowan sat back down in the bushes. Licking her doggie chops, Miss Lula watched me out of sight.

A block farther on, I saw Vivian Baxter out in her garden, hoeing. She wore a wide-brimmed straw hat and was completely enveloped, chin to ankles, in a brown cotton smock that made her look like Brother Cadfael. I climbed off my bike and leaned it against a tree.

"I'm looking for Khat," I said. "Have you see him?"

Vivian's face darkened. "If I had," she said shortly, "I'd have taken the flyswatter to his royal backside." She gestured. "Just look."

"Oh, dear," I said. I bent over and peered at a dozen small green plants — broken, mangled, and flattened, their roots drying pitifully in the sun. I picked a leaf and sniffed it. "Catnip," I said.

"You don't have to tell me what they are," Vivian said resentfully. "I planted them myself, a whole dozen, just yesterday. And this isn't the first time they've been destroyed. Last year, I put a few in a window box, but the cats climbed the wall and

Catnip (*Nepeta cataria*), is a member of the mint family. This perennial has been cultivated for centuries for both culinary and medicinal use. In England during the Renaissance, the fresh leaves were sprinkled on green salads and the dried herb, mixed with sage and thyme, was used as a seasoning rub for meats. Before Chinese tea became available, everyone drank a tea brewed from the catnip they grew in their gardens. In contrast to the stimulant quality of Chinese tea, catnip tea had a calming effect and was used to induce sleep, quiet upset nerves, and soothe upset stomachs. It was also used to treat colds and flu, reduce fevers, and bring on menstruation. (It shouldn't be used by pregnant women.)

All felines, from tiny housecats to large lions, are attracted to catnip by a chemical called nepetalactone, which induces a harmless physiological reaction that seems to be psychosexual. That is, catnip has both a euphoric and an aphrodisiac effect. Susceptibility, however, seems to be genetic, and varies from cat to cat. Some cats just don't get turned on, while others go . . . well, bananas.

English colonists brought catnip to North America. It adapted easily to its new home and now grows wild across the continent.

In the seventeenth century, it was thought that the root of catnip made people angry and fierce. Public hangmen were given the root to chew before they carried out their duties.

uprooted every plant in the box, along with two scented geraniums and some parsley. Last month, I set out another batch, and the next morning, the bed looked as if a tornado had romped through it. This time, I put chicken wire over the plants, but the durn cats tore up the wire, hid it behind the garage, and *then* tore up the catnip." She made a plaintive noise. "Wretched beasts. Why can't they leave it alone?"

"On behalf of Khat and his colleagues," I said ruefully, "I apologize. But the problem is that cats *can't* leave it alone, Vivian. They're genetically programmed to react to the volatile oils. If you want catnip, you might try raising it from seed."

Vivian leaned on her hoe, frowning. "From seed?"

I nodded. "Ever heard the old saying, 'If you set it, the cats will get it. If you sow it, they won't know it'?" When she looked doubtful, I explained. "If you set out transplants, the leaves inevitably get bruised. The oils are released and the cats come running. If you start catnip from seed, the plants may be able to grow to maturity before some passing kitty discovers them."

"I guess I could give it a try," Vivian said. She glanced at me from under the brim of her hat. "You say you've lost your cat? That big, beautiful Siamese?" She sighed. "He's no gentleman where catnip is concerned, but otherwise, he's a charmer."

"I haven't seen him for two days and I'm really worried," I said. "Call me if he comes around, will you?"

"Sure," she said. "By the way, would you tell Janet I'm looking forward to Friday's luncheon. I hear she's serving marinated bocci balls."

"Bocconcini," I said. "Mozzarella cheese balls."

"Is that what they are?" Vivian said dubiously. "Well, I'm

sure people will like them just the same." She frowned. "Probably."

By Thursday morning, I knew I had to do something more productive than simply riding my bike around the neighborhood. I scanned a photo of Khat into the computer, ran off several dozen flyers, and began posting them. My first stop was at Cavette's Grocery, a couple of blocks down Crockett Street.

Cavette's is one of those old family markets that have been almost completely obliterated by the Safeways and Krogers of this world—a small shop with wooden bins and wicker baskets of fresh fruit and veggies lined up on the sidewalk. The Cavettes buy organic produce from local growers, newly baked tortillas from Zapata's Tortilla Factory, and fresh herbs from my garden, in season. It always gives me a lift to see cellophane packages of fresh rosemary and basil and sage, prettied up with a green ribbon and the Thyme and Seasons label.

"Hello, China," young Mr. Cavette wheezed, straightening up from a box of fresh Fredericksburg peaches he was putting out. Young Mr. Cavette must be close to seventy and is bald as an onion. His father, old Mr. Cavette, who sits behind the old-fashioned cash register and rings up all the sales, recently celebrated his ninetieth birthday. The youngest Mr. Cavette, whom everybody calls Junior, is middle-aged and makes deliveries on his red motorbike. The three Cavettes, father, son, and grandson, live next door to the store.

"Hello, Mr. Cavette," I said. I held up my flyer. "Have you seen my cat?"

He took the flyer and held it up to his nose, peering near-sightedly at it. "Well, sure," he said. "This cat shows up whenever Old Pete brings in a batch of fresh fish. Has a special liking for catfish." He grinned and handed back the flyer. "Doesn't care for shrimp, though, or scallops. Just catfish."

"Have you seen him *lately*?" I persisted. "He's been lost since Tuesday."

"Oh, too bad," Mr. Cavette said, sounding sincere. "Lost, huh? Good-lookin' cat like that, somebody prob'ly cat-napped him." He looked down at the peaches in his hand. "Say, didn't Janet tell me she wanted me to save her some fresh peaches and melons for that lunch y'all are havin' on Friday?"

"I guess," I said, dispirited. I hated to think that anybody would be nasty enough to steal Khat. But it's certainly true that customers admire him. When they bend over to pet him, lots of them croon, "Would you like to come home with me and be my very own kitty?" Maybe somebody thought he said, "Yes." But I couldn't let that possibility stop me. "Is it okay if I post this flyer in your window?"

"Sure," Mr. Cavette said. "Pete's bringin' in some catfish this afternoon. If your cat shows up, I'll tell him to scat on home." He picked up a bag. "How many peaches do you reckon Janet wants?"

"A dozen," I hazarded.

He handed me the bag. "Tell her I couldn't get any of that bocorooni stuff she wanted."

"Bocorooni?" I asked. "Do you mean bocconcini?"

He frowned. "Whatever. Olives I can get, artichoke hearts, no problem. I even got them sun-dried tomatoes she wanted, even though they don't look like much to me. We got fresh ones a lot nicer. But botticelli, no way. Janet wants weird specialty stuff like that, she's going to have to drive to San Antonio."

"I'll tell her," I said.

An hour later, I had worked my way to Courthouse Square, posting flyers as I went. I only had two left, so I stopped at the Old Nueces Street Diner and asked Lila Jennings if I could put one in her front window. The Diner, which has a fifties look, is where you go when you're hungry for down-home Texas cooking. You can get breakfast all day, or meat loaf and gravy, chicken and dumplings, pot roast, fried catfish, and Lila's famous jelly doughnuts.

In answer to my question about posting the flyer, she said, "You just go right ahead, honey bun, and tape up that flyer." She swiped at the red Formica counter with a wet rag. With her ruffled pink nylon apron, red lipstick, and penciled eyebrows, Lila also has a fifties look. "I been missin' that sweet ol' tomcat, too," she added. "I always put out a little something for him around lunchtime."

"You do?" I asked, surprised. I hadn't realized that Khat was such an all-around Pecan Springs favorite.

"Why, sure. He's crazy about French fries and cream gravy. Goes after it like he ain't had a good meal in a week." She frowned. "He hasn't been around for a few days, though. Don't suppose he crawled off sick somewhere, do you? He could stand to lose a few pounds, if you ask me. It ain't good for cats to be too heavy, you know."

I agreed. But if Khat was eating Lila's French fries and cream gravy for lunch, I could see why his low-calorie cat food hadn't done a thing for him. "If you see him," I said, "please put him in a closet and call me right away."

Lila arched her skinny eyebrows. "Put that cat in a closet? It'd be like tryin' to shut a mountain lion into the privy. But if I see him, I'll sure let you know." She poured herself a cup of coffee and dumped sugar into it, giving me a quizzical look. "What's this I hear about Janet cookin' up some sort of married cheese stuff for the Friends of the Library?"

"It's marinated cheese," I said. "Little balls of mozzarella, soaked in basil vinegar. They go in a salad."

"Cheese in vinegar?" Lila gave a delicate shudder. "Don't sound just real good to me. Is that girl sure she knows what she's doin'?"

"Of course she does," I said defensively. "Janet's been to cooking school."

Lila gave me a look that said, plain as day, that cooking school was part of the problem. She leaned against the counter, sipping her coffee. "Well, if the Friends turn up their noses at married cheese, you just send 'em on over here. Friday is meat loaf. I ain't no gourmet cook, but nobody ever has a bad word to say about my meat loaf."

I was taping my flyer in the window when Hark Hibler came along, headed for a cup of Lila's coffee. Hark is the managing editor at the *Enterprise*, Pecan Springs's newspaper, which is owned by the Seidensticker family. A while back, he asked if I'd take over the Thursday Home and Garden page, so strictly speaking, he's my boss. Of course, he wouldn't be my boss if

LILA JENNINGS' FRIDAY SPECIAL MEAT LOAF

1½ pounds ground beef or ground sirloin
2 tablespoons bread or cracker crumbs
1 egg, beaten
3 cloves garlic, minced
1 small onion, chopped
1 teaspoon chile powder
1 teaspoon salt
Barbecue sauce

Mix all ingredients except for the barbecue sauce. Form into a large loaf and place in a baking pan. Pour barbecue sauce over the top. Bake for 90 minutes at 350°F. Let stand for 5 minutes before serving. Makes six servings.

the *Enterprise* had continued to be a weekly, as it had been for decades. But last year, Arlene Seidensticker decided that Pecan Springs deserved a daily, which means that Hark is always hard up for news. He frequents the Diner because it's the best place in town to plug into the grapevine and get an earful of the local stories making the rounds. Where the grapevine is concerned, Lila is like one of those old-fashioned telephone operators, sitting at a switchboard with a direct line into every household in town. What she doesn't know isn't worth knowing.

"Lost your cat, huh?" he grunted, glancing at the flyer I'd just posted. "I've got a hole at the bottom of tomorrow's page three. How about if I run a story on him?"

"Oh, would you?" I said gratefully. I handed him my last

flyer. "I'll go home and get the photo so Ethel can scan it into the computer." Along with becoming a daily, the *Enterprise* added a couple of computers. Hark wasn't happy about that, either, but he and Ethel Fritz, his assistant editor, couldn't put out even a little daily if they had to do it with old-fashioned equipment.

Hark peered at the photo. "I know this cat," he said. "He's not exactly the sort of animal you pass by without noticing."

"Everybody else in town knows him, too," I replied testily. "Mr. Cowan throws zucchini at him, Vivian Baxter is waiting with a flyswatter, Mr. Cavette feeds him catfish, and Lila makes sure he gets French fries and cream gravy for lunch." I was beginning to feel that Khat was public property. "So what's your connection to him?"

"Oh, no connection. I just mean that I saw him. Last night, maybe? No, it was this morning—I think."

I stared. "This morning! Where?"

"In a tree. On my way to the gym, maybe? No, on my way to work." Hark pulled at his moustache. You'd think that a newspaperman would have a head for dates and places, but Hark sometimes has a problem with details. "I can't remember exactly, but—"

"Try," I said urgently. Hark's bachelor pad isn't far from the *Enterprise* office, or from the gym, for that matter. Surely it wouldn't be too hard to remember where he'd seen a big Siamese perched in a tree.

Hark shifted from one foot to the other. "I think it was that pecan tree at the corner of Comanche and Pecos," he said finally. "Beside the vacant house—the old Gillis house." He paused, frowning. "Except it's not vacant anymore. Somebody moved in last week. I saw a moving van parked out front, and a woman carrying some boxes—"

But I was already racing for my bike.

The Gillis house is one of those places you'd love to inherit, if only it wouldn't take the entire national defense budget to make it livable. It's been vacant for three or four years, ever since old Mrs. Gillis died, and it needs a new roof, a new front porch, windows, doors, and probably a fortune in paint, plumbing, and wiring. But Hark was right. Somebody had moved into it. Sheets were hanging over the vacant front windows, and there was a pile of empty moving boxes on the front porch. The pecan tree was empty, however, except for a flock of Mr. Cowan's rabble-rousing grackles. There was no sign of Khat.

I knocked at the front door, waited for a moment or two, and then knocked again. No answer. I went around to the back, and found a car parked in the old garage—risky business, I thought, because the garage roof looked as if it could collapse if so much as a leaf fell on it. I knocked on the back door. No answer there, either. I made a fist and banged, loudly, and this time I thought I heard something. A meow?

"Khat?" I called anxiously. "Khat, is that you?" And then, when I heard a familiar, throaty meow and some urgent scratching on the other side of the door, I cried, "Khat, it *is* you! What are you doing in this house, you bad kitty? You come out this minute, do you hear? This is *not* your house. You don't belong here."

If you think I'm in the habit of lecturing delinquent cats through the locked doors of other people's houses, you're wrong. But in this case, I felt completely justified. And what's more, I felt equally justified in giving the door a very firm shove with my shoulder.

That did it. The old door opened with a shriek of rusty hinges, and I stumbled inside. The back entry was dark and so full of ancient dust that I had to sneeze. But there was Khat, winding himself around my ankles, butting his head against my calves, and meowing imperiously as if to demand, "What took you so long? I expected you two days ago!"

I bent over, scooped him up in my arms, and snuggled my cheek against his dusty fur. He might have been a bit lighter for having missed out on Lila's French fries and cream gravy for the last few days, but not noticeably so. He allowed me to caress and croon to him for a moment, and then jumped out of my arms, landing lightly on the floor. With a peremptory crook in his tail, as if to beckon me to follow him, he made for the dark stairway at the end of the hall.

That was when I heard it. A low, distraught moan, almost inaudible. Khat meowed again, more loudly, and again I heard the moan.

"Is somebody here?" I called. I fumbled for the wall switch beside the stairs and a bare bulb came on. "Do you need help? Where *are* you?"

"Mrrrow!" said Khat, and raised his paw as if to point.

That was how I found her. The narrow stairway to the second floor had collapsed, and the new owner of the old Gillis house—a heavyset woman in her mid fifties—had fallen through, all the way into the crawl space under the house. She was half-sitting, half-lying on the dirt, pinned down by a heavy wooden beam.

It took only a few minutes for the Pecan Springs Fire Department to answer my phone call, and by the time a couple of burly firemen had dug the victim out and hoisted her up, EMS was there to take her to the hospital.

Later, I learned that the woman's name was Ivy O'Toole, and that she had recently purchased the old house with the intention of fixing it up. But on Tuesday afternoon, as Ivy carried a big load of books up the stairs, the rotten wood had given way beneath her. Her injuries weren't terribly serious—a concussion, several cracked ribs, a broken ankle, and dehydration—but she was convinced that she would have died if it hadn't been for Khat.

"It wasn't just that he kept me company the whole time," she said when Hark, Khat, and I went to visit her in the hospital, "although that by itself was enormously cheering. He's a very companionable creature with a remarkable vocal range. It's almost as if he's talking to you." She turned to me. "But if you hadn't come looking for him, China, I have no idea how long it would have been before someone came looking for *me*." She gave a rueful laugh. "Weeks, probably. I don't know a soul in Pecan Springs."

"Look pretty," Hark said cheerily, and snapped a photo of Ivy sitting up in her hospital bed with Khat K'o Kung in her arms. Hark was pleased because a dinky little lost-cat story had developed into a much more satisfying cat-saves-human-life story, and was now front and center on Page One, under the banner headline, THE KHAT WHO BECAME A HERO.

When the *Enterprise* hit the streets the next morning, Khat was an instant celebrity. A day or so later, a television crew from Austin came to interview Ivy and me and shoot some footage of Khat, who assumed an air of imperial dignity, scarcely condescending to glance at the camera. For the occasion, Ivy gave him a new red-velvet cat collar, hung with a gold medallion that said HERO KITTY. Lila Jennings dispatched a plate of freshly fried French fries and some cream gravy, topped with half a jelly doughnut. Junior Cavette drove over on his motorbike to deliver a fresh catfish, Vivian Baxter brought an entire family of catnip mice, and even Mr. Cowan sent something—a half bushel of zucchini. I was just happy to have Khat K'o Kung back where he belonged, as sleek and inscrutable as ever, basking in the morning sunshine on the shop's front windowsill.

There was only one thing wrong. Janet hadn't had time to drive to San Antonio to look for the bocconcini, so she bought two pounds of mozzarella at Cavette's and cut it into cubes before she marinated it in basil vinegar with lemon juice, chopped fresh basil, and dried red pepper. Nobody seemed to notice the difference, although one of the Friends did ask about all those little red flecks sticking to the cheese.

"Looks like red paint," she said, poking it doubtfully with her fork. "Is it for decoration, or are we supposed to eat it?"

I won't tell you what Janet said.

The Recipes for Janet's Luncheon

SPICY TOMATO JUICE COCKTAIL

3 quarts tomato juice
½ teaspoon celery salt
½ teaspoon onion salt
1 tablespoon fresh snipped dill
1 teaspoon prepared horseradish
1 teaspoon lime juice
½ teaspoon Worcestershire sauce

Combine all ingredients in a nonreactive pan (glass or stainless) and heat thoroughly, stirring to mix well. Refrigerate for a day or so to allow the flavors to blend. Serve with a parsley garnish.

HERBED BREADSTICKS

2 cups white flour
About 1½ cups whole-wheat flour
1 package active dry yeast
1 tablespoon brown sugar
1 teaspoon celery salt
1 teaspoon garlic salt
2 teaspoons celery seed
2 teaspoons dill seed
1½ cups warm water
1 large egg
1 tablespoon water
2 tablespoons white sesame seed

Place the white flour, yeast, sugar, celery salt, garlic salt, celery seed, and dill seed in a mixing bowl. Add warm water and beat with an electric mixer for 4 to 5 minutes, until batter is thick and sticky. Mix in whole-wheat flour, ½ cup at a time, until the dough comes away from the sides of the bowl. Turn it onto a floured board and knead until a soft, elastic dough is formed, adding more whole-wheat flour as necessary. Place the dough in a lightly oiled bowl, turning to oil the top, and cover with a damp towel. Let rise in a warm place until double, about 1 hour. Punch dough down and divide into quarters. Divide each quarter into four pieces (making 16 pieces), and these into thirds (48 pieces). Roll the pieces into eight-inch sticks and place on greased baking sheet, one-half inch apart. For egg wash, mix egg and water and brush onto breadsticks. Sprinkle with sesame seeds. Bake in 400°F oven for 12 to 15 minutes. Makes forty-eight.

FRESH GREEN SALAD WITH CHERRY TOMATOES, MUSHROOMS, AND BOCCONCINI

½ pound arugula, fresh spinach, other greens
½ pound cherry tomatoes
½ pound button mushrooms, stems removed, caps wiped clean and sliced
½ pound bocconcini
3 tablespoons olive oil
4 tablespoons basil vinegar
2 tablespoons fresh lemon juice
½ teaspoon red pepper flakes
3 tablespoons fresh chopped basil
Croutons for garnish

Mix together the oil, vinegar, lemon juice, red pepper flakes, and chopped basil. Pour over tomatoes, mushrooms, and bocconcini and marinate for several hours. Just before serving, arrange torn greens on chilled serving plates, and add marinated tomatoes, mushrooms, and bocconcini. Garnish with croutons. Serves six.

CHICKEN IN SUN-DRIED TOMATO SAUCE, SERVED OVER PASTA

4 large chicken breasts, boned and skinned,
  cut into strips
1 tablespoon olive oil
3 tablespoons butter
3 tablespoons flour, mixed with ½ teaspoon paprika
2 green onions, chopped fine
½ cup sun-dried, oil-packed tomatoes,
  drained and chopped
½ cup white wine
2 teaspoons chopped fresh oregano
  (or 1 teaspoon dried)
⅔ cup half-and-half
Salt and pepper to taste
1 pound fettuccini, linguini, or wide noodles, cooked al
  dente in boiling water

Melt oil and butter in skillet. Toss chicken strips with flour-paprika mixture and brown over medium-high heat until just cooked. Remove to a plate. Add chopped green onions to the skillet and sauté over medium heat for one minute. Stir in sun-dried tomatoes, wine, and oregano, scraping up bits of chicken. Stir in half-and-half, bring to a boil, reduce heat, and simmer until the sauce thickens. Return chicken to skillet to reheat. Season to taste. Serve over cooked pasta. Serves four.

GINGER-PEACHY MELONS

6 fresh peaches, medium-size, peeled, pitted, and sliced

1 small cantaloupe, peeled, seeded, and cut into ½-inch cubes

1 small honeydew melon, peeled, seeded, and cut into ½-inch cubes

½ cup orange juice

2 tablespoons lemon juice

1 teaspoon grated fresh ginger

2 tablespoons candied ginger, chopped fine

1 tablespoon honey

Mint sprigs for garnish

Mix together the orange juice, lemon juice, grated ginger, candied ginger, and honey. Place the fruit in a large bowl and pour the juices over it, stirring gently. Refrigerate until serving time (up to 8 hours). Serves six.

THE ROSEMARY CAPER

COMPARED to my former life as a Houston criminal defense attorney, where every day was a battleground and every encounter a combat, my life in Pecan Springs flows as smoothly as that sweet sorghum molasses they make over in East Texas. But every now and then there's a hitch in our git-along, as we say around here, and something happens to remind me that ugliness happens in even the prettiest places.

One Tuesday morning last month, for instance, when Pansy Pride came into the store, distraught. Pansy is the president of our local herb club, the Myra Merryweather Herb Guild, which is named for the energetic lady who organized the Guild back in the '30s and whose memory is still much loved today. Pansy is a short, bouncy woman with short gray curls. She wasn't bouncy that morning, though. She was wringing her hands.

"China, something awful has happened!" she cried. "You've got to help!"

I went to the hospitality shelf, poured a cup of just-brewed lavender-mint tea, handed Pansy a ginger cookie, and told her to calm down. She was so panicked that getting the story was like teasing a pecan out of a smashed shell. But when I finally pried the details out of her, I had to agree. Something definitely troubling had happened.

That morning, Pansy had gone over to the Guild House, where the club has its office and holds meetings. She didn't notice anything unusual until she went up to the second-floor library. Most of the books aren't in the least remarkable—donated cookbooks, herbals, and gardening how-to. But the Guild owns one crown jewel: *Myra Merryweather's Cookery Book*, published in 1920. A book dealer in Houston appraised it for ten thousand dollars, because the author herself, a well-known Southern herbalist, had written notes in the margin.

"And *that's* the book that's missing!" Pansy wailed. "Myra's *Cookery Book* has been stolen!"

I frowned. "I thought the book was kept in the Guild's safety-deposit box at the bank."

"It was, until just a few days ago," Pansy said. "We took it out to put into the library."

China likes to offer refreshments to her customers at Thyme and Seasons. Here are the recipes for the cookies and tea she was serving on the day that Pansy Pride dropped in — luckily, as it turned out. As medicinal herbs, both lavender and ginger are often used for their calming, soothing effect.

SPICY GINGER COOKIES

1 cup butter or margarine
1 cup white sugar, plus extra for sprinkling
¼ cup unsulfured molasses
1 egg
1 teaspoon vanilla extract
2 cups sifted flour
½ teaspoon baking soda
1 teaspoon powdered cinnamon
½ teaspoon powdered ginger
½ teaspoon powdered cloves
¼ teaspoon salt

Preheat oven to 350°F. Cream the butter and 1 cup sugar until light and fluffy. Stir in molasses, egg, and vanilla and mix well. Sift together flour, baking soda, spices, and salt. Add by thirds to creamed mixture, blending thoroughly. Sprinkle extra sugar on a baking sheet. Drop dough by tablespoons onto the sheet, and sprinkle with more sugar. Bake approximately 15 minutes, or until golden brown. Cool on a wire rack, and store in an airtight container. Makes about two dozen soft cookies.

LAVENDER-MINT TEA

4 teaspoons fresh lavender flowers or 2 teaspoons dried lavender flowers
3 to 4 tablespoons fresh mint leaves or 4 teaspoons dried mint
4 cups boiling water

In a one-quart teapot, combine the lavender flowers and mint. Pour boiling water over the mixture; steep 5 minutes.

"Well, then, maybe somebody borrowed it."

"I'm afraid not," Pansy replied miserably. "It was in a locked glass display case. The book is gone and there's broken glass all over the floor."

"Then it's a job for the cops," I replied, reaching for the phone.

Pansy clutched at my arm. "But we can't call the police, China! The Guild has just been offered a pair of valuable floral paintings — but only if we have adequate security. If the donor finds out there's been a theft, we can kiss those paintings good-bye. That's why I've come to you. You have to help me get that book back — without letting any of the members know that it's gone!"

What could I say? I hung up my OUT TO LUNCH sign and took Pansy next door to the Crystal Cave, to talk to Ruby Wilcox. In her vivid imagination, my best friend is Nancy Drew and Kinsey Milhone mixed together, with a dash of Stephanie Plum tossed in to spice up the blend. If I went looking for clues without her, she'd never forgive me. Over six feet tall, with red hair and gingery freckles, Ruby is utterly unforgettable, especially when she's wearing one of her weird outfits. Today, she had on a slim ankle-length dress, slit to the knee and tie-dyed in various shades of indigo blue, with a tie-dyed scarf wound around her hennaed curls. She looked like a carrot in blue shrink-wrap.

"Omigosh!" Ruby gasped, when Pansy and I told her that the famous *Cookery Book* had been stolen. "Who would do a thing like that? Let's go have a look!"

The library is at the end of the second-floor hall of Myra Merryweather's old Victorian house, overlooking the Guild's famous knot garden, which is planted and maintained by all the Guild members. Pansy unlocked the library door and we followed her in. Sure enough, the display case was broken. There was glass on the floor, and the book was gone.

"How long has the cookbook been on display in this room?" I asked.

"We took it out of the safety-deposit box just a few days ago," Pansy said. "We never dreamed anybody would *steal* it!"

"How many people knew the book was here?" Ruby asked.

Indigo

Many herbs, such as madder, yarrow, goldenrod, woad, and weld, produce dyes and have been cultivated specifically for that purpose. Until the invention of synthetic dyes, indigo (*Indigofera* species) was perhaps the world's most valuable dye plant. Its beautiful deep blue color—the color of royalty—was laboriously produced from the fermented leaves, processed with lye, urine, and other agents, then dried and pressed into cakes. Medicinally, Chinese herbalists used indigo to reduce fever and alleviate pain, while in South Africa, it was used to treat toothache. In the islands of the East Indies, only postmenopausal women (the wisewomen of the village) were permitted to work with indigo.

"Only the members of the Library Committee. We're planning to have a public showing of the paintings, and we wanted to have Myra's book here, as well."

"How did the thief get into the house?" I asked. "I checked the front door as we came in. It didn't look as if it had been jimmied."

Pansy shook her head. "It wasn't. It was locked when I

arrived this morning. And the downstairs windows don't show any signs of forced entry."

"How many people have keys?" Ruby asked.

"I do, and so does Cora Demming, our secretary-treasurer. And our handyman, of course. Jerry Weber." She frowned. "I suppose Delia Murphy still has a key, too. She was president last year."

"And the library?" I asked. "Was it locked?"

"Yes. But everybody knows that the key is kept behind the pantry door." Pansy clenched her hands. "We've *got* to find out who took the book!"

It was time to start making a suspect list. "We'll start with the people on the Library Committee," I said, "since they're the only ones who knew that the book was here and not in the bank." I took a notebook and pencil out of my purse. "Names?"

"Well, there's Cora Demming—I mentioned her a minute ago. And Jane Clark and Delia Murphy. And me, too, of course." Pansy gave us a sideways glance. "But if I were going to take the book, I wouldn't have broken the glass, would I? I have the only key to the case. I keep it on my personal key ring." She held it up.

Ruby and I traded glances. Personally, I doubted that Pansy had stolen the book, but we couldn't rule her out. Sure, she might have a key. But if she had taken the book, breaking the glass would be a smart move. It would cover her tracks.

Pansy caught our glances. "You can't imagine that *I* did it!" she exclaimed in a horrified tone. "Why . . . why, that's absurd!"

"Please don't take it personally, Pansy," Ruby said. "We have to consider all the angles."

"I'll try," Pansy replied grimly. "But I'll also expect an apology when you find the *real* thief!"

Cora Demming's yard has been chosen Pecan Springs's Yard of the Week three times already this year, which makes a great many people envious. But Cora has two green thumbs and certainly deserves the honor. We found her in her garden, snipping herbs into a basket. She had already collected sprigs of lemon balm and lemon verbena, and was reaching for a lemon-scented geranium. She looked up when Ruby and I said hello, but she didn't smile. Cora Demming—a tight-lipped, suspicious woman—hasn't smiled since her husband disappeared last year, leaving her with a stack of credit card debts as tall as the Texas Tower.

Cora looked even more sour when I told her about the stolen cookbook. "I warned Pansy not to take that valuable book out of the bank vault," she said. "The locks at the Guild House are a joke." She gave a short, hard laugh. "Pansy promised to ask Jerry Weber to install new ones, but that's like asking the fox to guard the hen house."

"What makes you say that?" Ruby asked curiously.

"Don't be naive," Cora replied, with a scornful toss of her head. "Jerry's always hard up for cash, and since I'm the Guild's treasurer, he's continually pestering me to give him an advance on what we owe him for his maintenance work. But Pansy gets upset when I tell her that he's more trouble than he's worth to us." She gave us a tight smile. "In fact, she's so protective that I wouldn't be in the least surprised to hear that there's some-

Lemon-flavored and lemon-scented herbs are easy to grow, fun to cook with, and add a cooling touch to summer. Here are China's favorites.

- Lemon balm (*Melissa officinalis*). With its crinkled yellow-green leaves, lemon balm even *looks* cool. It's a hardy perennial and needs frequent clipping to keep it tidy. But that's just fine, because the trimmings are a tasty addition to herbal teas, as well as fish and chicken dishes.

- Lemon verbena (*Aloysia triphylla*), a tender, shrubby perennial, is pure lemon delight. Planted where it can get some afternoon shade and mulched or moved indoors during the winter, the plant will reward you with lots of lemony leaves for teas and desserts.

- Lemon-scented geraniums (*Pelargonium* species), such as "Lemon Crispum," "Mabel Grey," and "Frensham," lend their fresh scent to desserts, teas, and potpourris. In patio pots or in the garden, scented geraniums need sun and plenty of water. In late fall, take cuttings for next year's plants.

- Lemongrass (*Cymbopogon citratus*), a native of India and Sri Lanka, is a must for Asian cooks. Dried, the leaves are wonderful in soups and teas. And as a bonus, the pale green, slender leaves of this three-foot-high bunchgrass make a striking garden accent.

thing going on between the two of them. And I certainly wouldn't put it past Jerry to take that book."

I raised my eyebrows. Somehow, I didn't think Pansy would compromise herself with Jerry Weber. Still, despite his many shortcomings, he's a charming man—and Pansy seems to be always on the lookout for male companionship. Unfortunately, Cora's suspicion was something to consider.

"It looks like the thief got in through the Guild House's front door," I said. I paused and added tactfully, "Has anyone asked to borrow your key?"

Cora leaned over and snipped a leaf of lemongrass. "Of course not. Anyway, you don't need a key to get into that place. If you know how to jiggle the knob on the kitchen door, you can walk right in. Anybody could have stolen that book."

"*If* you knew it was there," I said. And only the members of the Library Committee had known that.

"A rare book is a strange thing to steal," Ruby remarked. "I mean, once you have it, what would you do with it?"

Cora picked up her basket. "Jane Clark can tell you about that. Her brother is a rare-book dealer. Of course, I'm not making any accusations," she added with a tight, meaningful smile. She glanced at her watch. "Now, if you'll excuse me, I'm expecting a delivery any minute now."

We thanked Cora and said good-bye. "So Jane Clark's brother is a rare book dealer," Ruby said excitedly as we got in the car. "And Jane is on the Library Committee! Maybe *she* took the book and gave it to her brother to sell."

"That's certainly what Cora wants us to think," I replied.

"And she'd also like us to consider Jerry as a suspect, too." I glanced up. "Hey, look at that!"

A truck from Blanchard's Furniture Store in San Antonio was pulling up in front of Cora's house. As we watched, a couple of brawny guys unloaded an elegant living room suite — several thousand dollars' worth of furniture.

"I thought Cora was supposed to be broke and in debt," Ruby said, wide-eyed. "Where'd she get the money for all that new stuff?"

"That," I said thoughtfully, "is a very good question."

"Cora Demming has a lot of nerve accusing me of stealing that book!" Jane Clark said angrily. She bent over to add the last bit of parsley garnish to a tray of stuffed mushrooms. Jane, a handsome woman of indefinite age, has a successful catering business and is always in demand for dinner parties. If you want to book her, you have to call her weeks in advance.

"Cora didn't accuse you," I said quietly. "She just mentioned that your brother deals in rare books."

"We thought he might be able to give us some ideas about how the thief might attempt to dispose of the book," Ruby added.

Jane ran a hand through her blond, Martha Stewart–style hair. "Sorry," she muttered. "I suppose Cora has a reason to distrust people. If my husband ran off and left me dead broke, I might be suspicious of everybody, too."

I thought of Cora's new furniture and wondered once again

JANE CLARK'S STUFFED MUSHROOMS

1 pound fresh mushrooms
6 tablespoons butter, divided
2 tablespoons fresh chives, chopped
1 egg, beaten
½ cup dry bread crumbs
½ teaspoon Worcestershire sauce
½ teaspoon dried thyme
¼ teaspoon garlic powder
Salt and pepper to taste

Wash mushrooms. Remove and chop the stems. Heat half the butter in a small skillet and sauté the chopped stems and chives. With a slotted spoon, remove to a bowl. Add egg, crumbs, Worcestershire sauce, thyme, garlic powder, and salt and pepper and mix. In the skillet in which you sautéed the stems, heat the remaining butter and sauté the mushroom caps. Place caps stem sides up in a baking pan and fill each cap with crumb mixture. Broil until golden. Serve hot. (You can prepare and refrigerate these, and broil them just before serving.) Serves four.

where the money came from. But I didn't mention this to Jane. Instead, I said, "How can we get in touch with your brother?"

"You can't. Eric is in Europe on a buying trip. He left two weeks ago and won't be back for another month." Jane picked up the tray and put it in the refrigerator. "Somehow I don't believe that anybody would steal the *Cookery Book* for the money. If you ask me, the thief wanted it for its own sake."

"Do you have any guesses?" I asked.

Jane pursed her lips. "You might talk to Delia Murphy. Her mother was Myra Merryweather's niece. Delia has always claimed that the cookbook belongs to her. Nobody believes her, of course, but I wouldn't put it past her to—" She shrugged, leaving the sentence dangling tantalizingly in the air. It was obvious that Delia was not one of Jane's friends.

"Cora says Jerry Weber might be involved," Ruby said. "What's your take on that?"

"Jerry?" Jane laughed scornfully. "He'd steal anything if he thought he could turn it into a dollar. But he wouldn't know how to sell that book for enough to make it worth stealing. And Cora herself is a possibility. She told me that she's thinking of running for Guild president in the next election. She might have taken the book just to make Pansy look bad."

After we left, Ruby and I compared notes. Jane had been very ready to accuse other people. But even though her brother was in Europe, she certainly could have taken the book and sent it to him. Pansy was still on the list. Jerry, too, in spite of what Jane had said. And Cora, who suddenly had extra money to spend—and a reason to put Pansy in a bad light. I'm always astonished at the ease with which even the most petty motive can become irresistibly compelling.

It was time to talk to Delia Murphy. Maybe she could throw some light on this mystery.

Delia, a heavyset woman with gray hair and snappy blue eyes, has a bead shop in the Emporium, the craft and boutique mall that occupies the big Victorian house next door to Thyme and

Seasons. She shook her head sadly when Ruby said that we'd come to talk about the cookbook.

"I really don't have anything to tell you," she said. "There's already been enough unhappiness about that dreadful old book. Frankly, I'm glad it's gone."

"What sort of unhappiness?" Ruby asked.

Delia opened a box, took out a plastic bag, and opened it. "Have you ever smelled anything so sweet?" she asked with a smile, taking out a string of large black beads. "They're rose beads. They'd make a lovely family heirloom."

Normally, I'd be interested in those beads, since I make my own to sell in my shop. But not today. "What kind of unhappiness, Delia?"

She put the beads back in the bag and tucked the bag into the box. "It's an old story. It doesn't mean anything to anybody but me."

"I understand that your mother was Myra Merryweather's niece," Ruby remarked. "How did that valuable book get out of the family? You'd think it would be the kind of thing that Myra would want her relatives to have."

Delia turned away to put the box on a shelf. "Well, I hate to disillusion you, but Aunt Myra just wasn't a very nice person. She and Mother didn't get along. Mother tried very hard to satisfy her, but—" She turned with a shrug. "Aunt Myra always insisted on having her own way. She fancied herself a matriarch, as her mother had been." Her smile was slightly askew. "To tell the truth, she was something of a bully, at least in the family."

"Still," I said, "it must have been a disappointment when she gave the cookbook to the Herb Guild."

In our grandmothers' time, everyone wore rose beads, beautiful black beads made from fresh rose petals. They took a long time to make—two weeks or more—and involved a great deal of work. China has found an easier way to make this old-fashioned herbal treasure. All you need is a cast-iron pot or large skillet and a few rusty nails. (Honest. The iron in the pot and the nails help to blacken the beads.)

ROSE BEADS

In a cast-iron cooking container, place a quart of fresh, finely minced rose petals, a cup of water, a few drops of rose oil to enhance the scent, and a handful of rusty nails. Simmer, covered, for 1 hour. Remove from heat, stir well with a wooden spoon, and let it stand overnight. Repeat the next day, and the next, adding water if necessary, until the doughy mixture has darkened. Then set aside until it dries to a claylike consistency that can be easily molded. Wet your hands and roll into balls a little larger than a marble. (They will shrink about 50 percent as they dry.) Place on paper towels. When they are partly dry, thread a large needle with dental floss, string the beads, and hang them to dry. Turn them regularly so that they don't stick to the floss. In a week, your rose beads are ready for their final stringing, alternated with small, pretty beads used as spacers. Add a clasp and store in an airtight container to preserve the scent. For more about the way roses were used in earlier centuries, read *Rose Recipes from Olden Times*, by Eleanour Sinclair Rohde.

Delia's chin was quivering and she looked as if she might be about to cry. "I don't mean to be rude, China, but I don't see that my family's history is any of your business. Anyway, all that unpleasantness is over and done with. I don't want to think about it."

"Do you have any idea who might have taken the book from the Guild library?" I persisted. I felt sorry for Delia and didn't want to cause her more pain, but the question needed an answer.

"Of course not," she said. Another customer came in at that moment, and she turned away with a bright "How may I help you?"

"Well, we certainly didn't learn anything from Delia," Ruby said as we walked back to our shops. "Except that Myra Merryweather's family thought she was a bully. That's interesting, although it doesn't take us any closer to finding out what happened to the cookbook."

"When you come right down to it, we haven't learned anything from anybody," I replied. "All our suspects just point their fingers at one another. Cora accuses Pansy and Jane. Jane accuses Delia and Cora. And everybody denies knowing anything."

"What about Jerry Weber? We haven't talked to him yet."

"We can try," I said.

Jerry is a charming man, a retired widower in his early sixties, trim and athletic. But our talk with him produced nothing more than a firm denial, a few shakes of the head, and the tart remark that if the Guild paid him a little more money, he'd be glad to fix that dang kitchen door so nobody would have to worry about folks walking in off the street and stealing valuable books. Jerry did, however, point out that he had been in Houston visiting his daughter when the theft occurred. According to him, he couldn't have stolen the book.

"Anyways," he said with a frown, "what would I want with a cookbook? If I get to hankerin' for serious home cookin', I go over to the Diner. Otherwise, I open me a can o' beans and cut up a weenie in it. Some onions and catsup, too, maybe a little chile powder." He grinned. "You can't get much better than that, no matter how many cookbooks you got."

Ruby and I had gone through the complete suspect list and had gotten exactly nowhere. It was time for a different strategy. If we couldn't pry the information out of somebody, maybe we could *buy* it.

"A reward?" Pansy asked dubiously. "You want the Herb Guild to offer a five-hundred-dollar reward?"

Ruby and I were sitting in the swing on Pansy's front porch when I made my suggestion. Pansy has planted a lovely silver garden beside the steps. The sharp, clean scent of lavender filled the soft evening air, with the spicy undertone of clove pinks. Bees were gorging themselves with happy abandon among the blue catmint flower spikes.

"For information leading to the identification of the thief or the return of the book," Ruby explained. "No questions asked."

"But the book is worth a lot more than five hundred dollars,"

Pansy objected. "If somebody intends to sell it, that's not much of an incentive."

"That's true," I replied, pushing the swing with my toe. "However, the thief has probably found out how hard it is to sell. He—or she—may be happy to get five hundred out of it. It's worth a shot, isn't it?"

Pansy shook her head. "But the book may have been sold already. You said that Cora just bought some expensive furniture. If she's the thief—"

I threw up my hands. Why was Pansy being so stubborn? Didn't she want Myra's book to be found? "We have to try *something*, Pansy," I persisted. "We've interviewed every one of the suspects and we still don't have a clue."

"The problem," Pansy said quietly, "is that we can't have any publicity, for the same reason that we couldn't involve the police in the first place. Since we don't want anybody but the Library Committee to know that the book has been stolen, I don't see how we can offer a reward without letting on that there's been a theft."

"Rats," Ruby said, and I echoed her. Both of us had for-

A fragrance garden, planted near a window or beside a porch, is a long-lasting source of sweet pleasure. Here are a few especially fragrant herbs you'll want to include:

Catmint
Chamomile
Clove pink
Lavender
Lemon balm
Lemon verbena
Mignonette
Pennyroyal
Rosemary
Roses
Scented basil
Scented geraniums
Thyme
Violets

gotten about that. I sat for a moment, swinging back and forth, feeling frustrated.

"I don't think I've ever seen that book," I said after a while. "What kind of recipes are in it?"

Pansy got up from her chair. "I'll show you," she replied. She was back in a few minutes, with a manila folder. "This is a photocopy of the book." She laid a few pages on the table so we could see them. "I copied it so I could study Myra's revisions and see if the Herb Guild might publish a second edition."

"That's a good idea," Ruby said approvingly. She turned a few pages. "These are interesting recipes, China. Here's one for lavender butter—I don't think I've ever heard of that before."

"For her day, Myra was an amazingly inventive cook," Pansy said. "She particularly loved rosemary. She grew lots of it—in fact, a few of her original plants still survive, in the herb garden behind the Guild House. She had all sorts of novel ideas for using it in foods."

Myra Merryweather's unusual lavender butter is easy to make. Just mix 1 tablespoon of lavender flowers (fresh, unsprayed) with a cup of softened butter or margarine. Cover tightly and refrigerate for a day before using. Serve on crackers with smoked turkey or cold chicken, or use in your favorite butter-cookie recipe.

I picked up a few pages, thinking with relief that we could scratch Pansy off our suspect list. I doubted that she would have bothered to photocopy a book that she intended to steal. I began to study Myra's handwritten notes in the margins of the pages. Many were changes in existing recipes—an ingredient added here, another subtracted there. Others were entirely new recipes, written in a tiny but legible script. A couple of unusual ones caught my eye, and I blinked. If the stolen book hadn't been valuable because of Myra's handwritten notes, it should be valuable because of these new recipes. Some were quite unique. I looked up. "Do you know if anybody else copied Myra's notes?"

"I don't think so," Pansy said. "The book has been in the vault since her death, so no one has had access to it. Why?"

"Because," I said, "I have an idea." I grinned. "A brilliant idea, if I do say so myself."

"An idea for publishing a second edition from Myra's notes?" Pansy asked.

"An idea about how to offer a reward without letting anybody know?" Ruby guessed.

"You're both wrong," I replied. "I have an idea about how to trap a thief—in a trap baited with rosemary."

Pansy looked confused. Ruby looked dubious. "What are you thinking?" she asked.

"I'm thinking that it's time for a cooking contest," I said. "The prize goes to the person who comes up with the most creative use of rosemary." When they still looked puzzled, I added, a little impatiently, "Don't you see? The person who took the book won't be able to resist submitting one of Myra's unique rosemary recipes. She'll give herself away!"

"Well, maybe," Pansy said slowly.

"What if she's too smart to fall for the trick?" Ruby asked.

I shrugged. "Then we've gone to a lot of trouble for nothing. But let's face it. We've come to a dead end. We have no eyewitnesses, no clues, and nothing but accusations from the suspects. Do you guys have any other suggestions?"

"You're right," Pansy said. "I'll get the word out. People can bring their entries to the next meeting."

"They need to bring their recipes, too," I said. "If we find one that exactly matches one of Myra's handwritten entries, we'll know we've got our thief."

"And then what?" Ruby wanted to know.

"We try to get it back," I said with a shrug.

It was a suspenseful week. I thought back over the conversations we'd had with the suspects, wondering if we had overlooked a clue. But no matter how hard I tried, I couldn't think of anything we'd missed. If our trap didn't work, Myra Merryweather's original *Cookery Book* was probably gone forever.

Judgment day finally arrived. Everybody was excited about the contest, and the downstairs meeting room at the Guild House was full. The contest entries were arranged on a long table, each dish accompanied by the recipe written on a white index card, the contestant's name on the back. While Mrs. Gates gave a talk on herbal liqueurs and everybody got to taste her famous Rosemary Orange Honey Liqueur, Ruby and I snooped among the entries, checking the recipes against the list I had made of the handwritten rosemary recipes in the margins of Myra's *Cookery Book*.

"Mabel Gordon has entered something called Kidney-and-Leek Pie with Rosemary Radishes," Ruby said, shuddering. "What was she *thinking*?"

With a grin, I checked my list. "Myra had better taste. That's not one of her recipes, so Mabel is in the clear." I picked

Herbal liqueurs make wonderful gifts for yourself or for friends, but you do have to plan ahead. Allow this liqueur to mellow for at least 6 months before you serve it.

ROSEMARY ORANGE HONEY LIQUEUR

4 large navel oranges
1 small lemon
6 sprigs rosemary
2 cups vodka
1 cup brandy
1⅛ cups honey

Rinse and dry the oranges and the lemon. Use a sharp knife or grater to scrape the skin (the zest) from the oranges and lemon, being careful not to scrape off the bitter white pith. Put the rosemary sprigs and the orange and lemon zest in a glass jar and add the vodka and brandy. Seal tightly and let steep for 3 days in a cool, dark place, shaking the jar once a day. Strain into a clean bowl and whisk in the honey until it dissolves and the mixture clears. Pour into a clean glass bottle or bottles, seal tightly, and allow to mature at room temperature before using.

up a card labeled ROSEMARY AND RHUBARB PIE—an interesting recipe, but not on the list either. And neither were the next four we picked up. I was beginning to get discouraged. Maybe Pansy and Ruby had been right. Maybe our thief was too smart to take the bait.

On the other side of the table, Ruby picked up a card. "Now, here's a rosemary dish I've never heard of," she remarked. "It's called Rosemary and Ripe Olive Pesto. Weird. Very weird."

I ran my finger down the list. "Rosemary and Ripe Olive Pesto!" I exclaimed. "That's it, Ruby! That's Myra's recipe. Who entered it?"

Without a word, Ruby handed me the card. When I saw the name, I shook my head sadly, thinking that I understood. But at least we'd caught our thief. Now the trick was to make her confess.

Back in the meeting room, Pansy held up her hands for silence. "If we're not quiet," she scolded, "we won't be able to hear China announce the grand prize winner of our Creative Cooking with Rosemary Contest."

I stood up. "After due deliberation," I said, "the judges have decided to award the prize to the creator of an original recipe that Myra Merryweather would be proud of. Rosemary and Ripe Olive Pesto, by Delia Murphy!"

There was a round of applause punctuated by a few disappointed sighs as Delia proudly stood and came forward. I presented her with a sealed envelope and shook her hand. Pansy hurried through the rest of the announcements and the meeting was over. Immediately afterward, I whispered to Pansy that Ruby and I would be in the library. A few minutes later, Pansy came into the room, followed by Delia. Delia was holding the envelope I had given her.

"I thought there was supposed to be a check in this envelope," she said, sitting down at the library table. "It's empty. How do I get my prize money?"

"You don't," I said regretfully. "What's more, we must ask

MYRA MERRYWEATHER'S ROSEMARY
AND RIPE OLIVE PESTO

1 cup large ripe olives, pitted
½ cup fresh basil
½ cup fresh parsley
¼ cup onion, chopped
¼ cup grated Romano cheese
¼ cup walnuts or pine nuts
1 tablespoon fresh rosemary, finely minced
3 cloves garlic, mashed
1 tablespoon extra virgin olive oil
3 teaspoons lemon juice

Process all ingredients in a food processor or blender until smooth, stopping occasionally to scrape down the sides. Refrigerate for at least 2 hours before serving; if it seems too thick, stir in a little more oil. Makes about 1 cup. Serve with your favorite cooked pasta.

you to return the *Myra Merryweather Cookery Book* that you took from this room."

Delia's eyes widened. "But I . . . I didn't!" she sputtered. "I had nothing to do with it!"

Ruby sighed. "Show her the proof, China."

I opened the folder containing the photocopies and put a page on the table. In the left margin, in Myra Merryweather's careful script, was written the recipe for Rosemary and Ripe Olive Pesto. "This is your great-aunt's original recipe," I said quietly. "It's the same recipe that won the prize."

There was a long silence. Delia bit her lip and swallowed. In a low voice, she said at last, "Great-aunt Myra promised that cookbook to Mother years ago. It was just plain spiteful of her to give it to somebody else." There were tears in her eyes as she glanced at Pansy. "Now I suppose you'll call the police."

Pansy shook her head. "All you have to do is return the book, Delia. We'll never reveal that you took it."

Delia's face fell. "Return the book? But it's *mine!* It belongs in my family!"

"Would you rather be charged with a felony?" Pansy asked.

Another long silence, as Delia wrestled with her options. "Oh, I suppose," she muttered at last. She took out a handker-chief and blew her nose.

"I'll go with you to get the book," Ruby offered.

"Well, come on, then." Delia sighed heavily. "Let's get it over with."

❧

Two days later, Pansy was back in my shop, all smiles. "We've repaired the display case and put the book in it, China. I'm very grateful to you for solving the mystery!"

"I wish there could have been a happier ending," I replied, putting a tray of crackers and a pot of appetizer on the hospi-tality shelf. "It was wrong of Delia to take the book, but I could understand how she felt about it."

"I know," Pansy said. "But we have the book back, and Delia will get something out of it. We've decided to make the Creative Cookery Contest an annual affair, with a plaque that goes from one winner to the next. Delia's name will be first.

And when we publish a second edition of Myra's cookbook, we'll put in a thank-you to her—and a special one to you."

"That's very generous," I said.

Pansy turned to leave. "Oh, by the way," she said. "Remember that new furniture of Cora's? It turns out that her ex-husband made good on his promise to repay her for taking some of his debts." She paused. "And Jerry put a lock on the kitchen door this morning."

"That's good," I said. I dabbed some appetizer spread on a cracker and handed it to her. "I've been experimenting with another one of Myra's recipes. Have a taste."

Pansy popped the cracker into her mouth. "Delicious!" she exclaimed, her eyes lighting up. "And very different. What *is* it?"

"Traditionally, it's called tapenade," I said. "It's a Provençal specialty. I've added rosemary to the dish and given it a different name, in honor of our recent experience."

"What's that?" Pansy asked.

"China's Rosemary Caper," I replied.

Tapenade is an Old World appetizer that looks something like caviar but tastes like anchovies, olives, and capers — a zesty combination spread on toasted French bread or sturdy whole-wheat crackers, or served as a dip for raw veggies. Add a spoonful of olive oil, some chopped fresh tomatoes, and toss it with hot cooked pasta. Versatile and different!

CHINA'S ROSEMARY CAPER

2 small (6- or 8-ounce) jars of oil-cured black olives
1/3 cup olive oil
1/3 cup tiny capers (nonpareil), drained
2 (2-ounce) tins flat anchovy fillets, undrained
1 tablespoon lemon juice
3 cloves garlic, minced fine
2 teaspoons finely minced fresh rosemary leaves or 1
     teaspoon dried
Pepper to taste

Pit the olives and place in a blender or food processor. Add olive oil and blend. Add capers, anchovies, lemon juice, garlic, and rosemary. Blend until smooth (or, if you prefer, until it's slightly grainy). Taste, and add pepper if you like. If the spread is too thick, add additional olive oil. Refrigerate for several days for best flavor. Serve at room temperature. (To store, pack in a large-mouthed jar and cover with olive oil. Cover jar tightly.)

IVY'S WILD, WONDERFUL WEEDS

One person's weed is another person's wildflower.

—Anonymous

WHEN I bought the old stone building on Crockett Street and opened Thyme and Seasons Herbs, the neighborhood looked quite a bit different. The trendy, upscale restaurant across Crockett Street was still just an ordinary house with a friendly front porch and a big green side yard. The two-story house beside it was occupied by a family with eight children, sixteen bicycles, and five dogs; now, it's the Love Family Funeral Home and Mortuary. And the big, seedy-looking house next door on the east has been fixed up and turned into a children's bookstore called the Hobbit House, owned by Molly McGregor. Neighborhoods are just like people — they grow up, get new jobs, get facelifts and tummy tucks. Or they grow old, get tired, and let themselves go to the dogs. The neighborhood around Thyme and Seasons is changing from mostly residential to partly commercial, which has not been an entirely bad thing. In the process, it's been facelifts and tummy tucks all around.

Except for the Craft Emporium, which is desperately in need of a facelift. The Emporium, at the corner of Crockett and Guadalupe, occupies a sagging three-story Victorian mansion built before the turn of the century and, in its heyday, one of the grandest residences in Pecan Springs. Now, it stands like a sadly weary and time-worn grande dame, not quite ready to throw in the towel but lacking the energy for anything else. Through time and misfortune, the old place has come down in the world, losing all of its dignity and most of its opulence to a haphazard succession of owners who failed to give it a facelift, or even a good coat of paint. Eight or nine years ago, Constance Letterman bought it and turned the large, high-ceilinged rooms into a warren of antique booths, boutiques, and tiny craft shops, providing a livelihood to about a dozen crafters, artists, and collectors.

One day a few months back, I went over to the Emporium. Gretel Schumaker sells handcrafted candles in the front parlor, and I wanted to buy a dozen lavender candles, a popular item at Thyme and Seasons. Afterward, with the box of candles under my arm, I poked my head into Olive Carpenter's Quilting

You can buy your herbal candles from Gretel or next door at Thyme and Seasons, or you can try making your own, which isn't as hard as you may think. Here are some simple directions for making four lovely lavender-colored, lavender-scented candles, using supplies you can purchase at a craft store or find at home:

1 pound paraffin
½ pound beeswax
4 (16-ounce) aluminum cans, washed, for melting wax
Pan, large enough to hold all four cans
Wooden chopstick (to stir the wax)
*4 tablespoons stearic powder (wax hardener, also called
     stearin, to make your candles burn longer)*
*4 molds (plastic candle molds, or clean cardboard or
     plastic cartons)*
Candlewick
*4 wooden sticks or pencils (to secure the wick at the top of
     the mold)*
*Duct tape or electrical tape (to secure the wick at the
     bottom of the mold)*
Lavender color chips (enough to color 1½ pounds of wax)
Essential oil of lavender (about 60 drops for 4 candles)

1. Cut the paraffin and beeswax into one-inch chunks, using a knife and exerting a strong downward pressure. If you work on a dishtowel, you'll be able to scoop up the pieces more easily.

2. Put a couple of inches of water in the large pan and begin heating it. Divide the paraffin and beeswax chunks equally among the four cans. Place the cans in the water and bring it to a gentle simmer. As the wax melts, stir it frequently, using the chopstick. When it is melted, add 1 tablespoon of stearic powder to each can.

3. To prepare the molds, begin by cutting four wicks to the proper length, long enough to extend through the bottom of your mold about one-half inch, and to tie around the pencil or stick that will rest across the top of your mold. Punch a hole in the bottom of each mold and pull the wick through. When you've pulled a half-inch through, tape it with a piece of duct or electrical tape, securing the wick and covering the hole. Tie the free end of the wick to the pencil or stick, making sure the wick is centered and taut.

4. When the cans are full and most of the wax is melted, use tongs or a hot pad to remove the cans to a non-scorchable surface. Cut the color chip in four pieces and add one to each can. Add 10 to 15 drops of lavender oil to each can. Stir. Pour the melted wax into the candle molds, reserving a few ounces from each to fill in the top of the candle when it has set.

5. When the candles have hardened, check to see if there is a depression around the wick. If so, remelt some wax and fill in the sunken area. Let the candles set over-night. Then cut the wick below the stick, and remove the candle from the mold. Trim the wick to one-quarter inch. Light, and enjoy the lovely lavender fragrance!

Bee, which occupies the dining room, and said hello to Olive. Then I stopped in to browse at Delia Murphy's Bead Boutique across the hall, and waved at Annie Walters, who has cleverly filled the old kitchen with antique cookware.

Most of these shop owners do pretty well, for the Craft Emporium is only a couple of blocks from Courthouse Square, close enough for even the most befuddled tourist to find it without a map. But I can't say the same for Constance Letterman, who reminds me of a small woman who has a very large and rowdy tiger by the tail. And to make things even more difficult, Constance (who is certainly not the best-organized person in the world) has an imagination that tends toward the titanic. In her mind, small problems grow to catastrophic proportions in the instant it would take somebody else to say, "Oh, it can't be as bad as all that."

Which is why I was not at all surprised to find Constance in the crowded broom closet that is her office, tugging at her hair in a state of near-hysteria.

"This is *impossible*, China!" she cried despairingly, wadding up adding machine tape and slam-dunking it into a plastic mop bucket. "Real estate taxes have flown through the roof, the plumber wants a fortune to fix a few leaks, and the property insurance has skyrocketed." Her voice rose to a wail. "And Olive just told me she's moving out by the end of the month! She says she needs more space."

"I'm sorry to hear about Olive," I said soothingly, putting down my box of candles. "But I'm sure you have a waiting list of people who are anxious to move in."

"Not anymore, I don't," Constance replied in a dire Chicken Little tone. "Everybody on the waiting list has found another place—and who can blame them? The Emporium needs a paint job, the sidewalk needs patching, and the landscaping needs . . . well, there isn't any landscaping. It's just a bunch of weeds out there." Her shoulders slumped and she shook her head sadly. "It's all just too much for me, China. I've decided I'm going to take Mr. Trout's offer."

I frowned. "Trout? Terry Trout, the real estate guy?"

"That's the one." Constance pushed her chair back. "A couple of months ago, he told me he had somebody who was anxious to buy the Emporium — for more than twice what I paid for it. All I have to do is pick up the phone and tell him I'm ready to sell."

I know Terry Trout, and I don't much like him. He has a local reputation for developments that are out of sync with the neighborhood — a big apartment complex on a street of single-family homes, a block of houses sacrificed to a chain grocery and parking lot. "A buyer?" I asked nervously. "What kind of buyer?"

Constance's eyes slid away. "Well, Mr. Trout didn't give me the details," she replied evasively. "But he did say that the buyer wanted to tear down the house."

"Tear down the house?" I was horrified. "And do what with the land?"

Constance squared her shoulders defensively. "Build a gas station, I think he said."

"A gas station!" Right next door to Thyme and Seasons? "But . . . but that would change the whole neighborhood!" I sputtered. "Think what it would do to property values! Imagine the traffic! Picture the — "

"Excuse me, China." Constance clenched her fists. "But since you don't have my headaches, I hardly see that you have anything to say in the matter." Her voice became plaintively self-pitying, and a couple of tears squeezed out of her eyes and trickled down her cheeks. "I don't want to sell, heaven knows. I've put ten years of my life into this place. But no matter how many things I get fixed, there's always something else that needs attention. You have Ruby to help you out, but I don't have anybody, and I'm just tired of trying to juggle all these disasters all by myself. And now I have to find a new renter to take Olive's place." Her voice quavered. "I'm going to sell out, buy myself an RV, and head for the desert. Then I won't have to worry about anything."

Somehow I couldn't picture Constance living alone in the desert in an RV—for one thing, she'd be too far from Bobby Rae's House of Beauty, where her curls come from—and I knew her well enough to know that she'd always be worrying about something. But I understood her motivation. And anyway, I'd done enough damage for one morning.

"I'm sorry," I said sincerely. "I know how you must feel." Constance was right. She was the one who had to decide what to do, and it wasn't fair for me to put pressure on her. "But I hope you won't make up your mind right away," I added with a shudder, thinking about the horrors of having a gas station right next door. "Would it help if I could come up with somebody to take Olive's space?"

"Well, it might help a little," she replied. "Maybe then I'd be willing to put Mr. Trout off for a few months." She gave me a hopeful look. "Who do you have in mind?"

Now I'd done it. Of course I didn't have anybody in mind,

and I had raised her hopes. I muttered an apology, grabbed my candles, and fled back to Thyme and Seasons, where Ruby was minding both our shops.

"You look worried," she said. "What's wrong?"

"Constance is thinking of selling out to Terry Trout," I blurted. "He has a buyer who wants to tear the Emporium down and build a gas station."

Ruby paled. "Terry Trout? That guy is a *shark!* He'll take her to the cleaners! She can't be serious!"

On another occasion, I might have snickered at Ruby's mixed metaphors, but this wasn't the time for joking. "She sure sounds serious to me," I said grimly. "In fact, even I might be tempted to sell out, if I had her headaches." Constance was right about one thing—having Ruby as a partner in our tearoom has made all the difference. Even a small business can inspire some pretty large problems, and it's a relief to have someone to share the challenges.

"Headaches?" a woman's voice asked. "Haven't I heard that feverfew is good for headaches?"

I turned around. "Hey, Ivy! Good to see you."

"I thought I'd have lunch in your tearoom," Ivy O'Toole replied with a smile, "and I was hoping you would join me." She put down a large cardboard portfolio and bent over to pick up Khat, who had roused himself from his nap on the windowsill when he heard her voice. "How's my hero?" she whispered against his fur. Khat purred and gave her nose a quick lick, which is a remarkable tribute, from him.

Ivy O'Toole was the woman I had found when I went looking for Khat, who had gone missing six weeks before. Ivy had just moved into the long-vacant Gillis house, and had suffered a bad accident that might have been disastrous if I hadn't found her when I did. I'd given her a ride home from the hospital, and Ruby and I had taken lunch to her house a couple of times. Ivy looked a great deal better than she had back then. She'd lost some weight, and she was wearing her blond hair long, so that it brushed her shoulders.

"Feverfew is good for a migraine," I said, going back to Ivy's first remark, "but I don't think it'll cure what ails Constance Letterman." I told Ivy what Constance had told me.

Feverfew (*Chrysanthemum parthenium*) is a perennial that produces mounds of white flowers that look like tiny chrysanthemums. It offers an interesting answer to the question, "What's in a name?" In the Middle Ages, the plant was known as *featherfoil*, because of the feathered edges of its leaf. Over the years, *featherfoil* was corrupted to *featherfew*, and finally became *feverfew*. Because of this name, some people thought the plant might be effective against fever, especially malaria, and it began to be used for that purpose. However, when cinchona bark (quinine) was discovered to be a superior remedy, feverfew was more or less forgotten. It wasn't until the 1970s that the herb was discovered to be an excellent remedy for certain kinds of migraine. Its active chemical ingredient, parthenolide, appears to inhibit inflammation. Researchers are finding it of use, as well, in the treatment of rheumatoid arthritis. For a full description of this useful herb and many other medicinal plants, see Michael Castleman's *The New Healing Herbs* (Rodale Press, 2001).

"I certainly sympathize," Ivy said philosophically. "I've had my hands full with that house I just bought. But I located a contractor who seems to know what he's doing. The big stuff should be finished in another week or so, and I can do the rest as I go along."

"I don't think it's the actual work that bothers Constance," Ruby said. "The problem is that she's not very well organized."

"And she goes around looking for things that are wrong," I added. "If Constance doesn't have a disaster every day, she thinks she's not living right. The trouble is, you can't always tell whether the sky is really falling, or it's just another bad-hair day."

Ivy glanced at me. "You say that one of the Emporium's tenants is moving out?"

I nodded. "I got the feeling that Olive's departure was sort of the final straw. Now Constance has to find somebody else to move into the dining room, and all of a sudden it feels like the San Francisco earthquake." I sighed. "But it'll be a disaster for the entire street, if Terry Trout brings a gas station into the neighborhood."

Ivy looked thoughtful. "Maybe I should drop in and take a look at that dining room."

"Why?" Ruby asked curiously.

In answer, Ivy picked up her portfolio, placed it on the counter, and opened it.

"Oh, wow!" Ruby gasped. "Ivy, these are *beautiful!*"

I pulled in my breath. Before us lay a dozen different botanical prints, in exquisite shades of greens and pastels, all on fine ivory paper. "Ivy," I said, "you didn't tell us that you're an artist." I picked up a print and studied it carefully. "Why, this looks as if it were made from an actual sprig of yarrow!" I picked up another. "And here's thyme!"

"And lavender," Ruby said. "Look, China! It's lavender, with purple blossoms! Ivy, how gorgeous!"

"Do you think so?" Ivy asked, looking pleased. "I really enjoy making them. And yes, they're plant prints, made by inking the plant material and pressing it on paper. It's a very old art—the earliest example I know of is found in one of Leonardo da Vinci's books. He made an inked impression of a sage leaf, and within a few years, lots of people were making prints of natural materials, primarily for scientific purposes."

"I can see why," I said, looking closely at the print of a sprig of sage, which clearly showed the delicate veining and the pebbly texture of the leaf. "For a scientist, the actual print of a single leaf would be worth a dozen artists' drawings. And the plants could be collected in the field and used immediately to make the print—especially important before photography came along."

"Exactly," Ivy said. "I collected some of these plant materials from my garden, but weeds are actually my favorites. And you can use lots of different things, not just plants, to make nature prints." She picked up an imprint of a large goldfish, perfect down to the fins and scales. "This is Sushi. He jumped out of his goldfish pond, unfortunately. I tried to revive him but it was too late, so I printed him. The Japanese have been doing fish rubbing since the early nineteenth century. They call it *gyotaku*."

I gawked at Sushi. "Amazing," I said.

"These are watercolor prints?" Ruby asked.

Ivy nodded. "But you can also print with colored inks. When you're just getting started, ink is simpler. And of course, you can make all kinds of things—notecards, giftwrap, calendars, fabrics. I've even used large leaves and fern fronds to print wall borders."

"I am definitely impressed," I said, looking first at one print, then another. "Are any of these for sale?"

Ivy cleared her throat. "I've always made them for my own pleasure. But lately, I've been thinking about selling them. Do you think they're good enough?" She hesitated. "Be honest, now. If you don't think so, say so. I can take it."

"They're wonderful!" Ruby said enthusiastically. "I'm sure you'll be able to sell them." She frowned. "The question is where."

I looked around. "I certainly want some cards," I said. "And I'd like to hang some of the prints here. But I don't have enough room to do your work justice. What you need is some gallery space, where the framed prints can be hung at eye level. And where you can display some of your other things—cards, fabric, giftwrap."

"Do you think," Ivy asked hesitantly, "that the Emporium might work for me?"

"It would be perfect!" Ruby said. "The walls are white, the floor is polished wood, and there's lots of natural light. It's ex-

Nature printing is a lovely way to preserve plant images. To get started, you'll need to collect some garden plants and weeds and press them (a telephone book makes a sturdy plant press). When you're ready to print, assemble the pressed plants (make sure they're clean), some newspapers, a few sheets of printmaking paper, newsprint, a flat glass plate, water-soluble ink such as Speedball (it's best to start with one color, say, green), an artist's brush, tweezers, and a few sheets of nontextured paper towel. Squeeze or scoop a small blob of ink onto the plate and brush it out evenly. Lay the plant material on the newsprint, veined side up. With the brush paint the ink evenly on the leaf, beginning at the center and working outward. Use the tweezers to gently lift the inked leaf and place it on the printing paper, veined side down. Place a paper towel over the inked plant and gently press outward from the center. (Don't rub—you'll move the plant and smear the ink.) Remove the paper towel and use the tweezers to lift the plant. Let your print dry, frame it, and hang it where others can admire it. For examples, ideas, and detailed instructions for creating stationery, cards, and printed fabric, read *Nature Printing with Herbs, Fruits, and Flowers*, by Laura Donnelly Bethmann (Storey Publishing, 1996).

actly what you need to display your prints." She paused and cast a questioning look at Ivy. "But I don't know how much the rent might be," she added.

"Money isn't really an issue," Ivy replied. "My husband died two years ago and left me pretty well off. I can do just about anything I want to do, except bring him back, of course." Her smile was just the slightest bit crooked. "If I want to hang out my shingle as an artist — well, that seems pretty reasonable to me, if maybe a little brazen. I'm not sure I'm that good."

"Not brazen," Ruby amended. "Brave. Anyway, you'll never know whether you're good until you put your work out where other people can see it." She began to put the prints back into Ivy's portfolio. "Come on — we'll introduce you to Constance, and you can take a look at the Emporium." She gave a little laugh. "If you promise not to turn up your nose at the peeling paint."

"And watch those porch steps," I cautioned.

The Emporium's cosmetic problems didn't seem to bother Ivy, and within the hour, the arrangements were made. To my surprise, Ivy and Constance hit it off amazingly well. Ivy chuckled at Constance's jokes, and Constance was visibly awed by Ivy's botanical artistry. By the time the deal was consummated, the two seemed well on their way to becoming friends. Ivy signed a six-month lease and gave Constance a check for the first and last months' rent.

"There are some things I'll want to do before I open for business," Ivy said, as we stood on the front porch, saying goodbye. "A new carpet, green, I think. The walls will need painting, and I might try printing some leafy borders, in different shades of green. I'll want new blinds for the large window, maybe those very thin bamboo blinds that diffuse the light. And a few wicker chairs and a couple of large plants." She smiled happily. "I want it to look just like a real gallery."

"It will *be* a real gallery," Ruby said.

"Well, then," Constance said with a gleam in her eye, "we'll have to plan a grand opening, won't we? After all, we want to give the new business the right send-off." She gave a critical look around. "I've been meaning to get these steps fixed. And I'll need to do something about the landscaping. All those weeds—"

"China and I were just thinking about that," Ruby put in quickly. "We were saying that it wouldn't be very much work to extend China's herb garden all the way across the front of the Emporium." She gave me a meaningful look. "Weren't we, China?"

"Oh, absolutely," I lied happily, as the gas station began to fade into the realm of remote possibilities. "How about a butterfly garden, with salvia and echinacea and fennel and yarrow and—"

"A butterfly garden!" Constance exclaimed, her brown curls quivering. "I swear, y'all are so full of ideas and energy, you're getting me excited, too! This is gonna be *fun!*"

Constance managed to maintain her excitement long enough to get the porch steps fixed and the sidewalk patched. Ruby and I worked evenings and a weekend, putting in the new butterfly garden. And when Olive moved out, we all pitched in to fix up Ivy's new gallery, which she was calling Wild, Wonderful Weeds. By the second week of the month, the grass-green carpet was laid and the walls were painted white and printed with fern-frond borders. Ivy hung her prints, arranged tasteful displays of her cards, fabrics, and giftwraps, and was ready for her grand opening.

"I'm so nervous, China!" she whispered as we stood near the door. She was wearing a sweeping green and white dress made of fabric she'd printed herself, and her pale hair was

Butterflies are nature's loveliest pollinators. You can lure them to your yard by offering their favorite plants. Here are some butterfly plants, listed with their hardiness zones. (Visit the USDA hardiness map on the Internet at *http://www.usna.usda.gov/Hardzone/ushzmap.html* or ask your librarian to help you locate a hardiness map.) Those that attract the greatest variety are starred.

Anise hyssop, Zones 3–9
New England aster, 3–9
Black-eyed Susan, 3–10
*Butterfly bush, 5–10
*Butterfly weed (larval host to Monarch), 3–10
*Button bush, 5–10
Chaste tree (*Vitex*), 7–10
Purple coneflower (*Echinacea*), 3–9
Coreopsis, 3–9
Fennel (larval host to Black Swallowtail), 3–9
Gayfeather, 4–9
Globe thistle (larval host to Painted Lady), 3–8
Hollyhock (larval host to Painted Lady), 3–9
*Joe-Pye weed, 4–9
Lantana, 9–10
Parsley (larval host to Black Swallowtail), 3–9
Sedum (especially varieties "Meteor" and "Carmen"), 3–9
Yarrow, 3–9

pulled back in a chic bun at the back of her neck. "What if they don't like my work? What if nobody comes?"

But there wasn't much chance of that. New businesses in Pecan Springs are always a big deal, and people come out of curiosity, if nothing else. Hark Hibler had interviewed Ivy and run a long article in Saturday's *Enterprise*, complete with photographs of her and her artwork. Helen Jenson, the president of the Chamber of Commerce, had strung a red ribbon across the newly repaired porch steps, and the entire Chamber wore their matching blue blazers for the ribbon-cutting and obligatory photograph. Within a half hour, the room was crowded with people who had come to get a look at Pecan Springs's first botanical art gallery and to chow down on a selection of Janet's tasty herbal hors d'oeuvres, courtesy of Thyme for Tea. The mayor was there, of course, and Madeleine Jordan, from the city council, doing their duty to encourage the local economy. Mrs. Love, of Love's Family Funeral Home and Mortuary, had dropped in, as had Molly McGregor, the owner of the Hobbit House, on the other side of Thyme and Seasons. As people began to wander in off the street, it looked as if we were going to have a full house, which would certainly bode well for Ivy's success. Something else might bode well, too.

I nudged Ruby. "Look at that," I said in a low voice. "Hark is turning on the charm." Over in the corner, he was talking intently to Ivy, who was smiling back at him with what looked like genuine interest. When he feels like it, Hark can manage a certain low-wattage charm. He's no Don Juan, but he's certainly not bad-looking, now that he's lost about forty pounds and cultivated a distinguished-looking salt-and-pepper mustache to go with his dark hair.

"Well, my goodness." Ruby giggled. "Looks like Pecan Springs's most eligible bachelor is seriously interested."

I glanced at Ruby, who, once upon a time, had dated Hark. But if she was jealous of Hark's attention to Ivy, she wasn't showing it. "Looks to me like he's seriously smitten," I remarked wryly. "And if you ask me, Ivy's enjoying every minute of it."

"Couldn't happen to a nicer pair," Ruby said with a shrug, and turned away to show Mrs. Love some of Ivy's work. Then Pansy Pride came over, making *ooh*-ing and *ahh*-ing noises over Ivy's botanical art, and bought three dozen hand-printed cards to give to her friends. And when the Garden Club showed up en masse, sales got even brisker. By the time everyone had left, the walls and shelves were all but empty.

Herbal hors d'oeuvres are easy, tasty, and attractive. Make a tray for your next party!

HERBED CHEESE IN A POT

4 ounces cream cheese	1 teaspoon dried summer
4 ounces grated Cheddar	savory
2 cloves garlic, crushed	1 teaspoon dried thyme
1 teaspoon dried basil	

Combine cheeses, garlic, and herbs and mix well. Spoon mixture into a small crock and press down firmly with the back of a spoon. Refrigerate for at least a day to blend flavors. Serve with crackers and a small knife. Makes 1 cup.

DILLED SALMON AND
CREAM CHEESE SANDWICHES

8 ounces light cream cheese, softened
1 tablespoon chopped fresh dill weed
1 tablespoon minced parsley
1 tablespoon chopped chives
10 slices white bread
3 ounces thinly sliced smoked salmon

In a small bowl, stir together the cream cheese, dill weed, parsley, and chives. With a serrated knife, trim the crusts from the slices of bread. Using a rolling pin, flatten each slice slightly. Spread about 1½ tablespoons of the cream cheese mixture over the entire surface of each slice of bread. Top with the salmon. Cut into squares, diamonds, or rectangles. Repeat with the remaining slices of bread. Arrange sandwiches on a serving plate, cover the top with plastic wrap, and refrigerate until ready to serve. Makes forty.

"It's a good thing I've got more items at home," Ivy said, looking around at the empty spots on the walls and shelves. "But I'm going to have to get to work—which means that I'll have to find somebody to mind the shop for a few hours every day." She laughed. "There's nothing like a few good sales to stimulate your creativity."

"I'll be glad to help out," Constance offered quickly. "It'd be fun. Give me something to do besides sit around and worry."

And that's what happened. With a new business breathing some life and energy into the old Emporium, Constance stopped imagining herself on the deck of the *Titanic* and began to fix things up. Ivy gave her the name of the contractor who had done the work on her house. He gave Constance a fair price on the repairs that needed to be made, including the plumbing and electrical, and he even fixed up the old garage at the back of the property, which Constance promptly rented out to a new shop specializing in antique garden furniture.

Things really seemed to be looking up as far as the Emporium was concerned, and I forgot all about Terry Trout and the gas station, until one day when I went over to the Emporium to buy some of Ivy's notecards. And there was Terry Trout, standing in the doorway of Constance's broom-closet office.

"Jes' thought Ah'd drop by," he was saying to her in that booming Texas voice of his, "and let you know my buyer's gettin' real antsy. Says he's figgerin' on lookin' somewheres else, if we cain't make a deal with you."

"Well, maybe he'd better do that," Constance said briskly, "because I've decided that I'm not ready to sell. I've got a few things I want to do around here."

"But Ah thought you wanted t' buy yerself an RV and move to the desert," Terry Trout said, in a tone of shocked surprise. "That's what you tol' me."

"Maybe someday," Constance said, "but not just yet."

Terry Trout didn't exactly gnash his teeth, but he jammed his white cowboy hat on his head and slammed the front door on his way out. I suppressed a grin, thinking that it was maybe just a little ironic that Ivy's wild, wonderful weeds had given Constance a new lease on life and saved the Emporium from being turned into a gas station.

DEATH
OF A ROSE
RUSTLER

Hope is like a harebell, trembling from its birth,
Love is like a rose, the joy of all the earth,
Faith is like a lily, lifted high and white,
Love is like a lovely rose, the world's delight.
Harebells and sweet lilies show a thornless growth,
But the rose with all its thorns excels them both.

—Christina Rossetti (1830–94)

IT all began with a trip to the cemetery.

I'm usually too busy at my herb shop to spend much time hanging out in cemeteries. But my partner and best friend, Ruby Wilcox, goes once a year to take flowers to the grave of her favorite grandmother, and this year I went with her, taking a lush green wreath of rosemary to place on the grave.

"This is so pretty," Ruby said, looking around at the spring flowers. "When I die, you can bury me right here." At the Pecan Springs cemetery, families can plant whatever they want without getting permission, so it's filled with fascinating cottage-garden herbs and flowers. Ruby pointed to a patch of spreading pink verbena. "And you can plant some of that on my grave, if you don't mind."

"Good choice," I said approvingly. "Verbena was one of the Druids' nine sacred herbs. They used it to exorcise devils and protect themselves from evil. They called it vervain."

"That's for me," Ruby declared with a grin. "Get all my friends together and throw a blanket of vervain over me. That should keep the ghoulies away."

"If you're really worried about being disturbed, we could plant some basil, too," I went on. "In India, in the days when families buried their dead under the floors of their houses, they kept pots of basil on the windowsills to make sure that everybody slept without being disturbed. There's a variety that is still called holy basil."

"I'll have basil, too, then," Ruby said. "There's nothing like a nice long nap."

Our laughter sounded uneasy. Giggles in a graveyard always seem a little—well, disrespectful. And cemeteries, however beautiful they might be, are spooky places. It's easy to imagine all sorts of things going on, some of them not very restful.

Ruby had already stopped laughing. "China," she said

Herbs That Honor the Dead

- Rosemary has been used for centuries as a funeral herb. Its evergreen needles symbolize our undying recollections of those we have loved and lost. Shakespeare called it the "herb of remembrance," and in the sixteenth century, Thomas More wrote: "As for rosemary, I let it runne all over my garden walls, not only because my bees love it but because it is the herb sacred to remembrance." Interestingly, researchers have begun to think that rosemary might actually *help* us to remember. Experiments suggest that a chemical in the herb may improve the memory of people suffering from early-stage Alzheimer's.

- Verbena is a trailing plant, about twelve inches high, with clusters of pink, red, or white flowers. In the south, you can grow it as a tender perennial. In cooler climates, treat it as an annual. The Celts knew it as vervain, which means "to drive away." The herb, revered for its ability to drive away the evil spirits, was often planted around sacred sites and burial places.

- Holy basil (*Ocimum sanctum*) is also known as *tulsi*. In India, where basil is considered sacred, some areas around the holy city of Pandharpur are restricted to the cultivation of *tulsi*. The fragrance of basil is a reminder of the purifying incense burned in memory of the dead.

- Wild thyme (*Thymus vulgaris*) was used in ancient Greece, where it was burned as a funeral incense, as well as being laid on the dead body. The playwright Aristophanes wrote: "Bury my body and pile a great heap of earth on it, and let the wild thyme cover the mound with its sweet scent."

quietly, "what's that over there? It looks like . . . somebody's feet." She pointed toward the life-size statue of a moss-covered angel that guarded the Hausner family plot. Protruding from behind the angel was what looked like a pair of women's shoes, with ankles attached.

"Definitely feet." I frowned. "Maybe she's taking a nap."

"On the wet ground?" Ruby asked nervously. "Maybe she's . . . dead."

"Ruby," I said reprovingly, "you always let your imagination get the better of you. But she might be sick. Let's see if she needs help."

The woman, dressed in a tweed skirt and heavy sweater, lay flat on her back, her head pillowed in a tangle of wild thyme. Her gray hair was unruffled, her hands were neatly arranged on her breast, and her face was peaceful. She looked like someone catching a quick nap.

I bent over and shook her. "Wake up," I said. But the woman's head turned limply to one side, and Ruby drew in a gasp.

"She *is* dead, China!"

We called 911, of course, and the EMS crew was on the scene in a few minutes, followed by a squad car driven by our friend, Chief of Police Sheila Dawson. Sheila took statements from Ruby and me. Then, since both of us had work to do, we went back to our shops, leaving the investigation in her capable hands.

The next morning, I dropped in at Ruby's house for breakfast. She poured me a cup of tea and handed me a plate with a

RUBY'S APPLESAUCE-MINT BREAD

2 cups flour
3 teaspoons baking powder
½ teaspoon baking soda
½ teaspoon nutmeg
½ teaspoon cinnamon
1 cup slivered almonds, chopped
1 egg, beaten
1 cup applesauce
¾ cup firmly packed brown sugar
¼ cup vegetable oil
¼ cup chopped fresh mint (best with fresh, but if you must
*   substitute, use 1 tablespoon dried)*

Preheat oven to 350°F. Sift the first five dry ingredients together, add almonds, and blend well. In a separate bowl, combine egg, applesauce, brown sugar, and oil and stir to mix. Add mint. Add wet ingredients to dry, and stir just until blended. (Do not overmix.) Pour batter into two small greased loaf pans and bake for about 45 minutes. Cool on rack.

fruity slice of some applesauce-mint bread she had baked the night before. "Have you seen this morning's *Enterprise*?" she asked.

I shook my head. "What does it say about the woman we found in the cemetery?"

"Not much," Ruby replied, giving me the newspaper. "The police know who she is, but they don't have any leads yet."

Quickly, I scanned the story. The dead woman was Rose Barton, a widow who had recently moved to Pecan Springs from Dallas and lived alone in a small house on Maple Street. She was survived by one sister, Sybil Sanders, of Bangor, Maine. There was no clear motive for the attack. It hadn't been robbery, because Mrs. Barton's wallet containing fifty dollars and several credit cards was found in her unlocked car a short distance away. According to the paper, Chief Dawson was confident that she and her investigators would turn up some new leads. "We'll have the case solved shortly," she declared.

But three weeks later, Rose Barton's death was still a mystery, and the police were no longer quite so optimistic. I was working in the garden outside the shop early one morning, when an elderly gray-haired lady came toward me. She introduced herself as Sybil Sanders, Mrs. Barton's sister. She said she had come to Pecan Springs to take care of her sister's affairs, and she'd been here ever since, hoping to see the police identify her sister's murderer.

"I must go back to Bangor," she said sadly, "but I hate to leave with so many questions unresolved. I understand that you've helped the police in the past, Ms. Bayles. I've come to ask if you'll see what you can find out about my sister's death."

I firmed the soil around the roots of the rosebush I had just planted—an antique rose named Ducher. I straightened up, frowning. Spring is a busy time at the shop, and I wasn't at all sure that Sheila would want me to get involved with the investigation. But at the same time, I knew how terrible Miss Sanders must feel—and I had to admit to a deep sense of unsettledness.

Ruby and I had discovered Rose Barton's body, but her killer was still a mystery. Reluctantly, I said, "I'll talk to Chief Dawson. If she says it's okay, I'll see what I can do."

"Oh, thank you," Miss Sanders said gratefully. "I'm staying at Rose's house for the next few days. If there's anything I can do to help, please let me know." She looked wistfully at the rose I had just planted. "My sister loved roses, you know. She had lived in her house for only a couple of years, but she already had quite a collection of favorites, and a small library of books about roses. She wrote me that she wanted to find plants that hadn't been named or identified yet. She seemed quite excited about making some of her own discoveries."

"Found roses can be fascinating," I agreed. I picked up my trowel. "I'm curious about one thing," I said. "Do you know why your sister went to the cemetery?"

Miss Sanders shook her head. "I have no idea," she said. "Our parents are buried in Maine, and Rose's husband—he's been dead for several years—had no relatives in this area." She shook her head again, sadly. "It's all a mystery," she said. "A very great mystery."

According to the American Rose Society, an antique rose is any rose that was introduced before 1867. But most collectors recognize as "antique" any rose that is seventy-five years old or more, as long as it exhibits the typical old-rose characteristics of hardiness, fragrance, beauty of form, and pastel color. In America, the effort to preserve old garden roses began in the 1930s, spearheaded by Ethelyn Keays. Ducher is the only white antique China rose. The flowers are cream-colored and softly fragrant, and in spring they cover the plant, which usually blooms in the summer and fall as well, earning it distinction as a "rebloomer." Early records date this lovely rose to 1869.

Sheila looked serious when I told her about Miss Sanders's request. "I have to confess," she said soberly, "that we haven't made much progress on the case. If you want to get involved—unofficially, of course—I certainly wouldn't have any objections." Sheila had come over for Sunday lunch, and she and I were in my kitchen, where I was cooking up a quick chicken and veggie stir-fry, using some of my homemade five-spice seasoning.

"How many suspects have you questioned?" I asked, stirring the sizzling chicken in the wok.

"None," Sheila said ruefully. She pushed her fingers through her blond hair. "We've canvassed the neighbors, questioned the sister, and searched the victim's house. But we haven't turned up a single substantial lead. The woman certainly doesn't seem to have had any enemies."

I added a cup of fresh green beans to the chicken. "Any friends?"

"None that we've found." Sheila sighed. "According to the calender on her desk, Mrs. Barton attended a club meeting on the first Wednesday of the month, but she just put down the word *club* and the time—seven-thirty. We thought we might be on to some-

"Found roses" are old roses discovered growing around abandoned cabins, in old cemeteries, or along country lanes. They are probably the offspring of an old rose, but have not yet been definitively identified. Until an old rose is identified, it is named for the person from whom it was collected. One famous found rose, which bears large pink blossoms, was collected from a homestead in northern Louisiana and is called "Maggie."

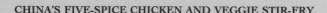

CHINA'S FIVE-SPICE CHICKEN AND VEGGIE STIR-FRY

To make Chinese five-spice seasoning, blend together and store in an airtight container:

2 teaspoons ground cinnamon
2 teaspoons crushed aniseed
½ teaspoon powdered ginger
½ teaspoon freshly ground pepper or ½ teaspoon Szechwan pepper
¼ teaspoon ground cloves

To make a marinade, mix together:
3 tablespoons soy sauce
2 tablespoons sherry
2 teaspoons five-spice seasoning
3 teaspoons honey
3 cloves garlic, smashed

Coat 1 pound thin-sliced chicken breasts with the marinade and refrigerate for 3 to 4 hours. In a wok or heavy skillet, stir-fry chicken until almost done, then add ½ cup vegetable stock and 3 to 4 cups of your favorite vegetables. Cook for another 3 to 4 minutes. Thicken the sauce with 1 tablespoon cornstarch mixed with 2 tablespoons water. Serve over rice.

thing there, but when we checked with the clubs that meet on the first Wednesday, we drew a blank. Nobody had ever heard of her."

"And you haven't found out what she was doing in the cemetery?"

"Not a clue there, either, I'm afraid."

"Maybe she was bird watching," I suggested, adding sliced peppers — green, red, and yellow — to the wok, along with sliced red onions. I put on the lid and let it steam for a few moments. "Was she carrying binoculars?"

Sheila shook her head. "When we searched the car, all we found was a canvas tote bag, a pair of clippers, and a bunch of zipper-top plastic bags with wet paper towels in them."

"Clippers, bags, and wet paper towels?" I asked, startled. I stared at her. "Sheila, I think I know what Mrs. Barton was doing in that cemetery! She was a rose rustler!"

Now it was Sheila's turn to stare. "A rose rustler? What in the world is *that*?"

"Rose rustlers are people who want to propagate old roses," I said, taking off the wok lid and adding a cup of sliced fresh mushrooms. "Mrs. Barton brought the clippers in order to take cuttings, and the wet paper towels to wrap around the stems before she put them into the plastic bags."

"So she came to the cemetery to collect roses," Sheila said in a wondering tone. "I never would have thought of that."

"And what's more," I said, "I'll bet I know exactly what club meeting she went to on the first Wednesday of each month." I reached for the phone, and by the time the stir-fry was finished, I had an answer. For the past year, Mrs. Rose Barton had been a faithful member of the Hill Country Rose Rustlers Club.

Sheila frowned. "So how come we didn't find out about that?"

"Because her sister didn't happen to tell you that Rose Barton was an avid rose collector," I replied. "And because the Rose Rustlers meet in San Marcos, not Pecan Springs." San Marcos, a much larger town, is about a half hour drive from Pecan Springs.

"Bully for you, Sherlock," Sheila said with a grin. "So where do you go from here?" She lifted the wok lid and sniffed appreciatively. "And when's lunch?"

"Anytime you're ready, Watson," I said, handing her a bowl and a pair of chopsticks.

The shop is closed on Mondays, so I drove over to San Marcos to talk to George Webb, the president of the Hill Country Rose Rustlers. He was a thickset man in his sixties with brown hair. His gold-rimmed glasses gave him a studious look, but he had an elfish smile. We had met at an herb conference a couple of years before, and he had told me all about the Rose Rustlers.

To take cuttings from a rose, select a pencil-thick, fairly stiff stem. (It is easiest to root a stem that has recently bloomed.) Cut a six- to eight-inch stem from the parent plant with a sharp knife, at a 45° angle. Dip in rooting hormone, then place in a plastic cup with holes punched in the bottom, filled with potting soil. Cover the cup with a plastic bag (don't let the plastic touch your cutting). Water well and place in a warm area with high humidity and indirect sunlight. Once the cutting has rooted (4 to 6 weeks), you can remove the plastic. Continue to water until the root system is well established, then plant outdoors. But do remember to take cuttings only from antique roses. Hybrid roses are protected by plant patents for twenty years, and propagating a patented rose without the patent owner's written permission is a violation of federal patent laws.

I found George in his large garden, putting a thick layer of mulch around the roots of several spectacular Bourbon roses, all of them in bloom. We chatted a few minutes, as he pointed out his favorites.

"What I like best about the Bourbons," he said, "is that

they're not only beautiful, but they're exceptionally hardy. That one over there, for instance. It's probably the most famous Bourbon of all—Souvenir de la Malmaison. I love it because it has such a beautiful blossom and fragrance. It propagates so easily, too. Every year, I have a dozen new plants to give to friends. That's one of the advantages of these old roses, you know." He grinned. "They haven't been patented."

After a few minutes, I brought up the subject I had come to discuss. "I wonder if you've heard that one of your members was killed a few weeks ago," I said.

"Oh, dear." He pulled his eyebrows together and his smile disappeared. "I've been visiting my daughter in New Orleans and haven't been reading the newspapers. Who was killed? An accident, was it?"

"Rose Barton," I said. "She was murdered."

"Murdered!" he exclaimed, shocked. "Why, that's terrible! Mrs. Barton seemed like such a nice person, even if she was a bit opinionated. She was very enthusiastic about collecting roses. If I remember right, she was especially interested in finding a new yellow rose." He smiled. "An old yellow rose, I mean. True yellow. The yellow rose of Texas."

> Propagation is the process of creating new plants, by seed, layering, grafting, or cutting. By controlling the pollination process, breeders cross desirable parents to propagate new hybrids from seed. (If your rose has hips, she's pregnant. The hip, or rose fruit, contains her fertilized seeds.) Breeders always patent their roses, to legally protect their plants and keep people from propagating them. However, old roses were never patented, and it is legal to propagate them freely. To obtain a cutting, all you need is the permission of the person on whose property the old rose is growing.

We were getting off the subject, so I told him about discovering the body, and the difficulties the police had run into with their investigation, and my theory about what Rose Barton might have been doing in the cemetery.

"Sounds reasonable to me," George Webb said reflectively. He picked up a pair of clippers and began to cut a few blossoms. "Spring isn't the very best time to go rose rustling—here in Texas, fall is better. But when we find a rose we want to collect, most of us take cuttings whether it's the 'right' time of year or not."

"I wonder if you know of any friends Mrs. Barton might have had," I said, nudging him back to the topic.

"Friends?" He scratched his head. "Well, like I said, Mrs. Barton had her opinions. Which might've been the reason she didn't seem to have many friends—among the club members, I mean," he added. "But you might talk to Mary Lewis. The two of them went rustling together a time or two."

I got Mary's address from Mr. Webb, accepted the large bunch of roses he thrust into my hands, and drove back to Pecan Springs. On an impulse, I stopped at Ruby's house, rang the doorbell, and gave her the roses.

"How lovely!" she exclaimed, sniffing them. "And how fragrant! Thank you." Then she frowned. "Is this a bribe? What are you up to now?"

"How'd you guess?" I grinned. "I want you to go to a crime scene with me."

"Who needs a bribe for that?" Ruby asked. "Wait until I put these fabulous roses in water." A few minutes later, we were heading for the cemetery.

The Pecan Springs cemetery was even lovelier than it had been a few weeks before. And now that I knew why Rose Barton had gone there, I could appreciate her interest. This particular cemetery was established when the town was founded, over 150 years ago. It's full of imposing granite monuments, like the massive stone angel that stands guard over the Hausner plot, where Ruby had spotted Mrs. Barton's body. It's also full of hundreds of very old rosebushes.

"Antique roses," Ruby said thoughtfully, when I had explained the concept to her. "Well, I guess it makes sense. Old things are often better than new."

"It makes sense because the old roses have survived for so long without special care," I said. I waved my hand. "Just look at all these bushes. They rarely get pruned or sprayed and nobody worries about black spot or other plant diseases. They just *grow*, without any coddling."

"So if Rose Barton was rose rustling," Ruby mused, "which rose was she rustling? And what makes you think that her interest in roses has anything to do with her murder?"

"I don't know," I admitted. "But everything else has turned into a blind alley. At least this alley has lots of pretty flowers in it."

We began walking around, looking at the plants. After a minute Ruby asked, "Mrs. Barton was just going to take cuttings, right?"

"That's right," I said. "A true rose rustler always leaves the plant intact. Why do you ask?"

"Because," Ruby said, "somebody has dug a hole beside the stone angel where we found the body." She pointed. "See?"

What we were looking at was a large spot of disturbed earth beside the Hausner granite monument. A clump of daisies had been planted and the dirt scraped back around their stems, but that didn't hide the evidence. Until fairly recently, a plant had grown there—a large, stiff bush, judging from the marks left by the branches as they had scraped against the monument. But the plant was gone. Someone had dug it up and put the daisies in its place.

A few minutes later, a conversation with the cemetery's caretaker confirmed this guess. He remembered the plant very well.

"Sure, I recall that rosebush," the old man said. "It was right purty. Had big yeller flowers. Smelled real sweet. I was surprised when I come along one day and saw somebody diggin' it up."

"You actually saw the person?" Ruby asked in surprise. "A man or a woman?"

"A woman," the caretaker said. "That there bush was good-sized, so she had her work cut out for her. O'course, she'd already pruned most of the branches way back, but it prob'ly had sixty, seventy years' worth of roots. I was gonna ask if she needed help, but the grave-diggin' crew showed up about that time, and when I come back, she was gone, and them puny little daisies was stuck in the hole."

"When did this happen?" I asked.

"When?" The caretaker looked vague. "About the time that

woman was found dead, mebbe," he said, scratching his head. "Reckon I cain't be more exact than that."

Ruby looked at me. "Do you suppose it was Rose Barton who dug up that rose?"

"If she didn't," I said, "who did? And why?" I tugged at her arm. "Come on. We're going to see Mary Lewis."

"Mary who?" Ruby asked as we walked away.

"A woman who went rose rustling with Mrs. Barton," I said. "Maybe she knows something about that rose, and whether it's connected to the murder."

Mary Lewis, a pretty, brown-haired woman with a delicate face, lived in the nearby town of New Braunfels, where we found her in the little craft studio behind her house. The walls were covered with herb wreaths and braids of chile peppers and garlic. Mary stood at a table, preparing roses to dry in silica gel. We introduced ourselves and told her why we had come.

"I was sorry to learn about Rose's death," Mary said. She selected a perfect half-open blossom from the basket beside her and cut off the stem about a half inch below the calyx. "It's too bad the police haven't been able to come up with any answers."

I agreed. "Mr. Webb says that you and she occasionally went rose rustling together," I remarked.

"We did, for a while," Mary replied, pouring an inch of silica gel into a plastic margarine tub. The gel, a drying agent, looked like sugar, with little blue flecks in it. "In fact, one day we found a really beautiful Prairie Rose, growing beside an old log cabin. The cuttings I took from it have already rooted, and every time

I look at them, I remember the afternoon we found that plant." She settled the blossom in the gel and began to spoon gel around it, covering it completely. "But Rose was getting into collecting in a big way, and she began going off on her own. I think she was looking for a particular plant, and didn't want anybody around when she found it."

"Really?" I asked curiously. "What was she looking for?"

Mary smiled. "A lot of people think it would be fun to find the original Yellow Rose of Texas." She put a lid on the container and wrote the date on it with a marker. "I think that's what Rose had in mind."

"But the Yellow Rose of Texas wasn't a rose at all!" Ruby exclaimed. "She was a slave girl named Emily Morgan who helped Sam Houston and his men defeat the Mexican army by stealing Santa Anna's battle plan. And then she—"

"And then somebody wrote a song about her," Mary took up the story. "But according to legend, there really *was* a yellow rose of Texas. Emily wore it in her hair."

"But there aren't any antique yellow roses," I said. "At least, no yellow shrub roses," I amended.

"That's right," Mary said. "Emily's rose is just a legend—or maybe the plant was lost. But there are plenty of rose fanciers who would like to discover an antique yellow rose. It might even be valuable."

"Mmm," I said, thinking of what the cemetery caretaker had told us. "Did Rose ever mention that she wanted to go collecting at the Pecan Springs cemetery? Did she say anything about looking for a yellow rose that might be growing there?"

"No, she didn't," Mary said. She picked up another blossom. "Why are you asking?"

"Because," I said regretfully, "it's beginning to look like that yellow rose might have played a role in her death."

"I'd be sorry to hear that," Mary said. She looked at the flower in her hand. "Roses are wonderful, but they're not to die for."

Ruby had to go back to the shop, so I dropped her off, then drove on. I had an idea, and now was as good a time as any to check it out, so I went to the office of the Pecan Springs *Enterprise*. I wanted a few words with Ethel Fritz, who knows everything there is to know about the history of Pecan Springs and its founding families.

"The Hausners?" Ethel asked, smiling. "Now, there's a family for you. Old Mr. Hausner's daddy's daddy was a mover and shaker in the old Republic of Texas, around the time of the Alamo. But there's only one family member left—Charlotte Hausner Thomas. She gives talks at the library on the early days of Pecan Springs." Ethel gave me Charlotte Thomas's address. I made a quick phone call, and a few minutes later, I was on my way again.

Mrs. Thomas lived in a comfortable frame house in an older section of town. As I walked up the porch steps, I noticed that several rosebushes had been newly planted beside the porch. They'd all been pruned back and were just beginning to put out some sturdy new growth. Behind them, leaning against the house, was a spade.

The woman who answered the bell was in her fifties, tanned

and athletic-looking with short-cropped gray hair. I introduced myself, and she gave me a welcoming smile.

"Please come in," she said, opening the door. "I was so excited when you called, Ms. Bayles. It's nice to know that the *Enterprise* would like to do an article about my family."

I felt guilty for making up a story, but I couldn't have told Mrs. Thomas about my real reason for coming to see her. So I followed her into the living room and took the chair she indicated. A teapot waited on a small table, together with two slices of pie.

Mrs. Thomas handed me a plate, and when I had taken a bite and exclaimed at the unusual taste, she said proudly, "It's vinegar pie—an old family recipe."

"Vinegar pie?" I asked, surprised. The pie was almost like custard, with a delicate rose flavor.

Mrs. Thomas nodded. "During the Depression, lemons were expensive and hard to get. So instead of lemon pie, people made vinegar pie. My mother made lots of herbal vinegars, and she often used them in her vinegar pie. I made this one with rose vinegar, just the way she used to do."

"It's delicious," I said. I listened for the next half hour or so, pretending to take notes, while she told me about her family's early days in Pecan Springs. She was obviously proud of being a descendent of one of the founding families and anxious to talk about this important connection. I was more interested, however, in the photograph album she brought out to show me. One of the pictures showed the stone angel standing guard over the Hausner plot. At its feet was a large shrub rose, smothered with yellow blossoms.

THE HAUSNER FAMILY RECIPE FOR
ROSE-FLAVORED VINEGAR PIE

½ cup softened butter
1¼ cups sugar
3 tablespoons rose petal vinegar*
4 eggs
1 teaspoon vanilla
1 unbaked 8" pie shell

**Cream together butter and sugar until light and fluffy. Add
vinegar, eggs, and vanilla; beat well. Pour into pie shell. Bake
in 350°F oven 45 minutes or until knife blade inserted between
center and edge of pie comes out clean. Makes eight servings.**

*To make rose petal vinegar: Steep 1 cup red rose petals (clean, freshly
picked, unsprayed) in 2 cups champagne vinegar for one week. Check the
flavor and steep for a longer period, if desired. Strain and rebottle. Store in
a dark place, tightly capped. Use for fruit salad dressing, in a sorbet, as a
facial splash—or to flavor vinegar pie!

After a time, I put away my notebook and thanked Mrs.
Thomas for her hospitality. Then, as she was showing me out,
I said casually, "I see that you've just planted a rosebush beside
the porch. I love roses. What kind is it?"

An uneasy look crossed her face. "It came from the cemetery," she said. She bit her lip and dropped her eyes. "I brought
it home because the poor thing never bloomed."

And that was that. But after Mrs. Thomas had gone inside
and closed the door, I stepped quickly off the porch and peered
at the spade that was leaning against the house. What I saw

sent me to my car in a hurry, where I picked up my cell phone and called Sheila Dawson.

"You want me to question a Hausner descendant about Mrs. Barton's death?" Sheila asked, surprised. "Why? Have you turned up some evidence to suggest that this woman had something to do with it?"

"I'm afraid I have," I said sadly. It was a shame. I liked Mrs. Thomas.

"Oh, yeah?" She was skeptical. "Like what?"

"A rosebush," I said. "And a spade."

There was a long silence. "Is that all?" Sheila asked finally.

"When you see the blood on the spade," I said, "you'll think it's enough."

It took Sheila a little while to round up a judge and obtain a search warrant. When the squad car pulled up in front of Mrs. Thomas's house, I left. I wasn't exactly anxious to hang around while the chief questioned this particular murder suspect. Anyway, I knew I'd hear all about it before long.

I was right. The next morning, as Ruby and I were opening our shops, Sheila stopped in.

"Well?" I asked somberly. "Did Charlotte Thomas tell you how she came to kill Mrs. Barton?"

"Yes," Sheila said. "When she was confronted with the victim's blood on the spade, she made a full confession. By the time she's arraigned, we'll have the DNA evidence."

"How did it happen?" Ruby asked, coming in with a plate of cookies and a pitcher of iced tea. She set them on the shelf where we put treats for our customers. There was a little sign on the plate that read CAUTION: HOT LIPS COOKIE CRISPS. "Did she *really* kill Mrs. Barton over a yellow rose?"

"Well, yes and no," Sheila said. "The way Mrs. Thomas tells it, she went to visit her mother's grave and surprised Rose Barton, who was digging up the rosebush. She told Mrs. Barton to stop, but the woman paid no attention. She took the bush out of the ground and put it into a tub she had brought. Then Mrs. Thomas lost her head — or at least that's what she says. She grabbed the spade and hit her."

"So she didn't intend to kill her," Ruby said quietly.

Sheila nodded. "She dragged the body behind the monument, put the tub and the spade in her car, and drove away." She sighed. "I think she was actually glad to get it off her chest."

"I hope she's got a good defense attorney," I said. "Sounds like manslaughter to me." And in Texas, where people take their family burial sites seriously, a jury might find it difficult to send her to prison for very long.

"Are you going to tell me what led you to Charlotte Thomas?" Sheila reached for a cookie. "Was it the Hausner connection?"

"Be careful of those cookies," Ruby warned. "They're a little spicy."

"Yes, it was the Hausner connection." I picked up the pitcher and poured a plastic cup of iced tea. "That, and the fact that the cemetery caretaker had mentioned that the rosebush that had been removed from the Hausner plot was a *yellow* rose."

"And Mary Lewis told us," Ruby chimed in, "that Rose Barton had been looking for a yellow rose. She intended to collect some cuttings."

RUBY'S HOT LIPS COOKIE CRISPS

1 cup soft shortening
2 cups brown sugar
2 eggs
1 teaspoon vanilla
1½ cups finely chopped cashews
1½ cups whole-wheat flour
1½ cups unbleached flour
½ teaspoon baking soda
1 teaspoon baking powder
½ teaspoon habanero powder*

Preheat oven to 325°F. Cream butter and sugar. Add the eggs and vanilla and mix well. Mix the dry ingredients together with the nuts, and stir into the creamed mixture. Form into a log about two inches in diameter and chill. Slice and bake until golden, 12 to 14 minutes. (Watch carefully—these cookies burn easily!) Yields four dozen.

*The habanero pepper is an incendiary chile with a fruity flavor. Look for the powder in a specialty shop that sells spicy foods.

"She was taking more than a few cuttings," Sheila said, and popped the cookie into her mouth. "She was digging up the entire—" Her eyes opened wide and filled with sudden tears. She grabbed the cup out of my hand and gulped it down. I poured another and handed it to her.

"You should have been careful," Ruby said, in an I-told-you-so tone.

"I was just caught off guard," Sheila replied. After a minute,

If you'd like to read more about old roses, here are three helpful books:

Old Garden Roses, by Edward A. Bunard (New York: Earl M. Coleman Publishing, 1978)

In Search of Lost Roses, by Thomas Christopher (New York: Summit Books, 1989)

Antique Roses for the South, by William C. Welch (Dallas, TX: Taylor Publishing, 1990)

For a wealth of pictures and information on-line, go to *www.antique roseemporium.com* and click on "A Guide to Old Roses."

she wiped her eyes and reached for another cookie. "What in the world did you put in them, Ruby? They're wonderful!"

"Thank you," Ruby said modestly. "They're made with habanero powder. I'm glad you like them. And I'm glad the case is solved."

"Yes," I said. "There's only one more thing to be decided."

"What's that?" Sheila asked.

"Who gets custody of that yellow rose?"

MUSTARD
MADNESS

*"I ain't too old to cut the mustard,
but I'm too tired to spread it around."*

—*Shel Silverstein*

*"Not only can't you cut the mustard, honey,
you're too old to open the jar."*

—*LaWanda Page to George Burns*

IN Pecan Springs, the big event of the summer is the annual Adams County Fair, which is held in late July and early August at the fairgrounds a couple of miles outside of town. The weather during fair week is al-

Mustard: The Herb

**Mustard is an annual herb that belongs to the genus *Brassica*
(the same family that includes cabbage, cauliflower, and Brussels
sprouts). It is usually described in terms of the color of
its seeds: black mustard (*Brassica nigra*); brown mustard
(*Brassica juncea*); and pale yellow mustard (*Sinapis alba*). The
black mustard plant can grow to nearly twelve feet high, but
the more restrained brown and yellow mustards top out at
three feet. Black mustard seeds are the smallest, brown are
middle-sized, and yellow are the largest. In terms of intensity,
however, the smallest (black) seeds are the hottest and the
largest (yellow) the mildest. Black mustard seeds are very difficult to find, since they must be harvested by hand and are
less viable commercially than brown and yellow mustard
seeds.**

ways hotter than a string of firecrackers, but folks don't seem
to mind. They look forward all year long to the Cowboy
Breakfast, the carnival, the calf-roping, and the big country
music concert in the Pavilion, not to mention Barnyard Babies
for the kids, performances by the Cowgirl Cloggers, and the
best old-time fiddlin' contests in the whole state of Texas.
Now, those of you who live in the city and are used to sophisticated entertainment—off-Broadway shows, foreign film
festivals, opera and ballet—may find these down-home doings
just a little too simple and folksy for your taste. But for people who live in Pecan Springs, this kind of entertainment
seems exactly right. It hits the spot.

And what especially hits the spot for most Pecan Springers is the Mad for Mustard competition, which takes place at the fair on the first Saturday in August—which just happens, of course, to be National Mustard Day. Bet you didn't know that, did you? National Mustard Day has been on the calendar since 1991, when it was first officially sponsored by the Mount Horeb Mustard Museum, in Mount Horeb, Wisconsin, the World's Mustard Mecca.

What makes this particular contest so interesting is the fact that many of the people who settled this part of Texas originally came from Germany, and Germans are notoriously fond of their mustard. A great many families have closely guarded heirloom mustard recipes. What's more, they don't just *make* homemade mustard—they *cook* with it, too. Which is why the Mad for Mustard competition is divided into two sections. In Division One, Gourmet Mustards, you can

Here's how the Mustard Museum describes itself: "The Mount Horeb Mustard Museum began when its founder, Barry Levenson, started collecting mustards on October 27, 1986. His beloved Red Sox had lost the World Series to the New York Mets that night and Barry was very depressed. He went to an all-night supermarket to wander the aisles. He turned down the condiment aisle and heard a deep resonant voice as he passed the mustards: 'If you collect us, they will come.' Barry bought about a dozen jars of mustard that evening and resolved to amass the world's largest collection of prepared mustards." From this inauspicious beginning, the collection has grown to more than 3,700 mustards. You can see them all at the Mustard Museum, 100 West Main Street, Mount Horeb, Wisconsin, or enjoy a virtual visit at *www.mustardweb.com*.

enter your home-cooked mustard in five different categories: classic mustards, sweet-hot mustards, herb mustards, spirit mustards (made with beer, wine, and hard liquor), and fruit mustards. In Division Two, Mustard Cookery, you can enter your favorite mustard-flavored dish in six different categories: appetizers, soups, main dishes, vegetables, salads, and desserts.

Now, the prizes in Division Two are always fiercely contested by quite a few very good cooks, and you can find several entries, each one unique and different, in any one category. (I can tell you this with confidence because Hark Hibler always asks me to write a Mad for Mustard story for my regular Thursday Home and Garden page in the *Enterprise* —which means that I get to sample all the entries.) But Division One is different. While the competition is every bit as fierce, it is concentrated between two people, Homer Mayo and Pete Hitchens, a pair of cantankerous senior citizens with temperaments as tart and tangy as their mustards.

These two fiery old geezers, now in their seventies, have come out on top since the contest began, although if you count up the ribbons, you'll see that Homer has won about twice as many as Pete. In fact, the two of them have won so many times that nobody else ever bothers to enter the Gourmet Mustard Division, leaving these two to divvy up the prizes between them. You'd think that this would be discouraging, and that maybe there'd be a move to get these winners to step aside and let other people have a shot. But while this has been hinted at a time or two, nobody seems to want to spoil the fun.

And fun it is, because Homer and Pete put on quite a show —the Grumpy Old Guys, people call them. They've been

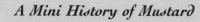

A Mini History of Mustard

For centuries, mustard has been one of the most widely grown and used spices in the world. It was cultivated in China some seven thousand years ago. In ancient cookery, the seeds and oil masked the off-taste of spoiled meat and added zest to an otherwise bland cuisine. The Romans were the first to make prepared mustards by grinding the seeds and mixing them with honey, vinegar, oil, and an unfermented grape juice called *must*—hence the Latin name *mustum ardens*, "burning wine," which eventually became the word *mustard*. In addition to flavoring food with mustard, the Romans used it as an all-purpose cure for everything from hysteria to the bite of mad dogs and the plague. Roman soldiers, who were especially fond of the condiment, took it with them to France, and Dijon, the ancient capital of Burgundy, became the center of the mustard world. In Tewkesbury, England, during Shakespeare's day, ground mustard seed was mixed with honey, vinegar, and horseradish. The thick paste was formed into balls, which were sold in London markets. (In *Henry IV*, Falstaff snorts, "His wit is as thick as Tewkesbury mustard.") To serve, the dried balls were broken apart and mixed with more liquid—vinegar, beer, wine, cider—along with sugar, cinnamon, or honey. This method of managing mustard seems to have fallen into disfavor around 1800, when a Mrs. Clements, of Durham, began grinding and sifting mustard seeds to produce a fine flour. She was followed by Jeremiah Colman, who marketed his ground mustard in the still-familiar yellow tin.

A Little Mustard Lore

Mustard, which is traditionally thought to be ruled by the planet Mars, has long been considered an aphrodisiac and a symbol of fertility. In northern Europe, mothers sewed mustard seeds into the hems of their daughters' wedding dresses in order to ensure the groom's desire and enhance the bride's ability to bear children. The Chinese, too, thought that mustard (like other spicy herbs) was an aphrodisiac. In India, mustard seeds were spread on door- and windowsills to repel evil spirits, and in Denmark mustard was grown around barns to protect the animals. In biblical times, mustard seeds symbolized faith and endurance, an idea that perhaps arose from the fact that mustard seeds, which have a hard outer shell, may lie dormant for decades, even as long as a century, before conditions are right for sprouting.

feuding for years, although I suspect that, down deep, they really like one another. All through the competition, they trade exaggerated glowers, glares, and insulting stares, like a pair of aging wrestlers showing off for the TV cameras. All this goes on behind the judges' backs, of course—they're all smiles and sweet as stolen apples when the judges turn around. Last year, Homer's cheering section (the regulars at Baker's Barber Shop) showed up with mustard-yellow T-shirts emblazoned with HOMER'S MUSTARD MAVERICKS in fiery red letters. Pete's backers, most of them members of the Pecan Springs Horseshoe Team, wore yellow MUSTARD HAPPENS caps and carried big yellow signs that proclaimed MUSTARD SÍ, MAYO NO.

But all their energies were to no avail. For the third year in a row, Pete took first prize in only one category, while Homer took first prize in four, bringing his fans to their feet in frenzied celebration and causing Pete's fans to swear that next year, their Mustard Mogul would sweep the field. Pete showed his displeasure by shoving his one blue ribbon and four red ones into his back pocket and stomping out of the judging tent in disgust, while Homer and his friends danced off to celebrate at Bean's Bar and Grill. This entertaining rivalry has turned an ordinary, ho-hum mustard contest into one of the big events of the year, and people line up early to get good seats.

That's why Ruby Wilcox was so pleased when she was asked to be one of the judges in the Gourmet Mustard Division, the very first woman judge, in fact. "At last," she said, "I'll have a chance to see what all the shouting is about."

"Better you than me," I replied, with feeling. While I always look forward to the spicy mustard-flavored dishes that show up in Division Two, I do not have Ruby's taste for great bowls of fire—or rather, hot pots of fire, since we're talking mustard here.

"I've always been curious about Homer and Pete," Ruby mused. "Are they really as good as everybody says they are?"

"Well, I guess you'll get the inside story," I replied. "I hope

---

The Strange Case of the Mistress of Mystery and the Mustard Club

Mystery fans are sure to recognize the name of Dorothy Sayers, the much-acclaimed author of the Lord Peter Wimsey and Harriet Vane mysteries. In 1922, as a young advertising copywriter, Sayers helped to create the Mustard Club, an advertising campaign for Colman's Mustard. Members of the fictional Mustard Club included its president, Baron de Beef; Master Mustard, Lord Bacon of Cookham; and the club's secretary, Miss Di Gester. Among the elements of the campaign: a filmed spoof in which a man is tried for allegedly attempting to eat a ham sandwich without mustard (he is found guilty and sentenced to be dunked in a mustard bath); and the "Recipe Book of the Mustard Club," also written by Sayers, an excellent cook.

you're ready, Ruby. Last year, I saw smoke curling out of the judges' ears. You'll need an asbestos tongue."

In answer, Ruby only gave me an anticipatory grin and rubbed her hands together. I sighed. Anybody who can come up with a recipe called Hot Lips Cookie Crisps, made with habanero chiles, deserves anything she gets.

The next day, I ran into Homer Mayo in the checkout lane at Cavette's Grocery. He was buying honey, several different kinds of vinegar, garlic, cloves, and allspice, and chile peppers.

"I see you're getting ready for the mustard contest," I remarked in a neighborly way.

Homer is a lean, leathery old man with a mane of white hair and very blue eyes—a blue which was intensified by the blue jumpsuit he was wearing, the zipper unzipped to show curling white hairs on his chest. He gave me a pitying look. "This ain't fer the contest," he said. "I cooked up my contest mustards a couple months ago. They gotta age, doncha know? You like yer mustard medium nippy, let it sit fer six weeks 'fore you put it in the fridge. You like it hot, give it four weeks, and double that for a good mild herb mustard." He frowned. "You oughtta know that, China. It's the secret to good mustard."

"Oh, I do," I said hastily. "Absolutely."

He waved an arm, waxing el-

Mustard by Any Other Name . . .

Mustard is also known as *rai* in India, *chiehi* in some areas of China, *biji sawi* in Malaysia, *san-ape* in Italy, *Senf* in Germany, *moutarde* in France, and *mosterd* in Holland.

oquent. "Mustard needs to settle down, hang out fer a while, get mellow. Folks don't think about that. They think, you cook up a batch o' mustard, it's hot to trot right that minute." He leaned closer and grinned flirtatiously, showing a gold tooth. "Mustard's like us old coots. Better when it's been around."

I grinned back, liking the sparkle in his eye. "There's something to that," I agreed.

"Want some o' my mustard?" he asked. "I give a lot away, y'know. Fam'ly, friends, anybody that asks." He put his hand on my arm, leaned closer, and whispered, "I spesh'ly like to give it away to pretty girls."

"I'm flattered," I said.

My encounter with Pete Hitchens wasn't quite as pleasant. He came tearing into Thyme and Seasons the next afternoon. "Mustard seeds," he puffed, heading for the shelf of bulk herbs. "Gotta have more mustard seeds." Unlike Homer, Pete is plump, red-faced, and mostly bald, with a fringe of gingery hair around his ears and a gingery mustache across his upper lip. He seems to be out of breath most of the time.

"I've got plenty of yellow seeds, and mustard powder," I said, "but I'm all out of brown seeds. I expect them in sometime next week."

"Next *week!*" he wheezed apoplectically. "I need them brown seeds *now!* I been studyin' on Homer's beer mustard, and I figgered out why it always wins. I aim to make me some jes' like it, only better. This year, I'm gonna get me a whole bunch of blue ribbons."

"I'm really sorry," I said. I wanted to ask why he hadn't made his mustard in time to age it, but thought it might inflame him further. "Whole Foods in Austin always carries mustard seeds. It won't take you more than an hour to drive up there and —"

Pete glared at me, his red face getting even redder. "I don't relish drivin' all day jes' fer a few seeds. That's what I get fer dependin' on small-time bidness folks. Shoulda known you'd let me down in my hour of need."

I rose to defend myself. "Around contest time, lots of people buy mustard to cook with. I had plenty yesterday, but —"

"You ain't got none now," he growled, "and that's what counts." Muttering under his breath, he paid for several ounces of yellow seeds and mustard powder and stalked out, slamming the door behind him.

"Are you all right?" Ruby wanted to know, sticking her head through the door. "What was all that ruckus?"

"That was one of your contestants," I said. "The hot-tempered one. Seems he's trying to copy his competitor's beer mustard and ran out of seeds."

"This is getting more interesting by the minute," Ruby said. "I can't wait to see how it turns out."

"Better wear your bulletproof vest," I advised. "If this guy gets as upset over losing as he does when he can't get what he wants, you might need it."

The day of the contest dawned sunny and hot, and the TV weatherwoman was predicting that the mercury would hit a hundred before the sun went down. But long before that, we'd know for certain who'd won the Mad for Mustard competition. Would Homer make a clean sweep of the field, or would Pete make a comeback?

The contest entries close at ten A.M., and the judging takes place between ten-thirty and noon. When I got there at nine, the tables for all the entries were lined up in a double row down the middle of the judging tent, with the Division Two dishes arranged on one side, and the Division One mustards on the other. With my *Enterprise* press badge pinned to my T-shirt (which was already pasted to my back with sweat) and my reporter's notebook in my hand, I strolled along, taking note of the variety of mouthwatering dishes.

It looked like this year's Division Two competition was going to be outstanding. Maylene Grudge had entered a salad made with oranges, red onions, avocado, and yellow peppers, with an orange–honey mustard dressing. Genevieve Schultz had entered her famous Grilled Chicken with Rosemary-Mustard Marinade, and Prissy Taggert had cooked up a dish of Spicy Sautéed Veggies that she'd learned to make when her husband, Alva, got sent to Bangkok for a year. Percy Grimes had entered—again—his family's old-fashioned gingerbread. Sniffing appreciatively, I made a note to get the recipes for some of these dishes. The judges were going to have a very difficult time selecting winners.

But on the other side of the table, it appeared that Ruby and the two other Division One judges might have things easy, after all. Pete had already brought his mustards and the contest monitor had set them out, one or two entries in every category, along with plastic cups filled with mustard, plastic spoons for the judges, and several bottles of water—also for the judges, who would certainly need them. But Homer's entries hadn't arrived yet. It was certainly odd for him to be late, especially since he'd filled out all the paperwork the night before. By nine-fifteen, everybody was beginning to frown at their watches and ask, "Where's Homer? How come he ain't here?"

A few minutes later, we found out why. Ollie Benbow dashed into the tent, waving his arms. "Homer's been in a wreck," he cried. "His pickup was run down by a garbage truck. It was totaled."

A dismayed chorus of *oh-no*s filled the tent.

"But Homer's gonna be okay," Ollie assured us. "Just a few broke bones is all, and some cuts caused by flyin' glass. The doc says he'll be outta the hospital tomorrow."

A sigh of relief swept the crowd. "Attaboy, Homer!" somebody shouted. "Way to go, you old sonuvagun," somebody else yelled. "Let's hear it fer Homer!" And all of Homer's Mustard Mavericks began to cheer.

Ollie stood there, waiting for quiet to settle again. "That's the good news," he said at last, his face gloomy. "The bad news is that Homer's contest mustards was riding in a box on the front seat. They're all smashed to hell and gone — nothing left of 'em but a puddle o' yella mustard and broke glass all over the pavement."

People stared at each other in stunned silence. "No mustard!" Ralph Rattle lamented. "Well, hell, we might jes' as well go on home. There ain't gonna be no competition this year."

And all of Homer's backers began to mumble and mutter and discuss things grimly among themselves. I couldn't blame them. They were no doubt vastly relieved that their friend was okay, but they had to be grieving the loss of all those wonderful, one-of-a-kind gourmet mustards, the fruit of Homer's hard work and creativity. And it certainly looked as if Ralph was right, and this year's competition was going down the drain. In the unforeseen absence of Homer Mayo and his mustards, Pete Hitchens would have his once-in-a-lifetime chance to grab a fistful of blue ribbons.

But that isn't how it turned out. Two minutes before the deadline, Pete hurried into the tent carrying a cardboard box filled with a half dozen or more pots of mustard. As everybody watched, speculating about what was going on, he handed the box over to the contest monitor. A few minutes later, the new entries — *Homer's* entries! — were arranged on the table, and Ruby and her three fellow judges were ushered in. And within the hour, to the delight of the Mustard Mavericks, Homer Mayo's mustards had taken all five blue ribbons.

I turned around, expecting to see Pete throw a temper tantrum, the way he'd done the year before, only more so. But as the prizes were announced, he just stood there with a big goofy grin pasted on his red face. And when the judges had given Pete his five red ribbons, all the old guys in the bleachers

MAYLENE GRUDGE'S MUSTARD GREEN, RED, AND ORANGE SALAD WITH ORANGE–HONEY MUSTARD VINAIGRETTE

3 slices bacon

1 red onion, sliced in rings

1 red bell pepper, seeded and sliced lengthwise

1 avocado, peeled and sliced lengthwise

3 small oranges or tangerines, peeled, sectioned, pith removed

3 to 4 cups young mustard greens, washed

3 ounces feta cheese

To make the vinaigrette, whisk together in a small bowl:

¼ cup extra virgin olive oil

1 teaspoon white wine vinegar

½ teaspoon orange rind, finely grated

1 tablespoon orange juice

½ teaspoon freshly ground pepper

1 tablespoon honey mustard

¼ cup finely chopped toasted almonds (optional)

Fry the bacon until crisp and drain on paper toweling. Gently toss together the sliced onion, bell pepper, avocado slices, and 3 tablespoons of vinaigrette. Set aside to marinate for a few moments. Arrange the mustard greens on four to six small serving plates. Place the orange sections on the greens, and add the marinated mixture. Drizzle with the remaining vinaigrette and crumble the feta cheese and bacon on top. Serve immediately.

GENEVIEVE SCHULTZ'S GRILLED CHICKEN WITH ROSEMARY-MUSTARD MARINADE

To make Rosemary-Mustard Marinade, combine in a bowl:

> *1 cup vinegar*
> *⅓ cup olive oil*
> *3 tablespoons Dijon mustard*
> *1 teaspoon yellow or mixed mustard seeds*
> *1 large clove garlic, minced fine*
> *3 to 4 tablespoons fresh rosemary, chopped, or 1 tablespoon dried*
> *Freshly ground pepper, to taste*

Marinate chicken (skinless breasts or other pieces) overnight. Grill, brushing frequently with remaining marinade.

PRISSY TAGGERT'S SPICY SAUTÉED VEGGIES

¼ cup vegetable oil
Black peppercorns (5 for a mild taste, 10 for medium-hot, 20 for oh-boy!)
1 tablespoon white sesame seeds
1 teaspoon whole cumin seeds
1 teaspoon yellow or brown mustard seeds
3 tablespoons freshly grated ginger
1 red onion, sliced lengthwise
½ teaspoon turmeric
½ teaspoon cayenne (reduce or omit for a milder taste)
½ pound fresh green beans, washed, ends trimmed
1 red bell pepper, seeded, cut into strips
1 yellow bell pepper, seeded, cut into strips
1 cup sliced mushrooms
2 teaspoons lemon juice
Salt to taste

In a wok or large nonstick skillet, heat oil over medium heat. Combine peppercorns, sesame seeds, cumin seeds, and mustard seeds. Add to oil and cover immediately, reducing heat to low. (Seeds will pop.) When seeds have browned (20 seconds or less), add grated ginger and onion. Turn heat to medium-high and sauté until onions are translucent. Add turmeric and cayenne and sauté for 2 minutes, stirring constantly. Add green beans, and sauté until beans are bright green. Continue cooking for 5 minutes, then add bell peppers. Sauté until peppers are slightly browned, then add mushrooms and cook 3 to 4 minutes longer, until vegetables are cooked but still crisp. Add lemon juice and salt to taste. Serves four to six.

THE GRIMES FAMILY'S GINGERBREAD

½ cup unsalted butter, softened
¼ cup dark brown sugar, firmly packed
½ cup dark molasses
1 tablespoon grated fresh ginger
1 teaspoon ground cinnamon
2 teaspoons orange zest, finely grated
1 teaspoon orange flavoring
2 teaspoons mustard powder
1½ cups flour
1 teaspoon baking soda
½ cup boiling water

Mix together butter, sugar, molasses, ginger, cinnamon, orange zest, orange flavoring, and mustard. Add flour, one-half cup at a time. Add baking soda to boiling water, then stir into mixture. Turn into a square baking pan, lightly greased, and bake at 325°F for 30 minutes. Cool 10 minutes before removing from pan to a rack.

stormed the floor, hoisted him onto their shoulders, and marched around the tables, shouting and singing, "He ain't too old to cut the mustard anymore." And then this band of grumpy old geezers, with Pete still riding on their shoulders, disappeared in the direction of the hospital, to take the champion his well-earned blue ribbons. And no doubt they'd manage to smuggle several six-packs of beer, a big bag of pretzels, and—of course—mustard into Homer's hospital room, as well.

And how did Pete just happen to have all those pots of Homer's mustard handy, exactly enough to replace the ones that got smashed in the wreck? Well, it took a bit of superior sleuthing on my part to dig up the details, but eventually I found out that Pete had been collecting Homer's famous mustards on the sly, from friends, family, wherever he could get his hands on them. He aimed to analyze them and try to figure out why they took so many blue ribbons. In the end, he had several pots of each of Homer's mustards. He'd boxed them up and brought them along with him to the competition, intending to dispose of them after the prizes were all awarded.

But that was only part of the explanation. So Pete had Homer's mustards. But he certainly didn't have to enter them in the competition, thereby spoiling his own chances of winning. Why did he do it? Some said it was because he didn't want to disappoint the crowd, which had come to see another no-holds-barred mustard competition. Ruby suggested that he did it out of a burning desire to test his mustards one more time against the best that Homer could offer. "What's a hot dog without mustard?" she asked rhetorically. "What's a contest without competition? What good is winning first place if there's nobody around to take second?"

Two Gourmet Mustards You Can Make

PETE HITCHENS'S BLUE-RIBBON BEER MUSTARD

1 cup dark beer
¼ cup yellow mustard seeds
¼ cup brown mustard seeds
1½ cups apple cider vinegar
1 small onion, chopped
6 cloves garlic, minced
½ cup mustard powder
2 tablespoons icewater
1½ teaspoon salt
2 teaspoons sugar
½ teaspoon ground allspice
½ teaspoon ground cumin
1 teaspoon grated fresh ginger

Pour beer over the mustard seeds and let soak overnight. In a nonreactive pan (glass or stainless), place vinegar, onion, and garlic. Simmer until liquid is reduced by two-thirds. Strain and chill. Mix dry mustard and icewater and let sit for 20 minutes. Stir in cold vinegar, salt, sugar, allspice, cumin, ginger, and soaked mustard seeds. Place in a blender container and blend until mustard seeds are coarsely ground, scraping sides often. Pour into a sauce-pan and simmer over very low heat 10 to 15 minutes, until it thickens. Cool, place in a glass jar with a tight lid, and let sit in a dark cupboard for 4 to 5 weeks before using. Refrigerate after opening. Makes about 1 pint.

HOMER MAYO'S HORSERADISH MUSTARD

½ cup mustard powder
½ cup hot water
½ cup white wine vinegar or rice vinegar
2 teaspoons salt
1 tablespoon prepared horseradish
2 cloves garlic, finely minced
1 teaspoon sugar
⅛ teaspoon black pepper
⅛ teaspoon ground allspice
Additional vinegar, if necessary

Mix the dry mustard and water and let stand for 20 minutes, stirring once or twice. In a blender container, combine the vinegar, salt, horseradish, garlic, sugar, pepper, and allspice. Process until the garlic and horseradish have been pureed, then strain through a fine-meshed strainer, pressing out the juice from any pulp in the strainer. Discard the material in the strainer. In the top of a double boiler, combine the strained liquid with the mustard-water paste. Cook over simmering water for about 5 minutes, until the mustard has begun to thicken (it will continue to thicken as it cools). Remove from heat and allow to cool. If the mustard is too thick, thin it with a few drops of additional vinegar. Place in a glass jar with a tight lid, and let sit in a dark cupboard for 4 to 5 weeks before using. Refrigerate after opening. Makes about ½ cup.

But I have a totally different idea. I think Pete did it because he knew that if the shoe was on the other foot, or the mustard was spread on the other side of the bread, Homer would've done the same for him. Deep down under their surface rivalry, Pete Hitchens and Homer Mayo shared an abiding respect, admiration, and, yes, even *love* for one another. When push came to shove, Pete just couldn't stand to see Homer go down to defeat by default, any more than he could stand to see himself come out on top by default.

And that's it. A true story of Mustard Madness, on National Mustard Day in Pecan Springs. But if you're sad that the story is over, don't be. Just make it a point not to miss next year's Adams County Fair. You can stuff yourself with flapjacks and bacon at the Cowboy Breakfast, enjoy an evening of live country music in the Pavilion, and admire the Cowgirl Cloggers as they clog up a storm. And you won't want to miss Homer Mayo and Pete Hitchens, going up against one another, no holds barred, armed to the teeth with some of the finest mustards you'll find anywhere in the great state of Texas.

"A tale without love is like beef without mustard, an insipid dish."
— Anatole France

For more about mustard, read *The Good Cook's Book of Mustard*, by Michele Anna Jordan, and *Mustard: Making Your Own Gourmet Mustards*, by Janet Hazen.

In the meantime, though, you might want to make some of Homer's and Pete's gourmet mustards for yourself. It's not hard to do, and once the word gets around, you'll find yourself and your mustards invited to every weenie roast in town.

THE
PENNYROYAL
PLOT

THANKS, China," Mary Burnet said as she gathered up the plastic bags of teas she had just finished blending. "That was a great workshop. I learned more than I ever expected to know about herbal teas—and about real tea, as well."

"I'm glad you enjoyed it, Mary," I replied with a smile. "I did, too."

Of all the classes I teach at Thyme and Seasons, the workshop on herbal teas—called From Garden to Teacup—is my favorite. We all troop out to the garden and

The black, green, and flavored teas that we think of as "real" tea come from an evergreen shrub (*Camellia sinensis*) native to China. The plant is closely related to the camellia and magnolia, and it is the young leaves and leaf buds that are used as tea. The Chinese began brewing tea some two millennia ago, and it rapidly became an important part of Chinese culture. "Black" tea and "green" tea are both made from the same plant; the only difference is in the processing. The only commercial tea plantation in North America is located near Charleston, South Carolina.

look at a variety of tea plants: mint, scented geraniums, lemon verbena, pennyroyal, lavender, and many more. We talk about how to grow the plants and how to harvest and dry the leaves. Then we go into the tearoom and I demonstrate how to blend and brew the teas, using a variety of dried herbs. We sample the brewed teas, then everybody gets a chance to create their own original blends, or purchase some I've made.

Mary smiled and held up a plastic bag full of herbs. "I can't wait to brew some of your Sweet Thyme tea. And I'm hoping the DreamyThyme tea will cure my insomnia."

"Well, I don't know about curing insomnia," I said. "But it'll make falling asleep a lot easier — and more pleasant."

I said good-bye to Mary and the others, and began cleaning up. I was putting the dried herbs back on the shelf when Ruby came in from her shop next door. She was wearing a crazy-quilt broomstick skirt and a black top, and her orange Orphan Annie curls were a frizzy mop all over her head.

"I just got a phone call from Paula at the Teen Center," she said sadly. "Old Mr. Pennyroyal has died."

"I'm sorry to hear that," I said, with genuine regret. I re-

Herbs for a Tea Garden

Strictly speaking, all teas are herbal, since the tea plant that gives us our black, green, and flavored teas is also classified as an herb. But when we talk about "herbal teas," we're usually referring to teas made from the leaves or seeds of garden herbs, brewed for simple pleasure or good health or both. Most tea herbs enjoy full sun, a not-too-rich soil, and a non-competitive environment—meaning that they'll appreciate it if you pull the weeds now and then. (For more details, read *Tea Gardens: Places to Make and Take Tea,* by Ann Lovejoy.)

Anise hyssop
Basils (especially lemon basil, cinnamon basil)
Bergamot
Calendula (petals)
Caraway (seeds)
Catnip
Chamomile
Costmary
Dill (seeds)
Fennel (seeds)
Garden sage
Horehound
Lemon balm, lime balm
Lemongrass
Lemon verbena
Lovage
Mints (spearmint, peppermint, orange mint)
Rosemary
Scented geraniums
Sweet marjoram
Thymes
Wintergreen
Yarrow

placed a big jar of dried sage. "He'd been sick for a long time, hadn't he?"

Ruby nodded. "I think he was ready to say good-bye." Her smile was crooked. "We're sad to see him go, but there's a bright side. He left his house to the Teen Center."

How to Brew a Pot of Herbal Tea

Begin with pure water (spring or distilled water), heated just to boiling (overboiling reduces the oxygen). Meanwhile, half fill the teapot with hot water, to take the chill off. Be sure that you know how many cups your teapot holds, so you'll know how much tea herb to use.

Put the loose herbs into your teapot, one level teaspoon of dried herbs per cup. Pour boiling water into the pot and allow to brew for up to 15 minutes. Set a timer for 10 minutes and taste your tea. If you'd like it stronger, brew for 5 minutes more. Pour through a strainer into a pretty cup and sweeten with honey. Here are some other teatime tips.

- To avoid a metallic taste, heat the water in a glass, enamel, or stainless steel pan, and use a ceramic teapot with a lid, to prevent the loss of the herb's aromatic oils.

- If you're using fresh herbs, use 2 teaspoons per cup. Fold the leaves in a paper towel and bruise with a rolling pin to release the oil. If dry, use 1 teaspoon.

- To reduce bitterness, strain out herbs immediately. To enjoy the tea later, refrigerate in a tightly capped jar and warm it gently in a nonreactive pan (glass or stainless).

- If you use a tea ball or infuser, choose one that's stainless and don't pack it too full. These are best used to make one cup of tea, rather than a whole pot.

- Many herbs have their own natural sweetness, but if you like sweet tea, add honey. Dip a spoon into the honey to film the spoon, then into your teacup. Stir and taste.

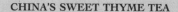

CHINA'S SWEET THYME TEA

½ cup dried pineapple sage leaves
½ cup dried chamomile flowers
½ cup dried rose hips
¼ cup dried lemon thyme
¼ cup dried lemon balm leaves

CHINA'S DREAMYTHYME TEA

½ cup dried chamomile flowers
½ cup dried lavender flowers
¼ cup dried catnip leaves
¼ cup dried strawberry leaves

**Blend herbs and store in an airtight container. To brew, use
1 teaspoon herbal blend to 1 cup boiling water. Steep 4 to 5
minutes, strain, and serve, sweetened with honey.**

"What a generous gift!" I exclaimed, surprised. The Pennyroyal house, which is located in a quiet residential neighborhood, is a famous Pecan Springs landmark, built back in the days when the railroad first came to this part of Texas, bringing an economic boom. The brick wall that surrounds it also encloses a lovely herb garden that Mrs. Pennyroyal planted years ago. After she died, the Herb Guild volunteered to take over its care. I added, "I hope the guild can continue to maintain the herb garden."

"I'm sure the board will agree," Ruby replied. For the past couple of years, she's been an enthusiastic member of the Teen Center's board of directors.

"What are you going to do with the house? Sell it?"

"Not on your life," Ruby said. "We'll use the lower floor for meetings and parties, and we're turning the upper floor into office space for the staff. We'll put some computers up there for the kids, too."

"What a great idea!" I replied.

"I wish all the neighbors agreed with you," Ruby said ruefully. "We've got to get a zoning variance, and Mrs. Jordan, who lives next door, isn't exactly thrilled at the prospect. In fact, she's threatened to oppose it." She brightened. "But I'm sure we'll be able to change her mind. After all, the kids need a safe place to hang out."

A few days later, several of us—all members of the Myra Merryweather Herb Guild—gathered at the Pennyroyal house, weeding the flower beds and adding a few more rosemary, santolina, and lavender plants to the knot garden. We tackle these pleasant chores every few months, and we all have a good time together. Today, though, we were subdued, because we missed our old friend.

> A knot garden is a geometric garden design that originated during the Tudor period in England. The pattern—a square, diamond, or circle—is outlined with a low border of dense, slow-growing plants, such as clipped boxwood, dwarf barberry, lavender, or santolina. The shapes defined by the borders can be filled in with a variety of neat, compact plants, such as violets, marigolds, sage, rue, pinks, thymes, and daisies, or with mulches (chips, sand, rock, shells). This kind of garden is suited to a flat, open space, and is both formal and intimate at the same time. For more information, consult *Knot Gardens and Parterres: A History of the Knot Garden and How to Make One Today,* by Robin Whalley.

There are two kinds of pennyroyal—the English (*Mentha pulegium*) and the American (*Hedeoma pulegioides*), a common wild plant. Nurseries usually offer English pennyroyal, but you'll want to check the Latin name to be sure, or ask. The English pennyroyal belongs in the mint family and has been used to treat many different ailments, from whooping cough to leprosy. Because of its reputation (not scientifically verified) as a flea repellant, it was traditionally planted around dooryards. Pennyroyal leaves make a fragrant and tasty cup of tea. If you're pregnant, though, you'll probably want to pass. Pennyroyal oil is far more dangerous to a fetus than is a tea made from the leaves, because it can cause uterine contractions. (In fact, pennyroyal was once a common abortifacient.) It is best for pregnant women to leave both the tea and the oil alone, and also avoid pet products (such as shampoos) that might contain it.

· In Scotland, pennyroyal is also known as pudding grass, because it is used to flavor haggis pudding (a meat pudding that we would think of as a sausage).

· Since antiquity, bee and wasp stings have been treated with a pennyroyal poultice, and the leaves were applied to carbuncles and boils.

· In the Middle Ages, pennyroyal in the garden was thought to repel evil forces. The dried leaves, stuffed into pillows and mattresses, were also believed to repel fleas, and the herb is used today in many pet products, such as shampoos, flea collars, and so on. In the Victorian language of flowers, pennyroyal means "you'd better go."

Even though Mr. Pennyroyal couldn't join in the weeding and planting, he used to love to talk with us while we worked.

The group finished weeding and left. I was lingering to set out a pennyroyal plant beside the walk, when Ruby came through the gate. With her was Jackie Peters, the president of the Teen Center board.

"Hi, you two!" I said cheerfully. I straightened up and brushed the dirt off the knees of my jeans. "Have you come to look over the house and start planning your renovations? I'll bet you're excited about getting this great place for the Teen Center."

"Looks like we might not get the house after all," Ruby said with a somber shake of her frizzy red curls.

"You're kidding!" I exclaimed. "Why? Don't tell me Mr. Pennyroyal changed his mind at the last minute!"

"That isn't exactly what happened," Jackie said, "but it's almost as bad." She looked as if she were about to cry.

"Well, what is it?" I asked impatiently. "Will somebody please explain?"

"Mr. Pennyroyal signed his new will just a few days before he died," Paula said. "He'd been planning to do it for some time, but he'd been pretty sick. The new will replaced the old one, which left the house to somebody else."

"So?" I asked, looking from one to the other. "There's a new will. What's the problem?"

"The problem is," Ruby said grimly, "that both of the signed originals have vanished." She waved her arms. "They're missing. Kaput. We've looked everywhere we can think of, but they're nowhere to be found."

Jackie frowned. "If you ask me," she said, "somebody took them."

"Tell me what happened," I said. "Jackie, were you there when Mr. Pennyroyal signed his new will?"

Jackie shook her head. "Mrs. Fisher, his housekeeper, says that the lawyer brought both copies for him to sign. Mrs. Fisher was one of the witnesses. The other was the next-door neighbor, Mrs. Jordan. This happened about a week before Mr. Pennyroyal died."

"Why didn't the lawyer keep at least one of the copies?" I asked. "That's the way it's usually done."

"That's what the lawyer suggested," Ruby replied, "but according to Mrs. Fisher, Mr. Pennyroyal insisted on keeping both copies. He said he planned to show the new will to his sister. He told Mrs. Fisher to put the originals into the top drawer of the desk in the library, where they'd be safe. After he died, the lawyer came over to pick them up. That's when they were discovered missing."

"Why did Mr. Pennyroyal want to show the will to his sister?" I asked.

"Because she thought she was inheriting the house," Jackie replied unhappily. "I guess Mr. Pennyroyal felt that he ought to explain why he changed his mind and decided to leave it to the Teen Center. After all, it's worth quite a bit of money."

"Not only that," Ruby said, "but the house has belonged to the Pennyroyals since it was built. He probably thought she might be upset that it wasn't going to stay in the family."

I sighed. "I hate to ask, but there's no doubt that Mr. Pennyroyal died a natural death—is there?"

"No doubt at all," Ruby said firmly. "Both his doctor and Mrs. Fisher were with him when he died."

"Thank goodness," I said, with some relief. "At least we're not looking for a killer."

"Right," Jackie said in a dark tone. "Just a thief."

Ruby looked at me. "What are we going to do?"

"We?" I asked.

"The board would be very grateful if you would help Ruby search for that will," Jackie said.

"You can't say no," Ruby said. "I'd hate to do this all by myself. I don't think it will be dangerous, but you never know."

"Well, if you put it that way," I said with a resigned sigh. I picked up my trowel and basket. "I know Hazel Pennyroyal, so I guess we can begin there."

"Oh, good," Jackie said, relieved. "Let me know as soon as you've found it."

I raised my eyebrows. "Don't you think you're counting on us just a little too much?"

"Why, not at all!" Jackie exclaimed. "I'm *sure* you'll be successful." She frowned. "You *have* to succeed, China. The Teen Center needs that house."

Mr. Pennyroyal's sister, Hazel, works as a volunteer at the Women's Crisis Coalition, so I know her slightly. She lives in a comfortable house with a gorgeous garden. As Ruby and I came up the walk, the multicolored daylilies were making an impressive display on both sides, and behind them, in the deep borders, bloomed several different varieties of salvia, including some beautiful Mexican sage in shades of purple and white.

Hazel Pennyroyal was wearing an apron when she answered the front door. She was a short, plump woman with a fresh-scrubbed face and bright white hair. She recognized me, and I introduced Ruby, as a member of the Teen Center's board of directors.

"I'm afraid that we need to talk to you about a rather difficult subject," I said. "It has to do with your brother's will."

Hazel nodded. "The best place for difficult conversations is the kitchen," she said firmly, and opened the door wider. "Anyway, I'm making soap and it needs stirring. Come on."

"Making soap?" Ruby asked curiously. "Isn't that a lot of work?"

"Not the way I do it," Hazel said. We followed her into the kitchen, where she went to the stove and picked up a spoon to stir something in a saucepan. The whole kitchen smelled of roses. "What's this about Howard's will?"

"I hope you don't mind our asking about this," I replied. "We understand that your brother signed a new will a week or so ago."

"That's right," Hazel said. "Howard decided to leave the house to the Teen Center." She looked at Ruby. "You surely know that by now, since you're on the board of directors."

Ruby nodded. "You saw the new will?"

"Howard showed it to me a few days before he died." Hazel dropped a handful of chopped rose petals into the pan, stirred it again, and turned off the burner. "He wanted to talk to me about the house. Once upon a time, it belonged to both of us, you see. He wanted to be sure I felt comfortable with it not being in the family any longer."

"Both of you?" I asked curiously.

"Yes. Our grandfather left it to us when he died. But I wanted to have my own home, so I sold my half to Howard. He always loved that house."

I gave her a searching look. "Did you feel comfortable with his plan to leave it to the Teen Center?"

"Of course," Hazel said. She began to pour the soap, which looked like pink whipped cream, into some small plastic molds. "Why shouldn't I? Howard had served on the Center's board ever since it began. It was something he felt passionately about. His daughter—his only child—started hanging out with the wrong bunch when she was a teenager, and was killed in a drag-racing accident on the old Austin highway. That was a long time ago, back in the fifties, but Howard always thought that if Felicity and her friends had had a place where they could dance and be with their friends, she might still be alive." She set down the pan and began to press the soap firmly into the mold with her fingers. "Anyway, he left me the family jewelry and a sizable cash bequest."

"I see," I said. It didn't sound as if Hazel would have a reason to want to take that will.

"I was a little concerned about how Mike might feel, though," Hazel went on. "I was going to tell Howard that he ought to talk to the boy, but he began to cough and I didn't want to trouble him."

"Who's Mike?" Ruby asked.

"Mike Rhodes, Howard's stepson. We're not very close, and

I don't know what plans Howard may have had for him. I do know that at one point, he'd talked about giving the house to the boy." She frowned. "I'm not sure, but I think that's how it was in the previous will. I don't have a copy, though."

"I can probably get it from your brother's lawyer," I said.

Hazel shook her head. "I'm afraid not. The lawyer who drew up the latest will is new. Howard's former lawyer died some time back. But Mike probably has a copy, since he was the beneficiary. You could ask him."

Ruby and I traded glances, and I knew what she was thinking. Had Mr. Pennyroyal's son made off with the new will, to make sure that the house would come to him?

> **HAZEL PENNYROYAL'S ROSE SOAP**
>
> Spray some small molds (try candy molds, which come in all sorts of pretty shapes) with non-scented cooking spray or grease with petroleum jelly. Grate 2 four-ounce bars of castile soap. Put the shavings into an enamel saucepan. Add 2 tablespoons of rose water and 12 drops of rose oil and heat slowly, stirring. When the soap has melted and the mixture looks like whipped cream, add 2 tablespoons of chopped red or pink rose petals. Quickly pour a small amount of the mixture into each mold, using your fingers to press the soap firmly into the mold so there are no air bubbles. Allow to harden overnight in the molds. Remove and let air-dry for a few days before wrapping.

Hazel looked at us. "Why are you asking all these questions? Is Mike making a fuss about not getting the house?" She went to the sink to wash her hands, adding over her shoulder, "He's a little hot-tempered and impulsive but he's harmless, really. You don't have to worry about him."

Maybe, maybe not. "We're asking because both copies of

the new will seem to be missing," I said regretfully. "It's important that we find at least one of them."

"Oh, dear!" Hazel turned around, a look of dismay on her face. "You can't imagine that Mike would have —" She frowned. "As I said, he sometimes acts impulsively, but he'd never deliberately go against Howard's wishes."

"Oh, I'm sure," Ruby said comfortingly. But when we left Hazel's fragrant kitchen, we both knew where we were headed next.

Mr. Pennyroyal's stepson, a slender, middle-aged man with gold-rimmed glasses and a ragged gray beard, lived in a second-floor apartment in a trendy, upscale complex. He answered the door in gray sweatpants and a T-shirt, holding a shallow terra-cotta pot containing what looked like a miniature rosemary, bonsai-shaped. Through the patio door behind him, I could see a balcony crowded with plants — a wooden half-barrel filled with herbs, pots of daisies, even a rose growing up a trellis. Obviously, Mike Rhodes was a container gardener.

"We're friends of your stepfather," I said, after I'd introduced Ruby and myself. "Do you have a few minutes to talk?"

Mike motioned for us to come into the living room and set down the pot with a thump. "Howard is dead. Died last week."

"We know," Ruby said. "We're very sorry."

"He was getting on in years," he said brusquely. "It wasn't unexpected."

"Still," I said, "I'm know it's a loss. Actually, we wanted to talk with you about his will."

"The will?" The frown deepened. "What about it?"

"We understand that your stepfather originally planned to leave his house to you," I said.

"That was quite some time ago," he said shortly. "Excuse me." He turned on his heel and went out onto the patio.

"He seems defensive," Ruby whispered. "Maybe he's hiding something—like the will!"

I went over to look at the rosemary. Yes, I'd been right—it *was* a bonsai. Its thick trunk, exposed roots, and complex branch structure gave it the look of an ancient tree clinging to a cliff face, sculptured by the wind. "Maybe we just caught him at a bad time," I said.

Mike came back. "I was watering," he said, a little more pleasantly. "Had to turn the hose off before it created a lake. Now, what was it you wanted to ask?"

"The original will," I said. "You were supposed to inherit the house, weren't you?"

"No," he said. "I mean, How-

Bonsai (pronounced *bone-sigh*) is the Japanese art of training a plant to resemble a full-size, ancient tree. The plants, which may be successfully maintained for several hundred years, are usually grown in a flat, shallow container. In traditional bonsai, long-lived, slow-growing trees are used, such as pine, maple, and elm, as well as holly and juniper, both of which are considered to be herbs. But many perennial herbs—germander, santolina, hyssop, southernwood, rosemary, and thyme are good candidates—can be used to create an herbal bonsai. For a history of bonsai, ideas, and detailed instructions for turning your favorite herb into a work of art, see *Herbal Bonsai: Practicing the Art with Fast-Growing Herbs*, by Richard W. Bender.

ard and I talked about that. But when he decided to give the house to the church, he gave me this place instead."

"This place?" Ruby asked, looking around. "He gave you this apartment?"

He grinned. "Actually, he gave me the whole apartment building."

"My goodness," Ruby said weakly. "It must be nice to have a wealthy stepfather."

"He was a generous man," Mike replied. "I was fourteen when my mother married him—lucky for me. He probably kept me from—I won't say 'a life of crime,' but he certainly helped to change my direction. I was a pretty impulsive kid when I was younger." He grinned ruefully. "I guess I just didn't know what to do with all my energy."

"Mr. Pennyroyal's sister didn't mention anything about a church," I said.

"Aunt Hazel?" Mike shrugged. "Well, maybe Dad didn't discuss it with her. He was pretty undecided there for a while. He had other interests, too—the Teen Center, especially. He served on their board and he'd already given them money to buy some new computers. But in the will he showed me six months or so ago, the church was supposed to get the house."

"Which church is that?" Ruby asked.

"The one just down the block from the house. The pastor is Juliet Giles."

"Thank you," I said. "I know Juliet. We'll have a talk with her. By the way, that's a great-looking bonsai. How old is it?"

"I started it about five years ago," he said. "I really enjoy bonsai—and all sorts of container gardening." He grinned. "In fact, if Howard had given me that house, I wouldn't have had a clue what to do with that huge yard. I just don't have the patience for vegetables."

We found Juliet Giles, the pastor of Mr. Pennyroyal's church, trimming the Bible garden beside the old stone building. Juliet and I have known one another since I came to Pecan Springs some years ago, and she's been a friend of Ruby's for longer than that. She's in her late thirties, a petite, dark-haired woman with large, dark eyes. When she saw us coming, she straightened up, a sprig of dill in her hand.

"Have you come to see how your garden has grown?" she asked with a smile.

Ruby turned to me. "Your garden?"

"I helped design it," I said.

"Don't be so modest," Juliet said with a laugh. To Ruby, she added, "China was the moving spirit behind the garden. She suggested the plants and sketched out the shape for us. Members of the congregation pitched in to do the planting."

"It really looks good," I said. I glanced around, admiring the many plants we had found room for. Garlic, mint, mustard, flax, and lots more, even a small fig tree. "Have you picked any figs yet?" I asked with a smile.

"Not yet." Juliet grinned and pushed her hair back. Her eyes were twinkling. "But I certainly have faith that we will, in God's good time."

"I'm afraid we haven't come to look at the garden," I said regretfully. "I'm sure you know that Mr. Pennyroyal has died."

People who love to garden and who also enjoy reading and studying the Bible sometimes create Bible or Scripture gardens, small gardens especially designed to showcase herbs and plants mentioned in the Old and New Testaments.

- Dill (*Anethum graveolens*) is mentioned in Matthew 23:23, where it is called "anise." In biblical times, it was both a culinary and a medicinal herb and was taxed under Talmudic law, indicating that it was grown and sold commercially. You may grow dill as an annual or a biennial. Sow the seed in sandy, moist soil where you want it to grow. If you don't harvest the seeds, you'll have plenty of dill next year!

- In Numbers 11:5, garlic is recalled with fond wishfulness by the wandering Israelites as one of the foods they ate in Egypt: "We remember the fish we used to eat in Egypt . . . the cucumbers, the melons, the leeks, the onions, and the garlic." The Egyptians also used garlic cloves as a form of currency.

- In Luke 11:42, mint is mentioned as subject to taxation: "You tithe mint and rue and herbs of all kinds, and neglect justice and the love of God; it is these you ought to have practiced, without neglecting the others." Biblical scholars believe that it was the horse mint (*Mentha longifolia*) that is the one referred to in this passage. The leaves were used in brewing tea, and the plant was used medicinally.

- Matthew 17:20 begins, "If ye have faith as a grain of mustard seed . . ." The mustard referred to here is probably black mustard (*Brassica nigra*), which was cultivated for its oil. The seed husk is very hard, which makes it possible for the seed to lie dormant for decades, even a century or more, before conditions are suitable for sprouting. The seed became a metaphor for endurance and faith.

- Flax, from which linen is woven, is the oldest known textile fiber and one of the earliest plants cultivated in Egypt and Palestine. Production was a lengthy process, involving submersion in water, drying, combing, spinning, and weaving. The first mention of it in the Bible is in Genesis 41:42: "And Pharaoh took off his ring from his hand, and put it upon Joseph's hand, and arrayed him in vestures of fine linen. . . ."

- You probably already know how fig leaves were used in the Book of Genesis (Genesis 3:7). The fig tree itself is one of the most important plants of scriptural times, and it is mentioned fifty-seven times in the Bible. It was extensively cultivated for its fruit. Since apples don't grow in the Near East, some scholars believe that the fig is the "apple" of the biblical Garden of Eden.

Juliet nodded. "We had the funeral here yesterday. He'll be missed." She glanced at Ruby. "You're on the board of the Teen Center, aren't you? You must be very excited about moving into the house."

"There's a problem," Ruby said. "The will can't be found."

"The will?" Juliet looked incredulous. "You mean, Mr. Pennyroyal's new will is missing?"

"Right," I said. "And unless it's found, it looks as if the estate will be probated under the old will, and your church will inherit the house. We hoped that perhaps you might have an idea what could have happened to the will."

"Uh-oh," Juliet said softly. "I hope you don't think—"

"Of course not!" Ruby exclaimed, horrified. "We know you wouldn't do a thing like that!"

Ruby might feel confident, but I wasn't so sure. Not that Juliet would stoop to steal the will, of course. But other people in her congregation might want to make sure that the church inherited the house. In fact, now that I thought about it—

"Juliet," I said, "isn't Mrs. Fisher a member of your congregation?"

Ruby whirled to look at me, a question in her eyes. "Mrs. Fisher? Mr. Pennyroyal's housekeeper?"

"She's one of our most dedicated members," Juliet said. "As a matter of fact, I think she was the one who suggested to Mr. Pennyroyal that he leave the house to the church. I'm afraid she was a little disappointed when he decided to give it to the Teen Center instead." She frowned. "But China, you can't possibly think that Mrs. Fisher would have—"

I sighed. "I'm sorry, Juliet. We have to consider every possibility. The person who made off with the will knew exactly what he—or she—was doing."

"Good Lord," Juliet breathed.

"I don't think God had anything to do with it," Ruby replied. "If you ask me, it was the other guy." She made a face. "You know who I mean."

Juliet was frowning. "I just can't believe that Mrs. Fisher would have taken those signed copies," she said. "She wanted the church to have the property, yes — but she wouldn't have done anything counter to Mr. Pennyroyal's desires. I'm certain of that. And she wouldn't even *think* of taking something that didn't belong to her."

"Then perhaps," I said, "you can suggest another possibility."

Juliet was silent for a minute, looking around the garden as if for inspiration. "Tell me what you already know," she said.

"There were two copies of the new will," Ruby replied. "Mr. Pennyroyal signed them, and Mrs. Fisher and a neighbor witnessed his signatures. Then Mrs. Fisher put both copies of the will into the desk in the library."

"In the *library*?" Juliet asked. A frown puckered between her eyes.

"That's right," I said. "What's this all about, Juliet? What do you know that we don't?"

She answered my question with another. "How much do you know about the opposition to Mr. Pennyroyal's plan?"

Ruby shrugged. "We understand that some of the neighbors are opposed to the idea of the Teen Center taking over the house. They don't want a bunch of kids around." She wrinkled her nose. "I guess they're worried about noisy parties."

Juliet nodded. "We've discussed the issues in some of our church meetings, but we haven't been able to change their minds." She looked at me. "Mrs. Jordan, who lives next door to the Pennyroyal house, is the most outspoken of all the neighbors. In fact, I think she's the one who's organized the opposition."

"Mrs. Jordan?" I looked at Ruby. "Wasn't she the other witness to Mr. Pennyroyal's will?"

"That's right," Ruby said.

"I don't want to accuse anybody," Juliet said, "but —" She pressed her lips together.

I could tell by the look in Juliet's eyes that she knew something important. "Let's go talk to Mrs. Jordan," I said. "Will you come?"

"Yes," Juliet answered. She looked around the peaceful garden. "Although I can think of a few other things I'd much rather do." She laughed sadly. "Pulling weeds, for instance."

"Oh?" Ruby asked. "It's that bad, is it?"

Juliet nodded. "Maybe I'd better tell you what I suspect." And that's what she did, as we walked down the street to visit Mrs. Jordan.

"Why, hello, Pastor Giles," the woman said, opening the door. She was tall, with a sharp, angular face framed by thick gray hair, her eyes magnified by thick-lensed glasses. She wore a hearing aid in one ear. "Would you like to come in?"

"These are my friends China Bayles and Ruby Wilcox." Juliet paused and added, meaningfully, "Ruby serves on the Teen Center's board of directors."

"On what?" Mrs. Jordan asked, fiddling with her hearing aid.

Juliet leaned forward. "On the Teen Center's board of directors," she repeated distinctly.

"I . . . see," Mrs. Jordan said. She glanced at Ruby, biting her lip. "Well, I . . . On second thought, maybe you'd better come back later. I'm pretty busy just now." She started to close the door.

Juliet put out her hand. "I think we need to talk *now*, Mrs. Jordan," she said firmly. "We won't take much of your time."

Reluctantly, Mrs. Jordan stepped back and Juliet went inside. Ruby and I followed the two women into a small old-fashioned living room. The slip-covered furniture was draped with crocheted doilies, the walls were crowded with framed photographs, and the room had a musty smell, as if the windows hadn't been opened in years. If there were a noisy party next door, I thought to myself, she probably wouldn't hear it.

Ruby and I sat down on the sofa, and Juliet took a chair. "May I bring you some tea?" Mrs. Jordan asked nervously, still standing.

"Thank you, but no." Juliet was resolute. "I think you know why we've come."

Mrs. Jordan perched on the edge of a chintz-covered chair. "Why, no," she said. She glanced at Ruby, then looked away. "I really can't guess."

"It's about Mr. Pennyroyal's will," Juliet replied. "The one you witnessed recently." She turned to me. "Tell her what's happened, China."

"The will is missing," I said loudly. "Both signed originals were taken from the desk in Mr. Pennyroyal's library."

"And without that will," Ruby put in, "the Teen Center won't get the house."

"I'm sorry, but I can't hear," Mrs. Jordan said. She stood up. "You might just as well leave."

"Sit down, Elvira," Juliet said. "You can hear us perfectly well. And if you can't, just turn up your hearing aid."

Mrs. Jordan sat down. "This is a good neighborhood, full

of decent people. We don't want gangs of teenagers hanging around. It's bad for property values."

"I knew you were unhappy about the idea of the Teen Center moving in next door," Juliet said sorrowfully. "But I had no idea you were so upset that you would steal Mr. Pennyroyal's will."

"I!" Behind her glasses, Mrs. Jordan's eyes widened. One hand went to her throat. "How can you say that, Pastor Giles? Why, I had nothing to do with it."

"Please don't compound your theft with a lie, Elvira," Juliet said quietly. "When you took the will, I was standing in the hall outside the library. I saw you open the desk drawer, take something out, and put it in your purse. Until China and Ruby told me where the originals were kept, I had no idea of the significance of what I'd seen. But now—" She held out her hand and said, in a clear, firm voice, "Give us the will. Both copies, please."

It took a few months for the Pennyroyal Teen Center to open, because the will had to be probated and then Jackie, the board president, had to go before the city council and request a zoning variance. To everyone's surprise, Mrs. Jordan—who had been the most vocal opponent of the idea—didn't put in an appearance, and all of the people who came spoke on behalf of the Center. With no opposition, the variance was approved.

"I just don't understand why Mrs. Jordan didn't show up," Jackie said in a mystified tone, as we walked out of the council chambers. "Without her, the whole thing was *easy!*"

Ruby and I traded glances. When Mrs. Jordan surrendered

the wills, Ruby, Juliet, and I had agreed that it would be best to keep the whole thing quiet. After all, we'd found what we were looking for, and that was the most important thing.

"It's a long story," I said.

"With a happy ending," Ruby added.

Jackie looked from one of us to the other. "I get the feeling that the two of you uncovered some sort of plot when you began looking for that will."

"I suppose you could call it that," Ruby said, tossing her head nonchalantly in an imitation of Kinsey Milhone, the alphabetic private eye. "Let's file this one under P."

Jackie frowned. "I'm not sure I see —"

"P is for Pennyroyal," Ruby said, with a dramatic flourish. "That's a catchy title, don't you think?"

I sighed. "If you've got to call it something, why don't you just call it 'The Pennyroyal Plot'?"

Ruby snapped her fingers. "That's it, China! The Pennyroyal Plot."

"Enough of this nonsense," Jackie said firmly. "I'm starving. Let's go get something to eat."

"Are you buying?" Ruby asked.

"Of course," Jackie replied expansively. "In fact, this one is on the Teen Center. We'll go anywhere you like."

"Wonderful!" Ruby said. "In that case, let's go to Thyme for Tea and see what's left from lunch." At my questioning glance, she shrugged. "Well, if Jackie's going to spend the money on us anyway, she might as well put it into *our* cash register, don't you think?"

"I guess I can't disagree with you there," I said.

A VIOLET
DEATH

H<small>EY,</small> fairies!" Energetically, Ruby Wilcox waved both arms. "Come on, fairies, show your stuff! And don't drag those wings, you'll tear them!"

A dozen six-year-old fairies in pastel tulle with gold crowns and gauzy, gold-flecked wings pranced across the grass behind Ruby and up onto the stage. Ruby herself was dressed as Peter Pan, with her ginger-red hair frizzed all over her head. She and Mavina Miles, a plump, fussy Wendy in blue dress, white pinafore, and white stockings, were in charge of the fairies.

It was May Eve, that magical evening when all the fairies in the world come out to celebrate the return of the flowers. As Ruby had just told our own wide-eyed group: "The Little People dance all night long on May Eve, and if you're very lucky you may catch a glimpse of one. You should never, never try to kidnap him, though, or steal his shadow, or you'll regret it the rest of your life." And then, as their eyes got bigger and bigger, she added, "The best thing to do is to leave a gift—a pretty seashell, something sweet to eat, or something glittery—under the oldest tree you can find, or beside a stream. But don't leave anything that's made of metal, for it might rob the Little People of their magical powers."

I'm sure that all this sounds pretty weird to you. You'll probably think we looked weird, too, since most of the grown-ups doing this gig were dressed up like various fictional characters—Peter Pan and Wendy, Alice, Peter Rabbit. I wasn't exactly in costume, but I was wearing a Fairy Festival T-shirt and a circlet of rosemary on my head.

Weird or not, it's all part of the annual May Fairy Festival, organized by the Myra Merryweather Herb Guild and held in the Pecan Springs Park on the weekend closest to May Day. On Friday night, the littlest fairies dance and the older children perform fairy-tale skits on the outdoor stage. On Saturday, there's a Maypole, free art projects for kids, and booths where local craftspeople and vendors sell their wares. The Herb Guild sells refreshments and puts the money into its scholarship fund.

The kids and their parents all have a great time playing make-believe.

By nine-thirty that Friday night, the party was over. The frazzled moms and dads had taken their sleepy fairies home, leaving Ruby and me and a half dozen other members of the Herb Guild to police our section of the park, picking up lost crowns and torn fairy wings and litter. Now that the lights were on and the magic had worn off, we all looked a little ridiculous in our costumes. Tired, too—and the festival wouldn't be over until tomorrow.

"I need your expert opinion, China," Mary Driscoll said, coming up with a plate of cookies. She was dressed as the Roman goddess Flora, with silk flowers sewn over a flowing gauzy tunic, and a honeysuckle circlet. "Tell me what you think of these," she said, offering me one.

I munched. "Yum," I said. "What's this?"

"The recipe calls them Lemony Basil Cookies," Mary replied, "but we're calling them Faerie Blossom Cookies. Do you like them?"

"They're great," I said, filching another one. "Be sure and leave one under a big tree. The Little People will love you for it."

Pansy Pride, the Herb Guild president, trotted up, carrying a

> Honeysuckle has been used medicinally for centuries. The Romans used it to treat many ailments, while Renaissance herbalists used it as a sore-throat gargle, expectorant, and laxative. Contemporary herbalists use the herb chiefly in topical creams, as an anti-inflammatory. Braided into the hair or worn as an amulet, honeysuckle was believed to ward off the powers of darkness, and farmers in northern Europe wound it around the horns of their cows to protect them from evil fairies who might want to turn the milk sour.

FAERIE BLOSSOM COOKIES

Enlist the children to help you to pick the herbs and wash them. They'll love to flatten the cookies, too.

⅛ cup sugar
¼ cup fresh lemon-basil leaves, packed down
¼ cup fresh lemon balm leaves, packed down
¾ cup sugar
½ cup butter or margarine, softened
1 egg
3 tablespoons lemon juice
3 cups flour

Preheat oven to 350°F and lightly grease two baking sheets. In a blender or food processor, process the fresh herbs with the ⅛ cup sugar and set aside. Using your electric mixer, beat butter or margarine until creamy, gradually adding the ¾ cup sugar. Add egg and lemon juice and blend. Add herb-sugar mixture, then flour, 1 cup at a time, beating to blend thoroughly. Shape into one-inch balls and place two inches apart on greased baking sheet. Dip the bottom of a glass in sugar and flatten each ball. Bake until golden brown, about 8 to 10 minutes. Remove to wire racks to cool. Makes about three dozen.

plastic bag full of trash. Pansy's Cinderella outfit was rumpled, her makeup was smeared, and she looked tired and cross. I couldn't blame her. Herding an unruly flock of fairies all evening is enough to wear anybody out. "Okay," she snapped, peering nearsightedly at Mary. "Whose idea was it?"

"Whose idea was what?" Ruby asked, joining us. She looked tired, too. Every year, those fairies seem to get a little harder to corral.

"Who decided to stage the make-believe murder beside the Maypole?" Pansy scowled. "Mavina and whoever else dreamed it up ought to be ashamed of themselves, considering that this is a children's festival. The kids see enough violence on TV, without — "

"Make-believe murder?" I asked, surprised. "What are you talking about, Pansy?"

"I'm talking about Mavina Miles," Pansy said. When we only stared at her blankly, she added, "Come on. I'll show you." We followed her to the grassy area of the park where, earlier that afternoon, we had erected the Maypole. A woman in a blue dress and white pinafore was lying facedown, a rusty stain between her shoulders.

Ruby gasped. "Pansy," she whispered, "put your glasses on. That's real blood!"

I knelt down and gently turned Mavina over, feeling for a pulse in her neck, hoping that she was still alive. But we had come too late. Her eyes were closed, her plump, round face was pale. In her hand, she was holding a crushed tussie mussie centered with a cluster of fragrant, dark-blue violets.

She was quite, quite dead.

It was midnight before I got home. McQuaid was sitting at the kitchen table with a book, a Lone Star longneck, and a grilled cheese sandwich. He glanced up at the clock when I walked in.

A tussie mussie is a small bouquet of herbs and flowers in a decorative holder. These nosegays were popular personal gifts in Victorian times, and every lady understood the special, secret meaning of each of the flowers. To make one, start with a single rose or a daisy, or a cluster of violets. Surround this center with a circlet of small green leaves, such as rosemary, thyme, fern, or laurel. Tuck in a few forget-me-nots, lilies of the valley, violets, and silvery lambs ears. Other silver-gray sprigs, such as artemisia, add a nice accent, while scented geraniums lend their sweet scent. Secure the stems with a rubber band and push them through a slit cut in the center of a lacy paper doily. For an elegant touch, use a silvery tussie mussie holder.

"A midnight revel with the Little People?" he asked, his dark eyes teasing.

"You might put it that way," I replied wearily. I went to the cupboard, got out some of my favorite DreamyThyme tea, and turned on the fire under the kettle. "On the other hand, you might say that it was a late-night date with murder."

He stared at me. "You're kidding."

"I wish." I put a teaspoon of tea leaves into a tea ball and dropped it into a cup. "Somebody shot Mavina Miles beside the Maypole. We found her about nine-thirty, but it took a while for the cops to get there and tape off the crime scene. They finally took the body away and allowed us to move the Maypole to a different location. The scene is still off-limits, of course."

"Mavina Miles? Do I know her?"

"Probably. She works at the Pecan Springs Library. The short, plump, middle-aged one who frowns a lot." The kettle, already hot, began to steam, and I poured the boiling water into my cup.

"Oh, yeah, that one. When she checks out my books, she looks at me like I'm *stealing* them." McQuaid leaned back in his chair. As he's a former homicide detective, crime isn't news to him. "Any leads? How about clues?"

"No leads," I said. "There might be a clue, if I could figure it out." I jiggled the tea ball in my cup, inhaling the lemony fragrance. "She was holding a tussie mussie. With violets."

McQuaid stared at me. "A what?"

"A little bouquet made up of herbs and flowers that have secret meanings," I replied. "Violets represent love and loyalty." I dipped a spoon into the honey, and then into my tea. "I wonder if the tussie mussie was a gift from a friend."

McQuaid raised one eyebrow. "Or maybe it was designed to decoy her to her death," he said alliteratively. He finished his sandwich and beer and I sipped my tea. We were both silent.

Finally, I got up and rinsed off our dishes. "I'm sure the tussie mussie must mean *something*," I muttered, frowning. "I just have to figure out what."

You might not think of the violet as an herb, but the plant has a long and interesting history of culinary and medicinal use. And while violets have come to be symbolic of steadfast devotion, they have also been associated with death. One ancient legend claims that violets sprang from the blood of the dying Attis, a Phrygian vegetation god who was slain beside a pine tree. In an annual ritual, the Phrygians hung an effigy of the god on a pine tree decked with violets. According to Sir James Frazer, in *The Golden Bough*, what we now know as the Maypole probably evolved from ancient pagan rituals celebrating the rebirth of plant life in the spring. Medicinally, violets were used to treat sore throats and respiratory ailments, and appear as the main ingredient in Hildegard of Bingen's famous remedy for external cancers.

McQuaid put his arm around me. "You will," he said, and kissed my neck softly. "I'm sorry about Mavina, China. She always made me feel like a criminal, but I'm sure she was a perfectly nice lady."

And with that, we called it a night.

The next morning was bright and cheerful, and when Ruby and I got to the park, a few people were beginning to filter in. We quickly set up our booth—herbal items from Thyme and Seasons and New Age-y things from Ruby's Crystal Cave—and settled down to the business of making sales and talking to people.

But not for long. We'd only been open for a half hour when Sheila Dawson, Pecan Springs's chief of police, put in an appearance at the booth. Actually, wherever Sheila goes, she puts in an appearance. She's tall, blond, and willowy, with the classy look of a Dallas deb. But don't let the look fool you. There's plenty of muscle power packed into that slender frame. Today, she was wearing plain clothes (if that's what you could call her silky pink slacks and embroidered tunic) and her badge wasn't visible. I gathered that she wanted to blend into the crowd, as much as she could, anyway. In Pecan Springs, where everybody knows almost everybody else, that's a challenge for anybody, especially somebody like Sheila.

"I need your help, China," she said, without preamble. "I want you to go with me to talk to Mavina Miles's niece. I thought she'd be more comfortable if you were there. You know her, don't you?"

"Esther?" I said. "Sure. She's over there, at the Children's Art Tent." I turned the booth over to Ruby, and Sheila and I went off together.

"I understand that Esther and her aunt didn't get along very well," Sheila remarked.

"They've been estranged for years," I said. I added, thinking of inheritance, "But she's still Mavina's closest relative." The estate probably didn't amount to much — a house, a car, a bank account. But in my former career as a criminal defense attorney, I had learned that most motives for murder can be spelled g-r-e-e-d.

Esther was helping three little girls make lavender hearts. She looked up as Sheila and I approached her. I introduced Sheila, who said, "I'm sorry about your aunt. Would you mind taking a break? I'd like to ask you a few questions."

Esther's pretty face darkened, but she only shrugged. "I'm afraid I can't tell you anything you don't already know," she said. "But I'll try."

We walked away from the booth and stood in the shade of a large live oak tree. "Were you here at the festival last night?" Sheila asked.

"I was at a friend's party all evening," Esther replied, "on Hawthorne Street. Lots of people saw me there." Her voice was a little sarcastic. "I guess that's what you cops call an alibi. Will it do?"

"It'll do for now," Sheila replied quietly, "if you'll give me your friend's name and address." She paused. "Did your aunt have any enemies that you know of?"

"Or admirers?" I added, thinking about the violets in that tussie mussie. "Someone who might have given her flowers?"

Lavender hearts are easy enough for children to construct. Here's what you need to make a pretty pair.

2-inch heart pattern, drawn on cardboard and cut out
4×6" sheet of foam, ¼ to ½ inch thick
White glue
1 cup dried lavender buds
Lavender essential oil
2 dried rosebuds
Small dried flowers and herbs
Scrap of lace
1 yard narrow satin ribbon, lavender
2 straight pins

Using the pattern, draw two hearts on the foam. Cut out (an adult may need to help with this). Coat the hearts with glue and cover with dried lavender buds, pressing for better contact. Add a few drops of lavender oil to the heart. Glue a rosebud to the center of each heart and surround with a miniature arrangement of dried flowers and herbs, glued on. Glue on the scrap of lace for a final decorative touch. Fasten the ribbons in the cleft of each heart with a dab of glue, and secure with a pin. Tie a pretty bow in the center.

Esther's smile was thin. "Aunt Mavina made it her business to know everybody else's business, and most people resented it when she poked her nose into their private affairs. She probably had dozens of enemies. And I can't think of a single admirer." She paused and added, coolly, "You probably already know that I'll inherit her estate, so I might as well tell you that it's substantial. Her father left her some real estate in San Antonio when he died twenty years ago, and it's worth quite a bit now." The smile got thinner. "It's a good thing I have that alibi, huh?"

And that was all we got out of Esther. Sheila walked with me back to the booth, where she bought a couple of herbal bath scrubbies. When I handed the bag to her, she said, "What do you think, China? About Esther, I mean." She paused. "San Antonio real estate makes a pretty substantial motive."

"Yeah," I said. "I suppose you'll check out her alibi."

"Right—although if the party was a big one, it's not much of an alibi. I'll let you know if we turn anything up. In the meantime, keep your ear to the ground, will you?"

"Glad to," I said. "Enjoy your scrubbies."

"Sure." She grinned. "Even a cop deserves a nice bath every now and then."

The next couple of hours were pretty hectic, with lots of customers stopping by the booth to talk about herbs and check out what I had for sale. By midmorning, I had sold every pot of basil I'd brought. I was also completely out of rosemary, which is not only a fragrant herb but a deer-proof landscaping plant, as well. The

China's Herbal Bath Scrubbies

Mix ¼ cup regular oatmeal with ¼ cup dried herbs and ¼ cup grated bar soap (unscented). Place ¼ cup of this mixture in a cotton bag and fold it inside a washcloth. You can use a single herb or mix several together; if you like, you can also add a few drops of essential oil. For a relaxing bath, use lavender, thyme, comfrey, or lemon verbena. For an invigorating bath, use rosemary, yarrow, jasmine, or lemon balm. When you're finished bathing, discard the contents of the bag, rinse, and turn it inside out to dry, then refill. (This recipe makes enough for three scrubbies.)

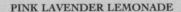

PINK LAVENDER LEMONADE

Lavender-hibiscus syrup:
2½ cups water
1½ cups sugar
¼ cup red hibiscus flowers, dried
1 tablespoon lavender flowers, dried

Lemonade:
3 cups cold water
1½ cups fresh-squeezed lemon juice (8 large lemons)
½ cup sugar (optional)
Thin lemon slices, for garnish

In a medium saucepan, combine the 2½ cups water and the sugar. Bring to a boil, stirring to dissolve sugar. Add hibiscus flowers, reduce heat, and simmer for 2 to 3 minutes. Remove from heat. Stir in lavender flowers. Cover and let steep until cool. Strain hibiscus-lavender syrup into a jar and chill. Make lemonade in your prettiest clear glass pitcher, and stir in the chilled syrup. If you like it tart, this will be fine. If you have a sweet tooth, add another ½ cup sugar and stir briskly to dissolve. Garnish with lemon slices.

resinous taste makes it unpleasant to the deer, while its fragrant blue blossoms attract every bee within commuting distance. Rosemary is a hands-down favorite around Pecan Springs, where it's a challenge to find a plant that you love but the deer don't.

Finally, sales slacked off a little and Ruby and I had time to pour a couple of paper cups of the pink lavender lemonade that she had brought. We sat down in our folding chairs, relaxing in the sunshine and listening to the music coming from a nearby booth. But the minute I sat down, my thoughts flew straight back to last night and the sight of Mavina Miles, clutching that tussie mussie. I thought for a few minutes, then put down my cup and stood up.

"That was a short break," Ruby said, surprised. "Where are you going?"

"To talk to a lady about violets," I said. "Hold the fort, Ruby. I'll be back in a few minutes."

Sandra Green owns Blooms and Blossoms, the only florist shop in town. Today, she was selling bouquets and individual flowers at her booth, only a few paces away. When I came up, a couple of young girls were buying a bunch of daisies. They walked away, giggling as they pulled off individual petals and whispering, "He loves me, he loves me not."

"If you're looking for daisies, you're out of luck," Sandra said, pushing her brown hair out of her eyes. "I've just sold the last one. Can I interest you in a bunch of carnations?"

Like many other herbs, daisies have been used in various forms of divination, like the "he loves me" chant you learned as a child, where the last petal is supposed to give you the correct answer. In another divination, close your eyes and pick a handful of grass and daisy stems. When you count them, you'll know how many years you have to wait for Mr. or Ms. Right to come along. If you want to get a glimpse of the person you're waiting for, put a piece of daisy root under your pillow and he or she will appear in a dream. And be sure to step on the first daisy you see in the spring. If you don't, it is said that the daisies will grow over your grave before the year is out! In another tradition, daisies growing on a grave were said to be a symbol of rebirth. Medicinally, the daisy was used to ease coughs; in lotion form, it was used to treat wounds and bruises.

One sixteenth-century name for the carnation was the inelegant "sops-in-wine," which reflects its use as a spicy flavoring for drinks. It was also used in soups, sauces, syrups, and vinegar, and the flowers were candied and preserved. To make your own carnation vinegar, use freshly picked, unsprayed flowers from your own garden (*not* from a florist!). Place 1 cup of loosely packed flowers in a quart jar and cover with 2 cups of room-temperature white wine vinegar. Add a cinnamon stick and a teaspoon of whole cloves. Cover and store in a dark place. Check the flavor after a week; and continue steeping until the desired strength is obtained. Strain into a pretty bottle. Use on a luncheon salad of crisp greens.

"I'm more interested in violets," I said. "Do you have any?"

Sandra shook her head. "I had two dozen last week, but they're all gone now."

"I see," I said thoughtfully. "Do you remember who bought them from you?"

"Of course," Sandra said. "It's not like Pecan Springs is a big city, you know. Alice Olsen bought most of them. Joe Keiffer bought what was left." She grinned. "Joe said he was buying them for someone he secretly admired, which I thought was cute. Joe must be sixty-five, if he's a day. His wife died last year, and I know he's been lonesome. I wonder who he's sweet on."

"Only those two? You're sure about that?"

"I've got the receipts back at the shop," Sandra said. "Why?" She shifted uncomfortably. "This doesn't have anything to do with Mavina, does it? I heard she was holding a bouquet of violets when she was found."

"It might," I said. Casually, I added, "Did you know her?"

A look of something—alarm, apprehension, I couldn't be sure what—crossed Sandra's face, and she half-turned away.

When she spoke, her tone was guarded. "Mavina? Of course I knew her. Didn't everybody? I checked out books from her at the library, and she came into the shop a couple of times a month."

"Did she ever buy violets?"

"Not that I recall." Her mouth tightened. "The last thing she bought was a single white rose."

It occurred to me that there might be something more to the relationship than Sandra was letting on. I filed the suspicion away and lowered my voice. "When you get back to your shop," I said, "it would be a good idea to put those receipts in a safe place. The police might want to have a look at them."

"Okay," Sandra said. She turned back to me. Whatever the look on her face had been, it was gone and she was smiling. "Hey, if carnations aren't your thing, how about a few nasturtiums?"

When I got back to the booth, I told Ruby what Sandra had said about selling violets to Alice Olsen and Joe Keiffer, and reported my suspicion that there was more to Sandra's relationship with Mavina than she was letting on.

Ruby took all this in, then asked, "Why would anybody bother to *buy* violets? Can't they just go out in the woods and pick them for free?"

Roses are among the favorite herbs of many cultures. Medicinally, roses have been used to enhance digestion, treat diarrhea, soothe headaches and earaches, and treat many other ailments. In the kitchen, roses appear in jams, jellies, and syrups, sweets of all kinds, and salads. They are prized for their scent in perfumes, soaps, lotions, and potpourris. In the Victorian language of flowers, the red rose represented love, and the white rose represented silence and secrecy.

"Not around Pecan Springs," I said. "It's too hot and dry here for wild violets. Anyway, the violets in Mavina's tussie mussie were cultivated violets, with large, dark blossoms. Wild violets are usually small and lighter in color." We didn't have time to discuss it further. Customer traffic picked up and we were busy until five, when the Fairy Festival closed and all the vendors began packing up.

Fortunately, we didn't have much to pack. Ruby had sold every single one of the dream pillows she had brought and most of the books, crystals, and magic wands. In addition to the potted herbs, my best-selling item turned out to be a spicy Kitchen Simmer Potpourri that makes the kitchen smell like cinnamon and orange spice. By five o'clock, our booth was almost bare, we had counted our money, and we were ready to pack the tables and our signs into the van.

When we'd finished loading everything, Ruby turned to me. "As it happens, Alice Olsen borrowed one of my astrology books when she was taking a class last month. Why don't we drop in on her? I can get my book back, and you might just casually ask her about those violets."

I slammed the van door. "Sounds like a plan worthy of Nancy Drew," I said. I was sure Sheila wouldn't object, since she's always complaining about not having enough trained investigators. And anyway, there was nothing to go on but my hunch about those violets—which wasn't enough to prompt Sheila to spend valuable police time investigating. Like all cop shops, hers is on a tight budget.

"Super," Ruby said happily. "Let's go."

So we climbed into the van and drove to an upscale part of

You don't have to go all the way to Pecan Springs to enjoy the fragrance of China's Kitchen Simmer Potpourri—you can make your own.

CHINA'S KITCHEN SIMMER POTPOURRI

Mix 2 tablespoons orris root (the dried root of the common blue flag, used to absorb and fix fragrance) with 6 drops orange oil, 4 drops cinnamon oil, and 3 drops clove oil. Then add the following herbs and spices and mix well:

½ cup broken cinnamon sticks
½ cup dried mint
½ cup bay leaves
¼ cup orange peel
¼ cup cloves
3 tablespoons star anise
2 tablespoons ground allspice
1 teaspoon ground nutmeg

Store in a tightly lidded can or jar. To use, shake the container, then put 2 to 3 tablespoons of the mixture into a pint of water and bring to a slow simmer in a stainless or glass saucepan. Be sure to include bits of all the different herbs, including the ground spices in the bottom of the container. If you'd like more fragrance, add more potpourri. Check the water often and add more as it evaporates.

town, where Alice had recently rented a new apartment. She was a cool, poised-looking woman, her hair swirled on top of her head in an ash-blond pouf. Her makeup was flawless, and she was dressed for a dinner date in a sleek, close-fitting white sheath. In my grubby jeans and Fairy Fest T-shirt, stained with some child's grape Kool-Aid and a smear of chocolate marshmallow ice cream, I couldn't blame Alice for looking at me like something that had blown in on a West Texas wind.

Ruby introduced me and explained about the book, and as Alice went to get it, I glanced around. The all-white living room was elegantly furnished with a sofa and stuffed chairs that looked brand-new. I didn't dare sit down, so I wandered around, looking at things. There was so much white that it made me want to squint, the way you do on a white-sand beach at noon on a summer day. The only relief in the entire room was a crystal bowl filled with a dozen deep-blue violets, sitting on a glass table.

"Those are beautiful flowers," I said when Alice returned with the book—something called *Read Your Romance in the Stars*—and handed it to Ruby.

Alice touched a petal reminiscently. "Violets are my favorite flower. They grew all around our house in Vermont. My mother used to make violet syrup for pancakes when we were children. It was a lovely springtime treat."

"But you haven't made syrup with those," I remarked idly.

"No," she replied. "I read somewhere that you shouldn't cook with flowers that come from a florist, because they may have been sprayed with something poisonous." She didn't look

To make violet syrup the way your grandmother used to do it, pour 2 cups of boiling water over 6 cups of washed violet blossoms (unsprayed), then place a saucer on top to submerge the flowers. Let stand for 24 hours. Strain out the plant material. Add 2 cups of sugar and 2 tablespoons of lemon juice to the liquid and simmer until the mixture is the consistency of syrup. Cover and refrigerate. Use within a week.

Violet conserve was a favorite confection. Flower petals were beaten to a smooth paste with twice their weight in sugar, then put into a jar and sealed.

To make violet vinegar, fill a sterilized jar half full of washed flowers, cover with white wine vinegar, and allow to steep for a week. Strain and pour into a pretty bottle. A lovely cosmetic vinegar, but also good on a spring salad garnished with fresh violet petals.

Violet honey was both a sweet treat and medicinal, as well. A cup of fresh, washed petals was added to 2 cups of honey and heated until the honey took on the scent of violets. A favorite on biscuits, or to soothe a sore throat.

up, and her voice had taken on a brittle edge. "I wanted them just to . . . remind me."

"At least I got my book back," Ruby said, as we climbed into the van. "Other than that, I'd say the visit was a loss. Wouldn't you?"

"I guess," I replied. I thought of Alice's poised coolness and the chilly white of her apartment, and shivered. "McQuaid's cooking Tex-Mex tonight. Let's take this stuff back to the shop and then go to my house and warm up over a plate of his enchilada casserole."

"Sounds like a plan to me," Ruby said happily.

As it happens, Joe Keiffer's house is a stone's throw from Thyme and Seasons Herbs, and as Ruby and I drove back to our shops, we saw Joe out in his yard, wearing dirty overalls and pushing an old-style rotary lawn mower. We left our van parked in the alley behind the shops, then casually walked over to talk to him.

Joe stopped pushing his mower and greeted us with his customary frown. "Careful where you put your feet," he said, pointing to a patch of freshly turned soil beside the fence. "I just planted me some epazote seeds and I sure don't need nobody trackin' in my fresh dirt."

"Are you sure you know what you're doing, Joe?" I teased. "That epazote spreads like a prairie fire in August." Epazote is used to flavor Mexican bean dishes and reduce the you-know-what that comes with beans. If it likes your garden (most epazote has never met a garden it didn't like), it will grow three or four feet high, then start eyeing your neighbor's garden.

"Won't matter none to me if it does," Joe said with a twinkle. "Ever'body needs a little epazote in the bean pot." He wiped his sweaty face with a red bandana. "What's on yer mind, China?" He pretended not to see Ruby. Joe's got a strong conservative streak, and she's too New Age for his taste.

"I was talking to Sandra Green this morning," I said. "She happened to mention that you bought some violets for a friend of yours."

"Yep," Joe said proudly. "Bought a whole half dozen. Set me back a good bit, too. Vi'lets ain't cheap, y'know."

I nodded. "It happens that I've got some violet bubble bath on special this week, and I thought your friend might like to have some of that, to go along with her flowers."

Joe raised both eyebrows. "Violet bubble bath," he mused. "Now, that's a thought." He leaned forward. "How much?"

"Just a dollar, for you," I said. "Who's your friend?"

He straightened up, frowning furiously. "None o' yer beeswax," he snapped.

I turned to go. "See you around."

"Hey!" he said. "What about that bubble bath? I reckon Charlene would like some. She did like them vi'lets I got her." He looked down bashfully. "Charlene Clark is her name. She works at the Quik-Wash Laundry. I bet you know her."

I do know Charlene, who is as sweet and kind as they come. I couldn't imagine her being involved with Mavina's death. And since Joe had given his violets to Charlene, we could scratch him off the suspect list. Now that I'd talked to him, I was ready to scratch him off anyway. I couldn't imagine Mavina unbending enough to give Joe the time of day. "I'll get that bubble bath for you, Joe," I said. "I'm sure Charlene will love it."

> Children love to help you make bubble bath. Grate a bar of castile soap into a quart of warm water. Mix with a whisk until you have a liquid soap solution (don't shake, or you'll end up with a jar of bubbly). Add 2 ounces of coconut oil and 1 ounce of glycerine (both are known for their skin-softening properties), then stir in 2 to 3 drops of essential oil of violets, or your favorite sweet scent. Pour into a pretty jar.

When Ruby and I went back to our unloading, I thought about Mavina's tussie mussie. Violets had been the central flower, but there had been others as well. Maybe they held a clue. Trouble was, I couldn't recall what they were.

But the answer to this mystery was as close as the Pecan Springs police station, where the tussie mussie was being kept under lock and key in the evidence room. With Sheila's permission, Ruby and I sat down and made a list of all the herbs and flowers in the bouquet. As we worked, I realized that these were unusual herbs, not the sort you're likely to find in a pretty bouquet. There was a sprig of rue, for instance, a leaf of sweet bay, a blossom of butterfly weed, a couple of leaves of garlic chives, and a tiny white rosebud. Oh, yes—there was a cypress twig.

Ruby looked down at the list, her forehead creased in a frown. "But what does all this *mean*, China?"

"I've got some ideas," I said. "But I have a couple of books that might help to confirm my suspicions. Let's go to my house." I looked at my watch. "And we'd better hurry. If McQuaid and Brian sit down to eat without us, there won't be a single tortilla chip left when we get there."

But the guys had waited. Along with the guacamole, chips, a green salad, and his enchilada casserole, McQuaid put a dish of *frijoles refritos* on the table, and the four of us pitched in. When dinner was over, McQuaid and Brian generously volunteered to wash the dishes. Well, McQuaid volunteered—Brian, who will soon turn fourteen, required a little persuading.

Ruby and I took our coffee and our list of tussie mussie flowers and headed for my studio, where I work on herbal prod-

ENCHILADA CASSEROLE

1 medium onion, chopped
3 cloves garlic, chopped
Vegetable oil
1 pound lean ground sirloin
2 cups salsa (homemade or purchased)
1/2 cup chopped green chiles, fresh or canned
2 teaspoons ground cumin
1/2 teaspoon salt (if desired)
10 corn tortillas, cut in half
2 cups shredded Cheddar cheese

Sauté the onion and garlic in a small amount of vegetable oil. When they're limp and translucent, drain off the oil and add the meat. Cook and stir until browned. Drain fat, add salsa, chiles, cumin, and salt, and simmer for 5 minutes, stirring occasionally. Layer half the tortillas in bottom of a greased two-quart casserole dish and cover with half the meat-salsa mixture and a layer of half the shredded Cheddar. Repeat. Cover and bake in a 350° oven for about 30 minutes.

FRIJOLES REFRITOS (REFRIED BEANS)

2 tablespoons olive oil
1/2 cup chopped onion
4 cloves garlic, crushed
4 cups canned pinto beans
1 teaspoon cumin
2 tablespoons lemon juice
1/2 cup grated Cheddar cheese
Sprigs of cilantro for garnish

Heat olive oil in a heavy skillet and sauté onion and garlic until translucent. Drain the beans (reserving half the liquid) and add to skillet. Heat, mashing with a potato masher. Cook, stirring frequently, for 10 minutes. Add cumin, lemon juice, and reserved liquid, if necessary, and cook for 10 more minutes. Sprinkle cheese over the top and let it melt slightly. Serve hot, garnished with cilantro.

SOUTH OF THE BORDER GUACAMOLE

2 cloves garlic
½ teaspoon salt
2 large ripe avocados
2 to 3 tablespoons grated onion
1 small ripe Roma tomato, chopped fine
2 tablespoons lime juice

Peel and mash the garlic cloves with the salt, making a paste. Mash the avocados and add the garlic, grated onion, tomato, and lime juice. Serve with a basket of warm tortilla chips.

ucts and keep all my reference books. I pulled three books off the shelf and we sat down with them, turning the pages.

"Let's see if I have this straight," Ruby said. "During Victorian times, people thought it would be cool to send secret messages to one another, and they decided to do it with flowers. Is that it?"

"Basically," I said. "It started in the seventeen-hundreds and was popular through the middle of the next century. But flowers and herbs have always had symbolic meaning. Violets, for example, have for centuries conveyed the idea of faithfulness. Napoleon loved them, and always gave a bouquet of violets to Josephine on their wedding anniversary." I made a face. "Although as I remember, he had a wandering eye. Anyway, his followers wore violets to show that they were eternally faithful to him."

Here are the three reference books that China and Ruby consulted, in case you'd like to do some of the detective work yourself:

Flora's Dictionary: The Victorian Language of Herbs and Flowers, by Kathleen Gips

The Meaning of Flowers, by Claire Powell

Tussie-Mussies: The Language of Flowers, by Geraldine Laufer

Ruby leaned back, sipping her coffee. "So that's where you got the idea that the violets in Mavina's tussie mussie came from an admirer?"

"That's right. But the other herbs and flowers in the tussie mussie are contradictory." I ran my finger down the list. "Rue, bay, butterfly weed, garlic chives, cypress, and a white rose."

Ruby frowned. "So? I have to admit that it's a little weird, but—"

"Weird is right," I said. I opened one of the books and flipped the pages. "Rue may be very pretty, but it represents repentance—being sorry for something. And a bay leaf stands for treachery."

"No, it doesn't," Ruby objected, leafing through another book. "It says here that it stands for fame and glory."

"That's the interesting thing about the language of flowers,"

I said. "There was a lot of disagreement. But you can see how the idea of fame is related to treachery."

"Yeah," Ruby agreed dryly. "Fame is treacherous—and bragging about it can get you into big trouble." She put down her coffee cup. "What about butterfly weed? What does it stand for?"

I turned several pages and found it. "Wow," I said. "According to this author, it means 'let me go,' or 'stop your pestering.'" I turned several more. "There's no entry for garlic chives, but garlic means 'hate.'"

"This definitely isn't a love letter," Ruby said firmly, "although roses stand for love, don't they?"

"The red rose means love," I said. "But the white rose symbolizes silence. Listen to this, Ruby. 'The white rose used to be sculptured over the door of banqueting rooms to remind guests that they should never repeat outside the things they had heard.'"

"Amazing," Ruby said, shaking her head. "And I suppose that cypress represents—"

"It represents mourning," I said, turning a page. "And death."

There was a long silence as we thought about this.

"So if we put it all together," Ruby said at last, "this tussie mussie says that somebody hates somebody else, and that there's treachery involved. And that somebody needs to stop pestering—"

"And keep quiet," I said. "Or die."

Ruby shuddered. "I suppose," she said, "since Mavina is the one who wound up dead, she was the one who was being warned to stop pestering and keep her mouth shut. It sounds as if she was blackmailing someone."

"Exactly," I said. "And if we can find her victim, we may have found her killer." I stood up. "Let's go."

Ruby jumped to her feet. "Go where?"

"I want to talk to Mavina's niece, Esther, again. She told Sheila and me that her aunt was always meddling in people's private affairs. Maybe she knows more than she was willing to let on — at least to Sheila." It's sad but true that even people who have nothing to hide don't want to share what they know with the police.

Esther lived in a small house on a dead-end street. As we came up the walk, I smelled the crisp, clean, citrusy scent of southernwood, and against the house, I could see the pale yellow blooms of St. John's wort. Through a window, we could see the television screen flickering in the darkened living room.

When Ruby knocked, the porch light came on. "Who is it?" Esther asked apprehensively, opening the door only a crack. But when we announced ourselves, she opened it wide and stepped back.

"You can't be too careful," she said, as if in explanation. She glanced at me. "Is this about Aunt Mavina?"

"Yes," I said. "I was hoping that you'd given a little more thought to the situation."

She laughed shortly. "Are you kidding? I'm about to inherit property that's worth in the neighborhood of a million dollars. It gives you a lot to think about." She paused. "I've got some iced tea in the fridge. Sit down. I'll be right back."

When she returned, she was carrying a tray with filled glasses garnished with mint and lemon slices and a plate of curry and cardamom cookies, deliciously fragrant, with an unusual taste. There was a brief silence while we all helped ourselves, and then she said, "I guess you want to know whether I've thought of anybody who might have wanted to kill her."

"Good guess," I said. "Have you?"

She put down her glass. "No. But I did find something that puzzled me. Maybe you can tell me what it means."

Ruby leaned forward. "What have you come up with?"

"My aunt had a talent for finding things out," Esther said. "I don't think she worked at it, but information just seemed to come her way." She laughed a little. "I used to think that, as a librarian, she was in exactly the right job. What are librarians called these days? Information specialists? That was Aunt Mavina, for sure. An information specialist."

"That's not necessarily bad," Ruby said tentatively.

"Of course not," Esther replied. "But Aunt Mavina was also a very self-righteous kind of person. She liked to see the guilty punished, and she always wanted the punishment to fit the crime." She smiled a little. "Once when I was a kid, I stole some candy. She doctored that candy with powdered chile pepper and made me eat it. I've never forgotten."

"I'll bet," I said with a shiver.

"So who was she punishing lately?" Ruby asked.

"I'm not sure," Esther replied. "But as I said, I've found something curious. I went to her house this afternoon to take care of her canary, and while I was there I went through the

CURRY AND CARDAMOM COOKIES

1 cup butter or margarine
2 cups brown sugar
2 eggs, lightly beaten
2 teaspoons vanilla
3 cups flour
1 teaspoon baking powder
½ teaspoon baking soda
½ teaspoon salt
2 teaspoons curry powder (sweet, rather than hot)
½ teaspoon cardamom
1½ cups chopped walnuts or pecans

Cream butter and brown sugar until light and fluffy. Add eggs and vanilla and beat until incorporated. Sift dry ingredients together. Add to creamed mixture, a third at a time. Stir in nuts. Divide dough into four rolls and wrap each in waxed paper. Refrigerate at least 4 hours (may also be frozen). Slice into quarter-inch slices and place on ungreased baking sheet. Bake in preheated 350°F oven until golden (12 to 14 minutes). Let cookies cool 2 minutes on baking sheet, then remove to racks and cool. Yields six dozen.

desk where she keeps her checkbook and business papers. I wasn't just snooping," she said defensively. "I needed to get her lawyer's name."

I took another cookie. "What did you find?"

"A check for a thousand dollars made out to an organization called Friends of the Faithful. It was in an unsealed envelope that Aunt Mavina had already addressed and stamped. I looked up the organization on the Internet. It's a nonprofit group that provides support and counseling for victims of marital infidelity." She paused. "I don't suppose it's important, but it did seem kind of curious to me."

"Who wrote the check?" I asked. "Your aunt?"

"No," Esther said. "I remember the name, but I didn't recognize it." When she told us who it was, I knew that we had discovered the identity of Mavina's victim—and her killer, as well.

When Sheila came into Thyme and Seasons a day or so later, she was shaking her head with amazement. "You two are incredible. I still can't believe that you unraveled the whole mystery from a little bunch of flowers."

"Oh, it was just some herbal sleuthing," Ruby said with a modest smile. "Easy when you know how."

"Actually," I said, "the answer to the mystery jumped out at us when Esther told us the story of the chile pepper powder her aunt used as a punishment—and mentioned the check that Alice Olsen wrote to Friends of the Faithful."

"But it might not have jumped out at us if we hadn't understood what was behind it," Ruby reminded me. "That's what we figured out from the tussie mussie."

"Let me see if I've got the story straight," Sheila said. "Mavina somehow discovered that Alice Olsen was having an affair with her boss. She threatened to tell Alice's husband unless Alice paid up, handsomely." She made a wry face. "So far, it sounds like a fairly ordinary blackmail. But the blackmailer didn't want the money for herself. She wanted her victim to make regular contributions to an organization that supports victims of marital infidelity."

"A fiendishly clever punishment," Ruby said. "It fitted Alice's crime to a T."

I thought back to Alice's all-white apartment and her brand-new furniture. "It turns out that Alice had recently separated from her husband and filed for divorce," I said. "There was quite a bit of money at stake in the settlement, and Alice quite naturally didn't want her husband to find out that she'd been having an affair while the two of them were still married. Rather than risk exposure, she was willing to pay up."

"But she must have been afraid that Mavina wouldn't keep her mouth shut," Sheila said.

I nodded. "The clue to that is in the tussie mussie. Alice designed it to lure Mavina to an out-of-the-way place in the park, including violets to make it appear that it was a token of love from a secret admirer. But when you look at the flowers and herbs, the message is altogether different."

"Right," Ruby chimed in. "The flowers say, 'I hate you. Stop pestering me and keep your mouth shut, or you're dead.' Short and simple and straight to the point."

"But Mavina didn't get it, of course," I said, "and Alice didn't intend her to. She was exercising her ingenuity, I suppose. And venting her feelings of anger and frustration."

"The tussie mussie might have been a clue to *you*," Sheila said, "but it was the check that broke this case. It gave us probable cause to get a warrant to search Alice's apartment. That's where we found the murder weapon—and those violets, of course. The magic number, in fact."

"The magic number?" Ruby asked.

"Remember?" I asked. "Sandra, at Blooms and Blossoms, originally had two dozen violets. According to Sandra, Alice bought most of them, and Joe bought the rest. He told us that he got a half dozen to give to Charlene, which means that Alice must have bought a dozen and a half. Right?"

"Makes sense," Ruby said.

"But there were only a dozen violets in the crystal bowl in Alice's apartment," Sheila put in. "The missing six—"

"—were in the tussie mussie in the dead woman's hand," I said. "Elementary, my dear Ruby."

"Wouldn't you think that grown people could find another way to sort out their differences?" Ruby asked, shaking her head. She started toward the door to her shop. "Well, guess it's time to get back to work."

"Hang on there," Sheila said. "Whose red Honda is parked out front?"

"Mine," Ruby said. "Why?"

"Because the meter's expired," Sheila replied, "and I just saw MaeBelle Battersby coming down the street. She's got her ticket book in her hand and a mean look in her eye. If the owner doesn't get out there and put some money in the meter—"

"Yikes!" Ruby cried, and scrambled for the door.

"I didn't expect to get that kind of reaction," Sheila said mildly.

"That's because you don't know about MaeBelle and Ruby and the parking tickets," I said. "You see—"

"Whoa." Sheila held up her hand. "Some stories are better off not told."

"Yes," I said, thinking about Alice Olsen and her boss. "I guess you're right."

A Deadly Chocolate Valentine

"Life is like a box of chocolates.
You never know what you're gonna get."

—*Forrest Gump*

Valentine's Day has always been my favorite holiday, but I've loved it even more since I met Mike McQuaid. Early in our relationship, we started a tradition of exchanging chocolate hearts and recycling the same valentine, not because we're too cheap to buy new ones, but because this was our first one. Each year, we write a love letter to en-

Yes, chocolate *is* an herb, and a New World herb, at that. It is a product of the cacao tree (*Theobroma cacao*), a native of Central and South America. The Mesoamericans ground up the cacao beans, which they considered sacred, and mixed them with water or wine, vanilla, pimento, and chile peppers. This bitter-tasting brew, called *xocoatl,* was used to treat diarrhea and dysentery, as an aphrodisiac, and as a source of quick energy. The Spaniards imported the cacao beans into Europe, and by the seventeenth century, the hot peppers had been replaced with sugar and the new drink was a sweet success.

"Inside some of us is a thin person struggling to get out, but she can usually be sedated by a piece of chocolate cake." — Anonymous

"Research tells us that fourteen out of any ten individuals like chocolate." — Sandra Boynton, in *Chocolate: The Consuming Passion*

close with the valentine, which is beginning to show the wear. Not that I'm sentimental or anything, but I've kept the letters, and after McQuaid and I got married, I put them into our wedding scrapbook, along with the herbs from my wedding bouquet and a few other special mementos.

Valentine's Day was just around the corner, and I was taking advantage of a lull in business at the shop to write my annual love letter to McQuaid. I'd just picked up the pen when the door opened and a blond, thin-faced man came in. He walked through the shop, glancing around, as if to make sure that we were alone. I frowned, not liking the furtive way he hunched his shoulders. Thyme and Seasons has never been held up, but there's always a first time. I was reaching for the phone, just in case, when he came closer and I recognized him.

> "All I really need is love, but a little chocolate now and then doesn't hurt." — Lucy (in *Peanuts,* by Charles M. Schulz)

"Jason Wagner!" I exclaimed, putting the phone down. "I didn't recognize you. I guess it's been a while since we've seen one another. Have you been out of town?"

Jason Wagner is a long-time friend of McQuaid's. He works in the computer lab at Central Texas State University, where McQuaid teaches courses in the law enforcement program. Every now and then, the three of us get together at Bean's Bar and Grill for barbecue and a game of pool. Ruby joins us sometimes, too, since she's known Jason since their high school days.

"No, I haven't been out of town," Jason said soberly. "I guess we just haven't been hanging out in the same places." He wasn't smiling, and his gray eyes had a bleak look.

I frowned. "Excuse me, but is there something wrong?"

"Yeah, as a matter of fact, there is. That's why I came." He dropped his voice. "Do you know Kaye Kennedy?"

Pecan Springs is a small town — of course I know Kaye Kennedy. "She's the woman you've been dating," I replied. Kaye is also a trainer at the gym where Ruby Wilcox and I occasionally work out. I'd always wondered about the relationship, which seemed a little like a mismatch. Jason is slender and shy and very sweet. Kaye is — well, she's a strong woman. Strong and assertive, with a habit of going after what she wants.

"Was dating," Jason amended. "Put that into the past tense. About three months ago, I started going out with somebody else, and it's been getting . . . well, serious." He grinned crookedly. "I told Kaye right away, of course. She didn't take it very well, and she wouldn't give up. She hangs around and—" He paused uncomfortably. "To put it bluntly, China, she's stalking me."

"*Stalking* you?" I asked, startled.

"Well, I guess that's the right word." He sounded embarrassed. "In the evenings, she sits in her car down the block, watching my apartment. She calls up in the middle of the night, and when I answer, she hangs up."

"If she hangs up," I asked reasonably, "how do you know it's Kaye?"

"The first time she called, she said—" Jason looked away. "What she said wasn't very nice." He swallowed. "To tell the truth, China, this stuff is really getting on my nerves. I'm not exactly afraid for myself—I can probably handle her. I'm more worried that she might try to harm my girlfriend."

Knowing Kaye, it wasn't hard to picture her doing what Jason described. And it wasn't difficult to imagine her pushing it just a little further—a little too far, in fact. But there was only Jason's word for it. I defended a man once against a harassment charge that turned out to be phony. The woman involved, who simply wanted to get him into trouble, was charged with making a false accusation.

"Stalking is a felony offense," I said firmly. "You need to talk to the police. But you'll need more evidence than a few hang-up phone calls. Real evidence, I mean."

"I don't want to get Kaye in trouble," Jason said uneasily. "Actually, I was hoping I could persuade you to . . . well, to talk to her. You've been a lawyer, China. You'd know what to say to convince her that she has to cut this stuff out."

I could understand where Jason was coming from, and I sympathized. But this wasn't the way to handle it. "I'd like to help," I said, "but you need to talk to her yourself, Jason. Warn her, and document your warning with a letter listing the dates and times that you've seen her sitting in her car. And make a log of those phone calls. Tape them, if you can. If she keeps it up, go to the police and file a complaint."

His shoulders slumped. "I suppose you're right. Thanks anyway, China." He gave me a crooked grin. "Hey, how about getting together for dinner at Bean's one night? I'd like you and Mike—and Ruby, too—to meet my girlfriend."

"Sure," I said in an enthusiastic tone, trying to pep him up. "Would Friday work for you? I'll check with Ruby to see if she's free."

"Friday would be great," he said, and raised his hand. "See you then. Meanwhile, happy Valentine's Day."

The next day, after we closed the shops, Ruby and I exchanged our annual handmade Valentine's gifts. She gave me a heart-shaped red bowl filled with rose potpourri, and I gave her a potted chocolate mint plant, decorated with a pair of chocolate hearts and tied with a red ribbon. We were exchanging thank-

Ruby's Rose Potpourri

In a large bowl, mix together 3 cups red rose petals and buds, 1 cup pink rose petals, ¼ cup carnation petals, and ¼ cup red globe amaranth blossoms. Mix 4 drops rose essential oil with 2 tablespoons powdered orris root (a fixative), and add to the flowers. Place in a covered container and allow to mellow for 6 weeks, shaking the mixture every few days. If scent fades, renew with rose oil.

you and you're-welcome hugs when McQuaid opened the door and came in.

"Happy Valentine's Day," Ruby said. She gave him a concerned look. "Hey, what's wrong? You don't look happy."

"I've just come from the hospital." McQuaid pushed back a shock of dark hair and turned to me. "Jason Wagner is in pretty bad shape. He's in a coma."

"A coma!" I exclaimed. "What happened?"

"The doctor says it was a heroin overdose," McQuaid replied glumly.

"Jason OD'd?" Ruby was shocked. "I never would've guessed that he'd do drugs."

"It's hard for me to believe, too." McQuaid's eyes were sad. "Jason's a health nut. He works out at the gym every day, and he's always careful about what he eats. I just can't understand why he'd do something like this to himself."

I was beginning to feel distinctly uncomfortable. "Jason came into the shop yesterday," I said slowly. "He was having some trouble. He asked me to help, but I told him it was something he needed to handle himself."

"Trouble?" McQuaid frowned. "What kind of trouble?"

"Girl trouble, I'll bet," Ruby said darkly.

"What makes you think that?" I asked. Ruby is uncannily

intuitive and she often sees things that other people overlook.

"I've noticed Kaye Kennedy hanging around him at the gym," Ruby replied. "He tries to brush her off, but he doesn't seem to have much luck. You know Jason. He's not very assertive. And Kaye—" She shrugged. "She doesn't take no for an answer."

"That's true," I replied thoughtfully. "When she wants something, she goes for it."

Ruby was eyeing me. "You don't suppose—"

"Of course not," I scoffed.

Chocolate mint is one of the many varieties of flavored mints. In general, mint is an easy-to-grow herb—too easy, sometimes, since it can be invasive. Growing it in a pot is a good way to be sure that it doesn't go wandering off into the next yard, or the next county! Chocolate mint lends itself to a variety of uses. Add a fresh sprig to the ground coffee beans when you're brewing coffee, or 2 tablespoons chopped fresh leaves to a packaged brownie or chocolate cake mix.

"Kaye may be upset because Jason broke up with her, but she'd never do a thing like *that*. Suppose he died? It'd be murder."

"A thing like what?" McQuaid looked from one of us to the other, scowling. "Murder? What are you two talking about?"

"Oh, nothing," Ruby said hastily. "We were just . . . weren't we, China?"

"Yeah, right." I pushed back my chair and stood up. "Did I understand that my husband is taking us both out to celebrate Valentine's Day?"

Ruby shook her head. "I'm invited to a party. You guys go out and have a romantic candlelight dinner, just the two of you."

"Romance," I said. "Great idea." I looked at McQuaid, thinking how nice it would be to drive down to San Antonio,

Like everything else under the sun, innocent plants can be put to harmful uses. This is certainly true of the opium poppy (*Papaver somniferum*), which ancient Greek and Egyptian physicians welcomed as a gift from Morpheus, the god of sleep, to ease human suffering. But this narcotic herb is powerfully addictive, and its derivatives — laudanum, morphine, opium, and heroin — have been the cause of enormous human suffering. If you would like to grow *Papaver somniferum*, check your state statutes and local ordinances and be sure to plant away from children. The poppy seeds available for culinary use do indeed come from the opium poppy, but have no narcotic effect because they are dried. Blue poppy seeds are traditional in many cakes, cookies, and Christmas breads. White poppy seeds are used in Indian cooking, to thicken and flavor sauces, lentils, and rice dishes.

where there's a wonderful little French restaurant. "Where shall we eat?"

"How about Bean's Bar and Grill?" McQuaid grinned. "I sure could get romantic over a plate of Bob's fajitas. And maybe we could shoot some pool afterward, huh?"

I made a face. Fajitas and pool at Bean's, with the jukebox playing "Mamas, Don't Let Your Babies Grow Up to Be Cowboys" in the background. Not exactly what I had in mind for a romantic dinner.

But McQuaid put his arm around me and nuzzled my ear. "Just kidding," he said. "Remember that French place you like in San Antonio? We've got reservations there. Let's go home and change, shall we?"

Fajitas are a speciality at Bean's Bar and Grill, a down-home eatery in Pecan Springs. But you don't have to drive all the way to Texas to enjoy this Tex-Mex dish. At China's request, Bob Godwin, owner and chief cook at Bean's, has modified his recipe to serve six to eight people.

BOB GODWIN'S FAMOUS FAJITAS

Marinade:
1 cup salsa (Bob makes his, but you can purchase yours)
2 cups vinegar-and-oil dressing (homemade or purchased)
1 onion, chopped
3 cloves garlic, chopped
1 (4-ounce) can jalapeño peppers
2 teaspoons cumin

2 pounds skirt steak
18 flour tortillas
Guacamole (homemade or purchased)
Onion, chopped
Tomatoes, chopped
Yellow cheese, grated
Salsa
Sour cream
Cilantro, chopped

Combine ingredients for marinade and pour over the meat. Cover tightly and refrigerate overnight. Pour off juices and reserve. Grill, pan-fry, or bake steak (if you bake, it takes about 45 minutes at 350°F), basting with marinade. Slice meat thinly, and roll into a warm flour tortilla. Smother with guacamole, onions, tomatoes, and cheese. Dollop with more salsa and some sour cream, and sprinkle with cilantro. Traditionally served with refried beans, rice, tortilla chips, and lots of salsa. Olé!

"Go to Jason's apartment?" I stared at Ruby over my morning coffee. "You've got to be kidding, Ruby. If you think I'm going to risk arrest just so you can play Nancy Drew—"

"We won't get arrested," Ruby said in a reassuring tone. "It turns out that my friend Ginger manages the apartment complex where Jason lives. I ran into her at the party last night. I told her that he was in the hospital, and that you and I needed to feed his cat. She agreed to let us in."

"His cat?" I frowned. "How do you know he has a cat?"

"If he doesn't, we can lend him yours." Ruby wrinkled her nose. "I told Ginger we'd be there on our lunch hour. Anyway, what are you worried about? I called the hospital. Jason's condition remains the same. They're still saying that he OD'd, so it isn't a crime scene." She took the last of Lila's irresistible jelly doughnuts off the plate and began to nibble at it.

I sighed. When Ruby makes up her mind to do something, there's no point trying to argue with her. Which is why, at twelve-fifteen that afternoon, I found myself unlocking the door to Jason Wagner's three-room apartment, on the first floor of an apartment complex on San Jacinto. The place was unusually tidy, considering that a guy lived there, although the air was stuffy and the potted herbs on the windowsill—thyme, chives, and parsley—were desperate for a drink.

"What do you suppose we're looking for?" Ruby asked, as I watered the herbs.

"You tell me," I said. "This was your bright idea." I paused. "Where's the cat?"

"I don't think a cat would be much help," Ruby said, looking around, "unless he had Koko's brains. What we need is an answering machine. Qwilleran always checks the answering machine to see if the villain has left any messages." But although we searched the entire apartment, we couldn't find one. "Go figure," Ruby said finally, sounding frustrated. "A good-looking single guy without an answering machine? Doesn't make sense."

I went into the bathroom, opened the medicine cabinet, and peered inside. "If Jason is into drugs," I remarked over my shoulder, "there's certainly no sign of it here. All I can find is a bottle of garlic caps and another of St. John's wort." I frowned down at the bottles in my hand. In my experience, people who take drugs aren't very likely to be involved with herbal medicine.

Ruby was rummaging in the drawer of the table beside Jason's bed. "Nothing here, either," she said. She went into the kitchen, and a moment later I heard her call. "China, I've found something!" She sounded excited. "Chocolate brownies!"

"Lunch first, dessert later," I called back. I picked up a bottle of ginseng caps. Ginseng is sometimes used by people who are worried about the harmful effects of toxic substances on the liver. Maybe Jason was into drugs, after all.

"I don't want you to *eat* them, silly," Ruby said impatiently. "I want you to *look* at them."

I went into the kitchen. On the counter was a small cardboard box, half-filled with what looked like homemade chocolate brownies.

"Do you suppose somebody sent him these?" Ruby asked. "If so, I wonder what else is in them—besides chocolate, I

Garlic, St. John's wort, and ginseng are three currently popular herbal remedies.

- Garlic has been used as a healing herb for centuries. It has broad-spectrum antibiotic properties and kills the bacteria that cause many infections. According to recent research, garlic helps to reduce blood pressure, lower cholesterol, and prevent the blood clots that cause strokes and heart attacks. It also reduces blood sugar levels and may help in the treatment of diabetes.

- St. John's wort (*wort* is the Anglo-Saxon word for *plant*) has made headlines during the past decade as a treatment for mild to moderate depression. Through the centuries, however, it has been used in a wide variety of ways, to treat wounds, asthma, sciatica, diarrhea, and menstrual discomforts. Recent research suggests that it may be helpful against some retroviruses, including HIV, as well as in the treatment of alcoholism.

- Ginseng has a centuries-old reputation as an energizer, a memory aid, an aphrodisiac, an antidepressant, and an immune enhancer. It seems to work as what herbalists call an *adaptogen*, a substance that helps the body adjust to change and stress. Ginseng may also protect the liver from the harmful effects of drugs and other toxic substances.

If you're interested in learning more about the healing properties of herbs, consult *The New Healing Herbs: The Classic Guide to Nature's Best Medicines*, by Michael Castleman.

mean." She looked longingly at the brownies, which were chocolaty-rich and inviting. "They certainly do look wonderful. And half of them are already gone. I suppose he ate them."

"We can ask McQuaid to get them tested at the DPS crime lab in Austin," I said. McQuaid has done a couple of jobs for the Department of Public Safety, and he knows almost everyone there. "An analysis would tell us the contents, for sure." I frowned. "But I think Jason would be suspicious of anything Kaye sent him, even if he loved chocolate. This must have come from somebody else."

"But who?" Ruby asked.

I bent over the garbage pail and pulled out a padded mailing envelope, being careful to hold it with the tips of my fingers. "Maybe this is our answer," I said. "It's addressed to Jason Wagner."

"Does it have a return address?" Ruby asked excitedly.

The ink was badly smudged, and it took a minute to decipher it. "The first name seems to be Phyllis," I said. "The last name looks like Anderson."

"The address?" Ruby asked. As I read it aloud, she copied it onto a scrap of paper. "Phyllis Anderson," she muttered. "Who the heck is *she*?"

McQuaid was headed into Austin that afternoon, so he took what was left of the chocolate brownies, and the mailing envelope as well. Back at the shop, Ruby phoned Ginger, the manager of Jason's apartment building, and learned that Phyllis Anderson was Jason's girlfriend.

She put down the phone and turned to me. "And guess

If reading about Jason's brownies is making you hungry, here's a recipe with almost enough chocolate to die for. But do try to keep those cravings in check until you've finished the story.

TWICE-AS-MUCH-CHOCOLATE BROWNIES

5 (1-ounce) squares bittersweet chocolate
¼ cup butter or margarine
¼ cup flour
2 tablespoons cocoa (unsweetened)
1 teaspoon baking powder
½ teaspoon salt
3 eggs
¾ cup granulated sugar
1 teaspoon pure vanilla extract
¼ cup sour cream
4 ounces chocolate chips

Heat oven to 325°F. Lightly grease a 9×9×2" square cake pan and dust with dry cocoa. In the top of a double boiler over medium-high heat, or in a microwave, melt chocolate and butter or margarine together. Stir until smooth. Sift flour, cocoa, baking powder, and salt together into a small bowl. In a medium bowl, beat eggs, sugar, and vanilla until slightly thickened. Add melted chocolate mixture and blend. Add sifted dry ingredients and stir to mix well. Add sour cream and blend, scraping sides and bottom of bowl with a spatula. With a spatula, fold in chocolate chips. Spread batter evenly in pan and bake about 40 minutes, until toothpick inserted in center comes out clean. Yes, you can leave a little in the bowl for licking, if you can't

> stand to wait for the pan to come out of the oven. But do try to allow the baked brownies to cool in the pan for 10 to 15 minutes before cutting and eating every last one of them. Yields twelve to eighteen.

where Phyllis works, China. At the drug treatment center! She might have had access to heroin."

"Aren't you getting ahead of yourself?" I asked, turning away from the shelf where I was stocking herbal soaps. "We have no idea what's in those brownies, Ruby. And why would Jason's girlfriend want to harm him? That doesn't make any sense at all."

Ruby was confident. "We'll find out when we talk to her. Let's go over after we close for the day."

"We can decide that *after* we've heard from McQuaid," I said firmly. "Chances are that those are just ordinary brownies, with nothing in them but a lot of chocolate."

But I was wrong. That evening, just as I was closing out my cash register, McQuaid called to confirm that the brownies we found in Jason's apartment had been liberally laced with heroin.

"Enough to kill a horse," he added grimly. "And the only prints on the mailing envelope belong to Jason. Whoever wrapped that package went to the trouble of wearing gloves."

"Thanks for the information," I said. I paused. "It's your turn to cook dinner tonight, isn't it? I'll probably be a little late. Ruby is giving me a ride home, and we need to stop and see somebody."

"China," McQuaid said in a warning tone, "we're not talking accidental drug overdose any longer. This is a case of attempted murder. It's a matter for the police."

"Yes, I know," I said quietly. "See you later, babe."

Phyllis Anderson lived in a small house not far from the clinic where she worked. When she answered our knock, her brown hair was disheveled and her eyes were red, and I knew she'd been crying. Ruby and I identified ourselves as friends of Jason and asked if we could talk.

Phyllis's eyes widened and she clutched at the doorknob. "He's not worse, is he? I was just on my way to the hospital."

"No," I said. "May we come in? This won't take long."

We talked for fifteen minutes or so. Afterward, as we walked out to the car, Ruby said earnestly, "China, I believe Phyllis when she says that she didn't send Jason any brownies. And I don't believe she would try to poison him. She seems to genuinely love him."

"She certainly gives every appearance of telling the truth," I said cautiously. Past experience has taught me that even the nicest people are capable of lying—and much worse. "But there's someone else we ought to see this evening," I said. "She doesn't live very far from here." Within five minutes, Ruby was parking her car in front of Kaye Kennedy's house.

Kaye lived in a large duplex, with window boxes planted with blooming pansies. Obviously, somebody in the house had a green thumb. Ruby rang the doorbell several times. Finally, it was opened a crack and a tremulous voice with a distinctive Southern accent asked, "Who is it? What do you want?"

In Pecan Springs and in much of the South, pansies bloom through the winter. You didn't know that this cheerful spring flower is an herb? In earlier times, the pansy was an important medicinal plant, and its juice was used to treat respiratory ailments, children's convulsions, and epilepsy. It was also considered a powerful love potion. If pansy juice were dropped on the eyelids of someone who slept, he or she would fall in love with the first person who came into view—who would most likely be the one who was administering the eyedrops. In Shakespeare's *Midsummer Night's Dream,* this little trick leads to some delightful romantic mix-ups. But the pansy was also taken seriously as a healer of broken hearts—hence, its common name *heartsease.*

"China Bayles and Ruby Wilcox," I said. "We've come to see Kaye. Is she home?"

"Wait here and I'll see," the woman said and stepped back, leaving the door partway open. From the rear of the house, we could hear voices. After several moments, Kaye Kennedy came to the door.

"Well?" she demanded brusquely. "What do you want?"

"You'd probably rather we talked inside," I said. "It's about Jason Wagner—and I don't think you want your neighbors to overhear."

A moment later, we were seated in the living room. The woman who had first answered the door came in. "There are soft drinks in the fridge," she said tentatively. "May I—"

"Thanks, Dora, but I don't think our guests are staying

long," Kaye said. "And didn't you say you have some laundry to do?" Dismissed, Dora dropped her head and obediently disappeared.

"So, what's all this about?" Kaye demanded. She was darkhaired, of middle height and muscular, and her dark eyes were intense. She glanced at Ruby, then at me. "Don't I know you?"

"We've met at the gym," Ruby said smoothly. "We're friends of Jason's. I suppose you've heard what happened to him."

If Kaye was disturbed by the question, she didn't betray it. "Somebody told me he was in the hospital," she said. "I didn't catch the details."

"It was an overdose of heroin," I said. "He's in a coma."

Something came and went in her eyes and she hesitated. But her voice was flat when she said, "I wouldn't have thought Jason would do drugs, but the quiet ones fool you every time."

"It was an *accidental* overdose," Ruby said. She frowned. "Accidental on his part, I mean—but deliberate on somebody else's. He received a package of brownies with heroin in them. He was poisoned."

Kaye's eyes widened. "Poisoned? You've got to be kidding. Who would want to poison Jason? He's such a sweet guy."

Who, indeed? I thought. "Fortunately for him, he ate only a few, which is why he isn't dead right now. The police lab tested the rest and identified the heroin." I paused. "Jason told me he was being stalked, so we suspect that it was the stalker who sent them."

Kaye's eyes slid away. "I don't know why you're telling me all this," she said.

"We thought you might be able to suggest who might have

wanted to kill him," I replied. "After all, you and he were close friends."

Kaye looked uncomfortable. "Yes, but that was months ago. He's seeing someone else now."

"Maybe it was somebody at the gym," Ruby suggested. "Can you think of anyone there who had a grudge against Jason?"

"Not a soul," Kaye said, shaking her head. "Everybody seemed to like him. I'm sorry I can't help," she added, her voice softening. "What Jason and I had was good, while it lasted. I hope they find whoever did it."

Ruby sighed. "Well, now that the cops know about the brownies, they'll be searching the apartment. I'm sure they'll find the audiotape, and the mystery will be solved."

I turned with a questioning look to Ruby, but Kaye beat me to it. "Tape?" she asked sharply. "What tape?"

"Jason told us that he taped the stalker's first phone call," Ruby replied. "Apparently what the guy said left no doubt as to his identity."

Kaye's eyes were fixed on Ruby's face. "The stalker was a man?"

"Actually, Jason didn't say," Ruby replied. "But we'll find out when the police turn up that tape." She stood up. "Thanks for talking with us, Kaye."

"Keep me posted," Kaye replied, rising as well. "I'm really sorry to hear what happened to him." Somehow, I didn't quite believe her. And on the way out, I noticed that the kitchen door was just swinging shut. Dora had been listening.

When we got to the car, I turned to Ruby. "What's all this

about an audiotape?" I demanded. "What do you know that I don't?"

Ruby put the key in the ignition. "Not a thing," she said innocently, starting the car and pulling away from the curb. "You know everything I know."

"Then why—" I frowned at her. "Where are we going?"

"To Jason's apartment, of course," Ruby said. "When you bait a trap, you want to be around when it's sprung, don't you?"

With a sigh, I reached in my bag for my cell phone. "I told McQuaid I'd be a little late for dinner. Guess I'd better call him and tell him to go ahead without me."

"I'm sure that Jason must appreciate you two taking such good care of his cat," Ginger said when we knocked on her door and asked her to let us into Jason's apartment again. She frowned. "Funny thing—I didn't even know he had a cat."

"It's just a kitten," Ruby said quickly. "In fact, I think I'll take her home with me tonight, so she won't be lonely."

"Good idea," Ginger said. She gave us the key and went back to watching TV.

It was just after eight when Ruby and I sat down at the table in Jason's shadowy kitchen. A streetlight outside cast lacy shadows through the window. I thought fleetingly, and hungrily, of those brownies. It had been a long time since lunch.

"So," Ruby said, "I guess we just sit here in the dark and wait, huh?"

"I suppose you're thinking that Kaye may show up," I said.

"Exactly." Ruby sounded smug. "She'll figure she's got to

get her hands on that tape to protect herself. Pretty smart, huh?"

"Well, maybe," I said. "Unfortunately, though, I don't think you've thought this thing through."

Ruby frowned. "What makes you say that?"

"Well, just for instance, what happens when Kaye shows up?"

"We grab her," Ruby said promptly. "I know she's strong, but there are two of us. After we've grabbed her, we call nine-one-one and report that we've caught a burglar."

I laughed shortly. "You've been reading too many Stephanie Plum mysteries, Ruby. So what if we capture her? There's no evidence that she sent those brownies."

Ruby frowned. "You don't think she'll confess? After all, if she's apprehended in the act of breaking and entering—"

"I doubt it," I replied dryly. "Unless Jason recovers and agrees to testify against her, we can't tie her to the stalking. And there doesn't seem to be any sort of physical evidence connecting her to the brownies. Without that—" I looked at Ruby, who had gone to the counter and pulled out the drawer beside the sink. "What are you doing?"

"I keep my unpaid bills in the utensil drawer," she said. "I was just thinking that maybe—" She riffled through a stack of envelopes, pulled out a piece of paper, and held it up in the dim light. "Hey, here's something interesting. It's about his telephone service." Then she looked at me, her eyes wide. "Did you hear that?" she whispered.

"I heard it," I said.

Somebody had come up the short flight of stairs and was

standing outside the kitchen door. Then we both heard the sound of something stealthily inserted in the lock.

"Jason must have given her a key when they were going together," Ruby whispered. The paper fluttered from her hand onto the floor. "Get ready, China! We need to grab her the minute she comes in." Quickly, she stationed herself to one side of the door, motioning me to take the other side.

But at that moment, a dog began to bark in the apartment next door. "What are you barking at, Renegade?" a woman called. More barking. "Is somebody out there?" the woman cried. "Go away, or I'll call the police."

The key was withdrawn from the lock and we heard the sound of footsteps clattering down the stairs.

"Rats," Ruby said in disgust. "That darn dog." She turned on the light. "I don't suppose there's any point in hanging around here any longer. After all that racket, Kaye won't be coming back tonight."

"It's just as well," I said. "Since she has a key, she could always claim she was just stopping by to get something she'd left here. She couldn't be charged with breaking and entering."

Ruby looked disappointed. "Too bad," she said. "What do we do now?"

I bent over to pick up the paper Ruby had dropped and scanned it. "Look at this, Ruby!" I said. "Jason Wagner was a subscriber to the telephone company's answering service. That's why we couldn't find an answering machine here in the apartment."

"Omigosh!" Ruby exclaimed. "Do you suppose that the

stalker—Kaye, I mean—might have left a message that Jason didn't get around to picking up?"

"If we can find the passcode," I said, "we can probably dial into the system."

"Maybe it's on the phone," Ruby suggested. She picked up the receiver. On it was a yellow sticker with four digits written on it. "Try this, China."

I took the phone and punched in the number on the paper Ruby had found. There was a recorded greeting—Jason's cheerful voice saying, "Leave a message and I'll return your call"—and then a prompt for his passcode. I punched in the number on the yellow sticker.

"It's working!" I said.

"What are you hearing?" Ruby asked anxiously, as I listened.

"The machine is saying that there are sixteen messages," I reported. "They must've been piling up since before Jason went into the hospital." I picked up a pencil and a scrap of paper and listened as a guy called with a reminder about a soccer game, a broker wanted to set up a meeting about an investment possibility, a dentist's secretary confirmed an appointment. Ordinary telephone messages, the kind that everybody receives all the time. And then there was a message that *wasn't* ordinary.

"What *is* it?" Ruby asked, watching my face.

"It's a warning," I said. I punched a button on the phone and the message—the last one on the machine—began to play again. I held up the phone so Ruby could hear it.

"Don't eat the brownies," the low, breathy voice said. *"They'll make you awf'lly sick."*

I pushed the star key to replay the message, and both Ruby and I listened again.

Ruby frowned. "That's not Kaye's voice."

"No, it's not," I replied. I hung up without erasing the messages. They'd be there until the police could check them out. "Didn't you recognize that Southern accent? We heard it just a little while ago."

Ruby snapped her fingers. "It's *Dora's* voice!" she exclaimed. "Kaye's roommate!"

"That's right," I said, and picked up the phone again. It was definitely time to call the police.

"Congratulations, you two," McQuaid said. "You pulled it off." He lifted his small glass of cranberry cordial—his Valentine's gift from Ruby. The bottle bore a handmade label that read "Cordially Yours."

"Thank you," Ruby said with a modest smile, raising her glass. "It only took a *little* cunning."

"We should be toasting Jason, too," I reminded them. "It's good to hear that he's feeling better."

Ruby sipped her cordial. "So Kaye actually confessed to sending him that deadly Valentine's present?"

McQuaid nodded and nipped one of Brian's chocolate-covered strawberries off the plate in the middle of the table. "After her roommate told the police that she'd seen Kaye baking those chocolate brownies and writing Phyllis Anderson's name on the package, she knew she couldn't get out of it," he said. "She probably figures that a guilty plea will get her a lighter

CORDIALLY YOURS:
RUBY'S CRANBERRY-ORANGE CORDIAL

1 (12-ounce) package fresh cranberries
2 tablespoons grated fresh orange zest (outer skin, no white pith)
1 cup sugar
4 whole cloves
4 whole allspice
2 cups light corn syrup
2 cups vodka plus ½ cup brandy (or substitute 2½ cups light rum)
1 cup water

Coarsely chop the cranberries. Mix cranberries, orange zest, and sugar in a large bowl until the berries are well coated. Using a mortar and pestle or a rolling pin, break the whole cloves and allspice into smaller pieces, but do not pulverize. Add spices to the cranberry mix. Stir in the liquids. Pour into a large glass jar, cover tightly, and store in a cool, dark place for at least 1 month, shaking every few days. Strain out the solids by pouring through a fine strainer or dampened cheesecloth. (If you use a cloth, gather and twist it to squeeze out as much liquid as possible.) Pour into a clean, dry jar for storage at room temperature, for up to 3 months. Refrigerate for longer storage. Makes about 1 quart. May be doubled.

sentence — and she's right. The DA is all for anything that saves him the cost of a prosecution." He frowned. "What I want to know, though, is what gave you the idea of checking Jason's answering service."

CHOCOLATE-COVERED STRAWBERRIES

Kids love to make this fruity treat. They can cool their confections by sticking the toothpicks into a piece of hard plastic foam, or laying the strawberries on waxed paper. Be sure the berries are perfectly dry, because even a drop of moisture can make the chocolate grainy. (Butter and margarine may contain water, and cooking oil can keep the chocolate from coating the berries. So do use shortening.)

1 (12-ounce) bag of chocolate bits
2 tablespoons shortening (not butter, margarine, or oil)
2 dozen large strawberries, washed and carefully dried
2 dozen toothpicks

Melt chocolate and shortening together in a microwave or the top of a double boiler. Make sure the strawberries are perfectly dry. Poke toothpicks into the strawberries and dip into the chocolate. Arrange to cool, then refrigerate.

Ruby and I exchanged glances. "Well," I said, "Ruby was snooping in the utensil drawer, looking for unpaid bills, when she found—"

"I was not snooping!" Ruby said heatedly. "I was just doing what any self-respecting PI would have done. And it's a good thing I did, especially since our trap failed." She scowled. "If it hadn't been for that stupid dog—"

"Trap?" McQuaid asked. He leaned forward. "What's this about a trap?"

"You don't want to know," I said hastily.

He gave me a thoughtful look. "Well, however it happened, you two were plenty smart. The police might not have thought to look for an answering service. Without that recorded warning, they wouldn't have questioned Dora directly. And without the threat of Dora's testimony against her, Kaye wouldn't have confessed. She's a tough cookie."

Ruby gave me a gratified glance and lifted her glass. "Here's to sleuthing!"

I grinned. "Have a strawberry," I said, and passed the plate.

BLOOM WHERE YOU'RE PLANTED

HAVE you ever noticed that people who live in big cities — Houston, for instance, where I came from — know very few of their neighbors? At least, that was true for me. There were probably five hundred residents in the upscale condo complex where I lived, but I couldn't have told you the name of a single one, except for some jerk named Troy who lived two doors down and was in the habit of nosing his vintage Jag into my parking space.

It's different here in Pecan Springs,

where every Pecan Springer seems to know all there is to know about everybody else—their life histories, their successes, their failures, their foibles. There are a couple of good reasons for this. For one thing, Pecan Springers have a habit of staying in the same place for a long time, so they put down roots and develop an interest in the community. For another, there aren't a lot of big events to discuss, since most of what happens around here is very small potatoes (the high school homecoming parade, for instance, or the Cowgirl Cloggers' foot-stompin' performance at the grand opening of the Senior Activities Center). Of course, there's usually something interesting going on up at the college—that's Central Texas State University, for those of you who don't know—but there's always been a strong separation between Town and Gown, so what happens on the Hill might as well be happening on Mars.

In the absence of local events of global significance, people in Pecan Springs tend to talk about what's up close and personal, which is mostly the neighbors. Gossip, some folks call it, with a sneering curl of the lip. More positively, others think of it as keeping tabs on what's going on in the neighborhood, like Neighborhood Watch. Watching the neighbors is everybody's civic duty.

Which is both good and bad. It's certainly nice when Diana Dabbs asks whether my cold is getting better, but it's disconcerting when she wonders whether I like the Taffy Cream hair color she saw me buying at Peterson's Pharmacy the week before (and which I was planning to keep a secret). It's sweet of Leona Love, of the Love Family Funeral Home and Mortuary just down the street, to send me a birthday card, even if it is a bit schmaltzy for my taste. But when her husband Dennis pops into the shop to inquire jovially whether I've hit the halfway mark yet, I am definitely not pleased. Sometimes people cross over the line between being caring and being curious, between looking out for a neighbor's welfare and invading her privacy. And sometimes it's just plain difficult to know when to stop.

I bring this up because, to a certain extent, it explains what happened after Molly McGregor failed to answer her telephone one Monday morning.

Molly McGregor is the owner and proprietor of the children's bookstore next door to Thyme and Seasons, on the east. The three-story frame house used to be owned by Vida Plunkett, who let her dog, a dedicated and devout hole-digger, run loose at night to excavate other people's yards. This practice did not exactly lead to serene neighborly relations, particularly since I am proud of the herb gardens around my shop. In fact, Ruby and I danced an elated jig when the For Sale sign went up on Vida's lawn. We were even more delighted when the new owner, a plump, plain-faced woman with dimpled elbows and an air of energetic and determined self-assurance, bustled into the shop and introduced herself.

"I'm Molly McGregor," she announced firmly, "and I've just bought the house next door from my aunt. I intend to turn the lower two floors into a children's bookstore and live on the third."

"A children's bookstore!" Ruby exclaimed, putting several of Janet's basil-pecan biscotti on a plate. "That's wonderful! Exactly what Pecan Springs needs."

Well, maybe, I thought skeptically. This is a tough time for a retail start-up, and there's a big chain bookstore in the shopping mall on I-35. However, the chain store is mostly staffed by college students whose acquaintance with books seems to be limited to the book covers, and the children's section is mostly stocked with comics. And while Houston and Dallas are still in the economic cellar, Pecan Springs's tourist-based economy seems to be in perennial bloom. If Molly McGregor knew what she was doing, she might make a success of her new venture.

"I'm calling it Hobbit House," Molly said, accepting the plate Ruby offered her. "I'm planning to have story times and book fairs and visits with authors and theme parties. I've been studying successful children's bookstores around the country to see what brings in the customers, and when Aunt Vida put her house up for sale, the price was right. And the location is perfect." She paused and added, in a practical tone, "I know this might not be the best time to start an independent bookstore, given the way the chains are taking over. But I've looked the situation over carefully, and I think there's a good chance of succeeding." She bit into a biscotti and added, "Anyway, I've always dreamed of having my own bookstore, and it's now or never."

I could only applaud the woman's determination, and it certainly sounded as if she'd done her homework. "If there's anything we can do," I said, "please let us know."

"As a matter of fact, there is," she said, munching apprecia-

JANET'S BASIL-PECAN BISCOTTI

Biscotti is an Italian word meaning "twice-baked," and that's exactly what biscotti are: traditional Italian cookies, twice-baked to give them more crunch. They're delicious in any language.

2¼ cups flour
1 cup sugar
2 tablespoons cornmeal
1 teaspoon baking powder
1 teaspoon salt
1 large egg, slightly beaten
¼ cup orange juice
½ cup butter, cut into small pieces and softened
¾ cup pecans, coarsely chopped (substitute walnuts, if you like)
1 tablespoon finely chopped fresh basil
Zest of 1 medium orange

Preheat the oven to 350°F. Lightly grease and flour a baking sheet. Blend flour, sugar, cornmeal, baking powder, and salt. Add egg and orange juice, and beat until a dough begins to form. Add the butter, beating until it is just incorporated. Gently stir in the nuts, chopped basil, and orange zest. Turn dough onto a lightly floured surface, flour your hands, and knead it several times. Divide in half. On the baking sheet, form each half into a three-inch log about twelve inches long, arranged at least three inches apart. Bake on the middle rack of the oven for 20 to 25 minutes, or until set and just beginning to brown. Remove the logs from the oven and reduce the temperature to 250°F. Cool logs on the baking sheet for 12 to 15 minutes, until just warm. Slice logs diagonally into three-quarter-inch slices. Arrange slices on wire cooling racks and return to the oven until crisp, about 15 minutes. Cool completely and store in an airtight container.

tively. "I was just admiring your garden. Could you help me design and plant a Peter Rabbit garden? I have a white rabbit named Peter, you see, and a cat I call Mrs. T—for Mrs. Tiggy-winkle, of course. And my name *is* McGregor, after all. I might as well get some good out of that wretched marriage." She grinned wryly, but there was a shrewd twinkle in her eye. "A Peter Rabbit garden would be a big attraction, don't you think? If the kids don't care about it, then their grandmothers will. And Granny is the one with the checkbook, after all."

I had to hand it to Molly McGregor. She had thought of everything. And I liked the idea of having a Peter Rabbit garden right next door. Over the years, I've created several theme gardens around Thyme and Seasons: a fragrance garden, a moon garden (Ruby's idea, of course), a Shakespeare garden, and a kitchen border next to the patio. I've always wanted to have a children's garden, but there just wasn't enough room. However, if the children's garden were in Molly's backyard, maybe we could install a gate in the fence and share it.

"I'd be delighted to help you with a Peter Rabbit garden," I said without hesitation. "When do we get started?"

"There's no time like the present, I always say," Molly replied cheerfully. "How about tomorrow?"

As Ruby and I got better acquainted with Molly McGregor, we learned that she was not a woman to let grass grow under her feet—or as we say in Texas, she moved faster than a prairie fire with a tailwind. Within the next few months, Hobbit House was painted and the lower two floors were remodeled to make room for bookshelves, display tables, reading corners, and child-sized tables and chairs. Upstairs, a round green door, with a shiny brass knob in the middle, opened into the Hobbit Hole, a large storytelling room, where children could gather for special events.

Outside, Molly had the front yard landscaped and then she and I turned the backyard into a Peter Rabbit garden. In the center, we hung a scowling hulk of a scarecrow named Mr. McGregor — "He reminds me of Max, my ex-husband," Molly said reminiscently. "See that frown? That's Max, to a T."

Over the handles of a rabbit-sized wheelbarrow, we draped a rabbit-sized blue coat and shoes. We planted the garden with the herbs, vegetables, and flowers that Mr. McGregor might have grown, and we built a small goldfish pond with a waterfall against the garage. On its bank, Molly placed Jemima Puddleduck, a plaster duck that she'd dressed in a pink-flowered shawl and bonnet. Beside Jemima, she put up a wooden sign, painted with red and white roses, that said BLOOM WHERE YOU'RE PLANTED.

"It's my philosophy," she explained as she pounded the stake into the soft soil. "You follow your bliss to where you're meant to be, and then you make yourself right at home."

And then McQuaid installed the gate in the low picket fence, Molly and I propped it open with a terra-cotta figure of Benjamin Bunny, and our garden merger was complete. Ruby's and my customers can enjoy the Peter Rabbit garden and buy books for their favorite children. Customers of the Hobbit House can simply step through the gate and follow the brick path through the herb garden to Thyme for Tea, for a refreshing plate of cucumber sandwiches, a slice of rose geranium pound cake, and a flavorful cup of English tea, after which they can shop 'til they drop at Thyme and Seasons and at Ruby's Crystal Cave. However you look at it, this shared garden is a happy and profitable arrangement for all three of us.

While Molly and I got our hands dirty together, I found out more about her. She had moved to Pecan Springs from Dallas, where her fifteen-year marriage ("to a Very Bad Person," as she put it, speaking in capital letters) had come crashing to a close when her husband was sent to prison for stock fraud. Shortly after the divorce was final, her mother died, leaving her a sub-stantial sum—enough to buy her aunt's house, finance the re-modeling and the purchase of inventory, and buy groceries and pay the bills until the Hobbit House began to turn a profit.

"And if it doesn't," she concluded practically, as we finished planting a row of lettuce, "then I'll go back to being a librarian." She stood up and brushed the dirt off the knees of her baggy green pants, giving me a sidewise look. "My daughter, Karen, thinks I'm crazy, giving up job security and health insurance and investing my nest egg in such a risky deal. But we only go around once, and life is too short to spend it doing something that shrivels the soul."

"If you're crazy, so am I," I replied. "And so is Ruby. Crazy as loons, all three of us. But we're having fun."

And with that, we washed our hands and adjourned to Thyme for Tea, for a cup of coffee and a slice of Janet's Lavender-Thyme Quiche, one of the most popular items on our menu.

MRS. RABBIT'S CUCUMBER SANDWICHES

Peel and slice 2 cucumbers very thin. Add 2 tablespoons grated onion and salt to taste and let drain in a colander. Trim the crusts from 6 slices of white bread, butter each slice, and cut on the diagonal. Arrange the cucumbers in an overlapping row, garnish with a sprig of parsley, and serve as open-face sandwiches.

❧

ROSE GERANIUM POUND CAKE

1 stick unsalted rose geranium–flavored butter, softened*
1½ cups sugar
6 large egg yolks
3½ cups cake flour
1 cup milk
2 teaspoons baking powder
1 teaspoon vanilla extract
2 tablespoons very finely minced rose geranium leaves

Preheat oven to 350°F. Butter and lightly flour a 13×9×2" baking pan. With an electric mixer, cream butter and sugar until light and fluffy. Beat in egg yolks one at a time. On low speed, add cake flour alternately with milk. Beat in baking powder and vanilla. Beat in rose geranium leaves. Pour into prepared pan and bake for 50 minutes, until cake tester inserted in center comes out clean. Cool in pan for 15 minutes, then turn out onto a platter and cool completely. Drizzle with Rose Geranium Glaze and garnish with a few rosebuds or lavender sprigs.

*To make rose geranium–flavored butter, wrap 4 to 6 washed leaves of rose geranium around a stick of butter. Wrap in plastic wrap and refrigerate.

> ⚜
>
> ### ROSE GERANIUM GLAZE
>
> **Place 3 washed rose geranium leaves in a microwave container, with 3 tablespoons water. Microwave on high for 2 minutes, let steep for 2 more minutes. Strain out leaves. Mix with ¾ cup confectioners' sugar and ½ teaspoon vanilla.**

As the months passed, it became clear that the Hobbit House was making a name for itself. Mothers and grandmothers went in empty-handed and came out with full shopping bags; children came for weekly story times, a Halloween Haunt, an Easter egg-painting workshop, a Celebrate Texas party, and book signings with four or five authors; and teens came to help out with the children and browse the shelves of young adult classics. There were picnics and Mad Hatter tea parties in the garden, and puppet shows and musical events in the big room upstairs. Molly hired a couple of part-time helpers, but she was still doing most of the work herself, which kept her so busy that Ruby and I rarely saw her. But we didn't worry about her. She was following her dream.

We didn't worry, that is, until the Monday morning when Molly failed to open her store or answer the telephone. We might not have noticed right away, but Ruby wanted to pick up a birthday book for her nephew. She came back wearing a puzzled look.

JANET'S LAVENDER-THYME QUICHE

9-inch unbaked pie shell

1¼ cups grated Swiss cheese

2 tablespoons butter or margarine, softened

1½ cups fresh mushrooms, sliced

4 large eggs, lightly beaten

1 cup evaporated milk

2 tablespoons fresh thyme leaves, minced, or 1 tablespoon dried thyme

1 tablespoon fresh lavender buds

½ teaspoon salt

⅛ teaspoon grated nutmeg

Preheat oven to 350°F. Prick the pastry shell to keep it from puffing and bake until it is set, about 15 minutes. Sprinkle ¼ cup of the grated Swiss cheese over the bottom of the crust and bake for 5 minutes more, or until the cheese is melted. Remove and cool.

While the crust is baking, prepare the filling. In a large skillet, heat the butter. Add the mushrooms and sauté, stirring. Drain and cool. In a large bowl combine the eggs, evaporated milk, thyme, and lavender, the remaining 1 cup of grated cheese, salt, and nutmeg. Stir in the mushrooms and pour the mixture into the crust. Bake for about 35 minutes, or until the top is just set. Serve warm or cold. Makes eight servings.

"The Closed sign is still on the door," she said, looking at her watch. "But it's almost eleven. Molly always opens promptly at nine." She picked up the phone behind my counter. "Guess I'll call her."

I handed her my cordless phone. "Here—use this. My answering machine's out of commission again."

One after the other, Ruby punched in both of Molly's numbers—the bookstore and the one that rings on the third floor, where she lives. But after letting the phone ring and ring, she gave it up. "If she's there," she said worriedly, "she's not answering."

At that moment, Constance Letterman stamped in. "What's going on at the bookstore?" she demanded. "I've been pounding on the door and nobody answers. I even went around to the back and checked the garage. Molly's car isn't there. Is she on vacation?"

"If so, she didn't tell me about it," I replied, thinking that it was just like Constance to go poking in Molly's garage. Next thing, she'd be telling us what Molly stashed there.

Sure enough. "You'll never guess what she's keeping in there," Constance said, leaning forward.

"I don't care what she's keeping in there, Constance," I said. "It's none of our business."

"But something is wrong, China," Ruby chimed in. "She doesn't answer her phones."

"Yes," Constance agreed. "Something is *definitely* the matter. I feel it in my bones."

I gave her a look. "Remember the time you felt in your bones that the Loves were running some kind of funeral home scam? Or when your bones insisted that Mrs. Tuttle, at the library, was pocketing the library fines?" Both of these non-events caused a great deal of embarrassment when Constance raised the alarm, but she hasn't yet learned her lesson. She still insists on imagining crises and disasters all around her—most of which never come true.

Constance glared at me. "I don't know why you're bringing up all that ancient history," she snapped. "You should be concerned about Molly McGregor. We all need to keep an eye on what happens in the neighborhood. It's our responsibility as citizens. Anyway, Molly is a friend as well as a neighbor. Don't you care what happens to her?"

Just then, somebody came in to buy some rosemary plants, and I didn't have to find an answer to the question. Constance stalked out, and that was the end of the conversation. It wasn't, however, the end of people's concern about Molly's welfare.

At noon, I left Laurel in charge of the shop and headed out to make the deposit and pick up some credit card slips. On the way, I stopped in at the *Enterprise* to leave my weekend ad with Ethel Fritz. She squinted at it, allowed as how it would probably do, and took my money. As she was writing me a receipt, she said, "What happened at the Hobbit House this weekend?"

I frowned. "Nothing, so far as I know. Why?"

She tore out the receipt and pushed it across the counter. "Because Diggety Dolittle came in just a few minutes ago. He said there'd been a break-in or something." Diggety is Pecan Springs's mail carrier. "He had a package to deliver and the shop was closed, so he went around the side and peeked through a window. The place was all torn up inside, like there'd been a fight, or maybe a break-in." Ethel's look was accusing, as if I should have been paying closer attention to what was going on at my elbow. "You mean, you didn't know?"

I wanted to say, "Am I my sister's keeper?" but settled for "Nope." However, I was beginning to feel definitively uneasy.

"Well, maybe you'd better check it out," Ethel said tartly. "Around here, folks keep an eye on other folks. We believe in Neighborhood Watch."

Feeling chastened, I went to the bank, where I headed for Bonnie Roth's window. Bonnie—a member of the Herb Guild and a regular customer at the shop—is my favorite teller. Fingers flying on the adding machine, she began to work on my deposit. Without looking up from the checks, she said, in a low, worried voice, "China, what's going on with Molly McGregor?"

"I'm not sure," I said cautiously, thinking about what Diggety Dolittle had seen when he peeked through the window. "What makes you think there's something going on?"

Bonnie leaned closer, her brown eyes anxious. "I know I shouldn't be telling you this, but I was on the drive-up window Saturday afternoon about four, when Molly drove up and wanted to cash a check. A *big* check."

"Oh?" I cleared my throat. "How big?"

Bonnie looked to the right and the left, then wrote $10,000 on a slip of paper and slid it through the window. "Of course," she said, watching my eyebrows go up, "for a check that size, I had to phone Mr. Carson. He was watching the UT-Oklahoma game on TV." She made a face. "It was overtime, the score was six to six, and UT was inside Oklahoma's ten-yard line. When I interrupted him, he was mad enough to spit nails."

"I'll bet," I said. Carl Carson, the bank president, used to be a cheerleader for the UT football team. He's one of the Long-horns' biggest fans. "Did he approve the check?"

"Finally, after UT kicked a field goal. He had me tell him Molly's balance." She frowned. "It worried me, though. Because of that guy."

"What guy?"

"The guy in Molly's minivan, with her. He looked like a *gangster*." Bonnie shuddered. "Big and square, with muscular shoulders and a day's growth of beard. Huge hands, with black hair on the back. Very sensual lips."

Bonnie certainly had seen a lot through that drive-up window. "Not everybody can look like Tom Hanks," I protested mildly. "Had you ever seen this man before?"

Bonnie shook her head. "A total stranger," she said, her voice ominous. "Molly took the ten thousand out of the caddy and that thug grabbed her arm and said, 'I'll take that.' In a really nasty voice."

I frowned. "And then what happened?"

"And then he said, 'Let's get the hell outta here,' and they drove off."

"I suppose," I said, "that there are all kinds of explanations for this."

"I can think of one." Bonnie's mouth was set and grim. "That gorilla kidnapped her at gunpoint, made her drive to the bank and withdraw that money, and then—" She stopped.

"And then what?"

She shuddered. "I don't want to think about it," she said, and looked over my shoulder. "Next!"

Back at the shop, I grabbed a sandwich from the tearoom and went in search of Ruby. I found her on her knees in her front window, setting up a display of Tarot decks. I filled her in on what Diggety Dolittle had seen through the side window at the Hobbit House this morning, and what Bonnie Roth had seen through the bank's drive-up window on Saturday.

"Ten thousand dollars!" Ruby's eyes popped wide open. "Why in the world would Molly give that kind of money to some strange thug, unless she was coerced?"

"Bonnie only thought he looked like a thug," I pointed out. "He might be a perfectly respectable person, for all we know." But even to my ears, I didn't sound convincing. I sighed. "Let's go next door and see what Diggety was talking about."

We went through the garden gate, and I took the key to Molly's back door out of its hiding place behind the loose shingle. Ruby and I let ourselves in. The back room, where Molly keeps the science and nature books, looked perfectly neat. But when we went into the main room, we could see right away that something was wrong.

Ruby gasped. "What a *mess*!"

That was almost an understatement. Books had been knocked from the shelves and lay open on the floor. Potted plants had been pushed from the windowsills, the soil spilled all over the floor, even tracked across the pages of books. The blinds hung askew, posters were crooked, and the toys were scattered in the play area. It looked as if a tornado had ripped through the place. And on the carpet in the middle of the room, we found a big smear of dark, dried blood.

"We'd better call the police," Ruby said through clenched teeth. "There's obviously been a fight of some kind. Maybe that gangster beat Molly up."

"Let's check upstairs before we call," I said, heading for the stairs. But the second-floor rooms were untouched, and Molly's living quarters on the third floor—a cute little three-room apartment—looked just the way they usually did. Except that the table had been set for two and not cleared after the meal was eaten, Peter Rabbit's cage door was open and Peter was gone, and there was no sign of Mrs. T, Molly's large calico cat.

"Molly's been kidnapped," Ruby said grimly.

"Maybe she's just . . . gone away somewhere," I said, trying to think of alternative explanations.

"And left Peter's cage open and the place in a mess?" Ruby snapped. "No way." She reached for the phone. "I'm calling the cops."

In Pecan Springs, phoning the cops usually gets you Tommy Ryan, who handles the calls in our part of town. Because it was Ruby calling, however, we also got Sheila Dawson, the Pecan Springs chief of police and a close friend of ours. Sheila and Ryan showed up in a matter of minutes. After a look around, she dispatched Ryan to check the windows and doors for signs of forced entry, then opened her notebook and asked us what we knew about the situation.

"Actually, we don't *know* anything," I said. By this time, I was feeling very defensive. "All we can do is guess. And we don't have much to go on."

"That's nonsense, China," Ruby replied tersely, and told Sheila what Ethel Fritz and Bonnie Roth had told me. "Obviously," she concluded, "Molly's been kidnapped by some big gorilla of a guy, who forced her to withdraw ten thousand dollars from her bank and—"

"Ruby," I said, "I don't want to throw cold water on your theory, but we don't know that anybody forced Molly to do anything. All we know for sure is that she made a withdrawal and—"

"And now she's gone," Ruby interrupted. "Her rabbit and her cat are also missing, the downstairs has been totally wrecked, and there's blood all over the carpet. Those are *facts*, China, not guesses."

"We'll check everything out," Sheila said, standing up. "And I'll ask the DPS to keep an eye out for her vehicle."

We gave her a description of Molly's van and found a photo of Molly on the bedroom dresser. We couldn't find an address book, unfortunately, and none of us knew exactly where her daughter, Karen, lived. Ryan came back to report that none of the windows or doors had been jimmied, and Sheila called for somebody to come and check out the blood on the floor. "Let me know if you hear anything," she said. "I'll keep you posted on our progress."

For the rest of the week, the neighborhood could talk about nothing but the mysterious absence of Molly McGregor. The news of her disappearance traveled up and down the streets faster than a computer virus, and each of the Neighborhood Watchers had a different view of the situation.

"She ran off with the UPS delivery man," Mr. Cowan told me with obvious relish when I met him in the alley the next morning, where he was walking Miss Lula. "I saw 'em together, out there strollin' through that garden o' hers." Miss Lula yapped vociferously, and he added, "Oh, yeah. Miss Lula wants me t' tell you that she chased that white rabbit outta the yard last night."

"Last night?" I asked.

"That's what I said, ain't it?" Mr. Cowan snapped. "Whatsa matter? You hard o' hearin' or something?"

"Before Mrs. McGregor ran off to Mexico, she turned her calico cat loose," Vivian Baxter lamented, coming into the shop to buy some more catnip. "The wretched beast destroyed my catnip last night!"

Last night. So both the cat and the rabbit were still in the neighborhood. Which didn't solve anything, unfortunately. It only added to the mystery.

"I never believed that story about Molly McGregor inheriting money from her mother," Leona Love told me, when I saw her on the street. "If you ask me, there's something *ve-ry* crooked going on here. Maybe she and that gangster stole some money together, and he tracked her down and forced her to hand over his share."

And so it went, each neighbor embroidering an already disturbing picture with one more bit of speculation. It would certainly have been helpful if the police had been able to track down Molly's car or get a fix on her whereabouts, but they seemed to have drawn a complete blank. A few questions did get answered, however.

The smear of blood on the carpet turned out to be animal, not human blood, and a likely explanation emerged when I discovered Mrs. Tiggywinkle nonchalantly washing her paws on my back patio and saw that her shoulder had been badly nipped. When Ruby found Peter Rabbit hiding under the holly bushes, there was enough dried blood on his white fur bib to convince us that he had been the nippee. And as we straightened up the Hobbit House, we decided that the mess was probably made by Peter and Mrs. T. Peter's cage must have come unlatched, and he and Mrs. T, normally best buddies, had gotten into a spat that had escalated into full-blown war, Mrs. T employing claws and fangs, Peter using his strong back feet and his sharp front teeth, perfectly honed for carrot-crunching. If the two of them had had access to nukes, there's no telling what would have happened before they made their exit through the kitty door and down the alley.

It was the next Monday morning, however, before we learned what had happened to our friend Molly—and by that time, the neighbors were thoroughly sick of their own gossipy tales and wild for some real information. I was in the shop, unpacking a box of crescent moon–shaped, satin-covered dream pillows that my friend Carol had made for me, when the door opened and Molly herself stepped in.

"Hey, China," she said. "I'm back."

China's Dream Pillows

Dream pillows date back to the times when herbal fragrances were used to summon sleep, invite pleasant dreams, and fend off nightmares. You can make fancy shapes and fabrics, like the crescent-shaped, satin pillows that Carol makes for China's shop. Or you can do it the easy way, by using a 3×5″ cotton drawstring bag. Fill it with ¼ to ½ cup of a dried herbal blend and add a few drops of essential oil. At night, place your dream pillow inside your pillowcase; during the day, keep it in a zippered plastic bag. To renew the scent, just add a few more drops of oil. Here are some traditional herbs, in the order of their prominence in the blend:

- For pleasant dreams: lavender, roses, mugwort, peppermint, rosemary, chamomile, with a few drops of lavender oil

- For romantic dreams: roses, violets, mugwort, yarrow, catnip, lavender, marjoram, passionflower leaves, with a few drops of rose or violet oil

- For psychic dreams: mugwort, jasmine flowers, catnip, hops, calendula, rosemary, marjoram, lemongrass, peppermint, fennel seed, cinnamon chips, with a few drops of jasmine oil

"Molly!" I exclaimed, jumping to my feet, scattering pillows and knocking over a display rack with a loud clatter. "It's really you!"

"Well, of course it's me," Molly said wearily. She sat down on the window seat and kicked off her shoes. "Boy, am I bushed. I've been driving all night."

Hearing the commotion, Ruby dashed in from the tearoom, where she'd been talking to Janet. "Molly!" she cried excitedly. "Where *have* you been? We've been worried sick!"

"Why, I've been to Oklahoma City to see about my daughter," Molly replied, surprised. "I told you I'd be back today." As we looked at her uncomprehendingly, she frowned. "What's the matter? Don't tell me you didn't get my message!"

Ruby and I traded looks. "What message?" she asked.

"I left a message on China's answering machine last Sunday night," she said. "Didn't you pick it up?"

I shook my head. "My answering machine was dead on Monday morning," I said. "I had to replace it. What did your message say?"

"That my ex and I were driving to Oklahoma City to be with Karen, who was having emergency surgery. She's going to be okay, but it was really scary for a while." Molly shook her head. "Poor kid, she didn't have hospital insurance, so I had to dig into my piggy bank to help her out."

"Good grief," Ruby said. "So Max was the gangster in the car with you when you cashed the ten-thousand-dollar check at the bank?"

"That's right," Molly said. She gave Ruby a startled look. "Gangster? That's Max, for sure, especially when he hasn't shaved in a while. But how in the world did you find out about him—*and* that check?"

Ruby sighed. "It's a small town. Nobody has any secrets."

"I thought Max was in prison," I put in hurriedly.

"He served his term and was released," Molly replied. She

folded her arms, scowling. "Okay, you two, answer my question. How did you know about Max and the money?"

It took us a few minutes to explain to her about Constance Letterman, Diggety Dolittle, Ethel Fritz, Bonnie Roth, the chief of police, and the Neighborhood Watchers. Then it took a few minutes more to get Molly's side of the story.

It seems that when Molly and Max got the news about Karen, Max (newly released from a prison near San Antonio) had taken the bus to Pecan Springs. When he arrived, he and Molly went to the bank to pick up the money, then drove non-stop to Oklahoma City, to get there in time for Karen's surgery. Before they left, Molly had hastily locked Peter Rabbit in his cage with a generous supply of bunny niblets, poured enough food in Mrs. T's bowl to tide her over until Monday morning, and hung the Closed sign on the door. Then she called and left a message on my machine, asking Ruby and me to take care of the animals and explain to people why the Hobbit House was closed for the week. Sometime over the weekend, Peter Rabbit must have escaped from his cage and he and Mrs. Tiggywinkle went to war.

"Well, it's a good thing those cops didn't find us," Molly said with a wry laugh. "Max would have had a heart attack. He'd probably have thought they were going to drag him back to prison."

"Your daughter's going to be all right?" Ruby asked worriedly.

"After some recuperation," Molly said. "She wanted me to stay and help her out." She sighed heavily. "In fact, she's begging me to move my bookstore there. She's found a place she thought would be even better than the situation here. And of course she fancies that her father and I might get together again."

"Are you tempted?" I asked. I wouldn't blame her if she decided to move, now that she knew what Pecan Springs was really like.

"Not on your life," Molly said, shaking her head decisively. "This may be a gossipy little town, but at least people care." She gave a little shrug. "Anyway, you know my philosophy. Bloom where you're planted. And I'm planted *here*."

"Well, we're glad you're back," Ruby said, giving Molly a hug.

"Right," I agreed. "And next time you have to go somewhere unexpectedly, leave a note on the door." I paused to consider the possibilities—Constance Letterman, Diggety Dolittle, Mr. and Mrs. Love, Mr. Cowan and Miss Lula—and thought better of it. "No, don't do that. Somebody might read it. You'd better phone both Ruby and me. But don't leave a message."

Ruby grinned. "Better yet," she said. "Don't go."

"Now, there's an idea." Molly stood. "And here's another, China. How about helping me plant a new garden?"

"Sure," I said enthusiastically. "Where are you going to put it?"

"In the space beside the garage." Molly's face became determined. "We'll build a tall fence around it so nobody can see in. We'll call it the Secret Garden. And when we want to do something that we don't want the Neighborhood Watch to know about, we'll do it *there*."

"I'll get my spade," I said.